After the End

ALEX KIDWELL

Dreamspinner Press

Published by
Dreamspinner Press
5032 Capital Circle SW
Ste 2, PMB# 279
Tallahassee, FL 32305-7886
USA
http://www.dreamspinnerpress.com/

After the End

Cover Art by Brooke Albrecht
http://brookealbrechtstudio.com

ISBN: 978-1-62380-307-0
Digital ISBN: 978-1-62380-308-7

Printed in the United States of America
First Edition
January 2013

For my most beloved Robin.
Whatever stuff our souls are made of,
I know only that ours are the same.

Chapter 1

IT WASN'T that I didn't want to be there. Really, the bar wasn't that horrid type, the kind with the pounding bass and the waitresses in too-tight everything, offering up breasts and asses to the desperate throng of singles that filtered through the hopelessly chic stained-glass doors. No, this was more a quiet kind of dying. The artfully bare décor, the abstract paintings that stood for nothing at all, the dim lighting, the polished wood of the bar; it all nearly went together in a way that didn't. Like someone had once seen a picture of what they wanted very much, in a dream, while high, and then attempted to recreate it while none of those things.

But in the end, it wasn't the worst way to spend an evening. Tracy would never forgive me if I didn't follow through, anyway. Apparently I was "exuding loneliness," whatever that meant. Therefore, my happy, newly wed best friend had taken it on to her shoulders to find me a man. What was it about settling down that turned everyone into meddling matchmakers? I felt a little like an extra in *Fiddler on the Roof.*

You'll love him, Quinn, I promise. He's just what you need.

And what is that?

You know, breathing. Walking. Talking. Come on, trust me. It'll be fun.

I bet General Custer had promised his men the same thing. "Come on, guys, just one more fight. It'll be fun."

But here I was, showered and dressed and shaved as promised. I was sitting at the bar staring down at the vivid pink concoction the bartender had pushed under my nose. For nerves, he'd said, with a cute, flirty wink I was positive had charmed many an outrageous tip from men and women alike. It'd certainly worked on me.

"That looks positively dreadful." The amused drawl came from over my left shoulder, and I turned, eyebrows raising. "Please don't tell me that's your usual. Even I think that might be too flaming for an everyday drink."

The man was taller than me, hair a purposeful mess of blond curls and product, brown eyes glinting as he spread perfect lips in an even more perfect smile. He had that kind of graceful, knowing wink about everything he did: how he moved, how he held out his hand for me to take.

"Quinn O'Malley, I presume?" he asked, again with that grin.

I nodded, slipping my hand into his, surprised at the firmness and strength there. "You must be Brady Banner."

Brady wrinkled his nose and collapsed elegantly onto the barstool next to me. "Don't make fun of the name," he sighed, raising one long finger and waggling it at me in playful warning. "My mother liked things to match. I have three sisters, Brittany, Belinda, and Beatrice."

It did sound like something you'd put on a fake ID or use as a stage name for a stripper. But I smiled politely and shrugged, asking, "Can I get you a drink?"

"Not if you're going to order me one of those," he said with a mock shiver, poking the plastic spear of rum-soaked fruit standing proudly out from the drink. "Can I ask what possessed you to order a Care Bear in a glass?"

Feeling a little awkward and a bit defensive, I shrugged. "The bartender suggested it. I, um, I don't go out much. Normally, I just have a beer at home if I'm going to drink."

"Now that sounds excellent." He smiled at me and gestured for the bartender. Beers in hand, pink drink abandoned, Brady led the way to our table. It was a quiet little booth in the back, tucked away and private. Candles flickered in the dimmer light there, one on each table, and I realized all at once this was a date. Not that I hadn't known before. Of course I did; I was the one on it. It was just a little more real with soft glow and cozy seating and Brady there.

To his credit, Brady seemed to pick up on my discomfort. Without missing a beat, he leaned across and blew out our candle. Handing me my beer, he leaned back in his seat and smiled, pushing a menu across to me. "So, how long have you known Tracy?"

I settled in, trying to not look as stupid as I felt. Of course I was on a date. Everyone said it was high time I started doing that again. I'd agreed to it, after all. Very silly of me to care if there was a candle on the table. But I appreciated that Brady had blown it out anyway.

"We grew up together. Tracy was kind of my big sister. She said I was hopeless without someone looking after me." I half smiled, shrugging. Relaxing a bit, talking about a mutual friend, which, I realized, was probably Brady's goal. "She was right, of course."

"Tracy's always right," Brady said somberly, with a glint in his eye. "That's the first rule of dealing with her. She's always right, and she'll more than happily point that out the second you forget it."

I breathed out a laugh, a little startled by the sound. It'd been a while since anyone had been able to make me do that. "So, how do you know her?" I asked, curious. I'd never bothered to find out. "Tracy's been telling me about you for a few weeks, but I can't say I asked how you and she met."

"Only a few weeks?" Brady smiled, holding his hand over his heart, feigning hurt. "I'm devastated. Here she's been telling me about you for months. Apparently you are the last good man in the entire state, and I will die desolate and alone if I don't at least agree to dinner with you. Which, as you can see"—he gestured at the menus—"I am more than willing to do."

Off my wide eyes, he paused, finger going to his lips as he winced. "And you had no idea she was shopping you around, did you?

Oh, God, I'm so sorry. Really, she's just very sweet, and she knew I was kind of horrified by the whole club scene anymore. I promise, this is not a meat market or anything."

"I'm probably going to kill her," I said conversationally, wishing the ground would swallow me up. "Really, I asked her not to...." Sighing, I scrubbed my hand across my face. "Sorry. I promise, about half of what she told you was pure exaggeration, and the other half was probably all the things I never wanted anyone else to know."

"All she told me was that you were worth getting to know." There was the weight of his hand on my own then, and I looked up to find those brown eyes, warm and sweet, staring into mine. Brady smiled, this one softer, none of the flash and mirth and charm of earlier. It was just a smile, one that crinkled the corners of his eyes and made me feel a little less like jumping in front of a bus.

"Well, that's true," I managed with a faint shadow of a grin, only to be rewarded by Brady's laugh sending soft little goose bumps along my skin.

"And I know Tracy through work." Brady was fiddling with the menu, paging through it. It was the first sign of nerves I'd seen him have all night, and that alone had my interest.

"You're a lawyer?"

Another laugh, this one not quite as warm, but there was no bitterness in there. Just genuine amusement. "Tracy really didn't tell you much, did she?" he asked with a grin.

"Just that I was going to die alone and be eaten by my cat if I didn't take the chance to meet you." This time I was the one who smiled at him, less hesitant and shy than before.

"And are you regretting that daring leap of faith?" Brady's hand, I realized all at once, was still on mine. Heart in my throat, I turned my palm over, letting the cool slide of his fingers settle in beside my own.

"Not so far," I admitted and he laughed, loud and infectious.

"Now that's what I call a rousing endorsement," he teased. We turned our attention back to the menus, though I found it hard to concentrate on anything other than the feel of his fingers curled around mine. It'd been a long time since I'd done this. I almost felt guilty about it, until I remembered the empty bed at home, the single chair at the kitchen table. This was what I was supposed to be doing. There wasn't any reason to feel guilty.

When the waitress appeared, Brady opened his mouth to order before hesitating, turning to me. "Please don't tell me you're the type of guy who will judge me for ordering mozzarella sticks on a first date."

"Only if you refuse to share," I returned, lips curving upward.

Brady beamed at me, squeezing my hand and sending little hop skips of tight warmth through my chest. He ordered the fried cheese and a salad, a strange dichotomy I found amusing and intriguing by turns. Off my glance, after I'd ordered a BLT and we'd turned our menus over to the waitress, he shrugged. "Life is all about balance," he informed me with a wink. "Indulgence is only ever really fun if it's tempered with restraint."

"How very progressive of you," I responded dryly. He laughed and our fingers tightened together; it was all so *normal*. So different from what I'd learned to live with.

Once the food arrived, Brady took his hand back. I tried not to miss it. He didn't say anything when I carefully removed the tomato from my sandwich, but I could feel his eyes on me as I meticulously rearranged the bacon and lettuce back onto the bread, removing the middle slice of the three-layer club.

"I don't like to bother the kitchen," I explained with a tight upward twitch of my shoulders, feeling out of place and defensive again. This was the part I'd forgotten, the part that was always so hard to do: figuring out a new person, their little tics and oddities, finding out if you fit.

"That's… kind of awesome," Brady told me quietly, and I looked up, startled, to find him beaming that gentle smile at me again. "I mean, most people wouldn't think about it like that."

The acceptance made me feel even more awkward, but the tightness in my posture eased as I carefully cut a section of the sandwich. "They have a lot more to do than fuss over my tomatoes," I said, then took a bite. He was grinning at me again, looking at the knife and fork in my hands, but he didn't say anything. Just carefully dribbled dressing across his greens and vegetables and took a bite.

We shared the mozzarella sticks, our hands bumping together as we reached for them. It happened more than once, and I began to suspect Brady was doing it on purpose. A theory supported by the Cheshire cat grin I caught on his face the fifth time our fingers tangled together. That time, though, he didn't let go. He just tugged me in a little closer, leaning across the table to kiss me, lightly, gently. It was barely more than a brush of our lips, a faint hello of a touch. My cheeks burned with color and I stared at him, stunned, fingertips going up to touch my mouth.

Heat bloomed across my gut, a lurch there like I'd just stepped off a cliff.

"You ready to get out of here?" Brady asked, and all I could do was nod dumbly, still overwhelmed. He paid the bill, ignoring my fumbling for my own wallet. Normally, I would have insisted, but it was nearly impossible to get my brain to form single words, much less an articulate sentence.

I walked most places. Driving made me nervous, and public transportation was too crowded for short trips. We ducked out of the bar, my mind finally kicking back into gear, only to find it was pouring out. And I was six blocks from home.

Fantastic.

"I'm sorry," I said, managing to get my cell phone out of my pocket without injuring myself or others. "I didn't realize it was so late. I should get home."

It was an excuse, a lame one, but Brady took it with good grace. "At least let me walk you to your car," he asked, hand resting at the small of my back. I could feel it with every inch of my body, that gentle, faintly protective touch of his fingers. Strange how such a small thing could become so overwhelming.

"I don't have a car," I told him, holding up my phone. "I was just going to check the bus schedule. I think there's a stop around the corner."

He looked positively scandalized. "Okay, well, while you do that, I'm going to pull up right here. And then you're going to get in and I'm going to drive you home."

I spluttered out objections, but he held up his hand, one eyebrow cocked. "You are far too cute to die of pneumonia," Brady informed me, smirking at my immediate blush. "And I'm not an ax murderer or a stalker. Let me drive you back to your place."

I glanced back at the sheetlike downpour and sighed, relenting. "Fine. But I…."

"Nothing's going to happen," Brady reassured me, his hand gripping my shoulder lightly before his fingertips went up to brush across my cheek. My throat jumped at the tender movement, but he didn't back away. "You need to go slow. I get it. Don't run away just because I messed up."

"You didn't—" I started, but he cut me off.

"Honey, you were bolting for the door the second I kissed you," he said with a rueful little smile. "I misread you, and I'm sorry. But I do like you, Quinn. You're sad, but you're sweet, and I think you need someone like me. So I'm going to drive you home."

With that he was gone, dashing out into the rain toward his car. A few moments later and he'd pulled up, as promised, pushing the door open for me from the inside as I darted out to collapse inside in a mess of soaked limbs and dripping hair.

"You're even cute when you're a wreck," Brady teased me as he revved the engine and pulled out onto the street, flipping the heat onto high. "No one should have eyes like yours, I swear. They're unfair to the rest of us mortals."

I blinked said eyes at him, startled. "I…." Sadly, I never had been good at this part.

"They're just so blue," Brady explained with a grin. "Add that to the brown hair and the little upturned nose and honey, you are delicious."

Shifting in my seat, I frowned slightly, running my hand through my hair and grimacing at the messy tangles. "Do you really just *say* things like that to people?" I asked, a bit startled. "I mean, is that kind of your thing? You say stuff no one else will?"

"Does it make you uncomfortable to be complimented?" Brady returned, following my indication to turn at the light. "You really are adorable. That's just a fact."

Shrugging, I nodded to the street ahead. "You can park right there. That's my place."

The nonanswer didn't faze Brady. He bounded out of the car as if the rain didn't matter, coming around to pull open my door for me before I could manage to figure out the handle. Then I was faced with the awkward situation of having him there with me as I walked inside. I could hardly leave him out in the rain, and he was far too soaked through to send him on his way. With a sigh, I tilted my head toward the door as I unlocked it. "Come on in. I'll make you some coffee and you can towel off before you go."

To his credit, Brady did his best to look innocent, as if that hadn't been his plan all along. He dripped cheerily onto my rug as I rushed around to get us towels, peeling off his sweater with a squelch to wring it out over the sink. He was left in jeans, slung low on his hips and wet enough that they left very little to the imagination, and a white T-shirt that clung to his slim frame, giving me an eyeful of what would lie underneath.

Cheeks on fire, I turned away, busying myself with undoing my own clothes, the dress shirt wrinkled and soaked. All at once, Brady's hands were there, helping to coax out the stubborn buttons, gently smoothing the shirt from my shoulders. I looked up, eyes wide, as he smiled at me, as we moved closer still. He didn't touch me; we simply stood, trembling, bodies poised on the brink of falling. His heat was shared, was made my own, our breaths mingling in ever-shorter pants. He didn't speak, didn't tease me for my blush or my self-conscious stumble of almost words. We just looked at each other, the rain making a heavy drumbeat that nearly matched the grinding rhythm of my heart.

When he moved away, letting the connection fade, I let out a slow, trembling breath. Brady collapsed gracefully down onto my couch, bare feet and bared arms somehow looking completely at home there. He laughed when I shooed him up to get a towel laid down, but he took my fussing good-naturedly, helping to get a second towel arranged so I could sit as well.

"I like your place," he commented, picking up a blue porcelain whale I'd gotten during one sun-soaked vacation to the Florida Keys. "It's very... you."

I arched an eyebrow at him. "And what does that mean?"

Laughing, Brady shrugged, somehow still looking completely at ease and put together despite being only partially dressed and squelchy. "It's surprising. You have a leather-bound copy of *The Adventures of Sherlock Holmes* next to a cheesy tourist souvenir whale."

Frowning faintly, I shifted, glancing around my living room, gaze half-betrayed. "And how is that like me?"

He leaned over, catching my cheek with the rough pads of his fingers, letting his touch slide back to tuck a strand of hair behind my ear. "Because you, Quinn O'Malley, are surprising. Unexpected. A strange contrast of things I'm quite enjoying trying to figure out."

"I'm not a contrast," I protested, feeling the burn in my cheeks as his touch lingered against my skin.

"You've been giving me the 'kiss me now' look since I made you laugh in the restaurant," he murmured, shifting closer. I suddenly couldn't find it in me to protest he was now getting the couch wet. "But you blush when I touch you and you get more nervous the closer I get." He paused, eyes widening. "You're not a virgin, are you?" Interpreting my stunned silence as a yes, he hastened to add, "It's okay if you are! I just... I didn't expect to—"

"Jesus, no," I cut him off, having to laugh at the absurdity of the question. "No, definitely not."

A grin curved up Brady's lips. "Good. 'Cause I haven't been with one since I *was* one and I wouldn't have been sure how to do this next part."

"What next part?"

I really shouldn't have asked. I'd seen it coming the second he'd helped me take off my shirt. Brady leaned in, catching my lips, my question, and teasing them lightly with his. I sighed into it, an exhale that rumbled through my whole body, reaching up to catch my fingers into the wet fabric of Brady's shirt. He took that as the "yes" it definitely was, drawing me in closer, the wet press of his tongue against my lips making me shudder.

"Wait," I whispered, and to his credit, he immediately did. He rested his forehead against my own, soothing soft strokes down my back, rubbing a thumb along my cheek.

"Yeah?" he asked, then grinned slowly, nudging our noses together. "Hey."

"Hey," I murmured back, heart thundering, a smile threatening my own lips. "I just… I'm sorry, it's been a while."

"It's fine." Brady pressed one last kiss to the bridge of my nose before leaning back, his hand still making slow paths up and down my back. "That was kind of incredible, just like that."

It had been. Acknowledging that made me feel exhilarated and guilty all at once. But the guilt—I knew, I thought, I kept telling myself—was foolish, so I tried to concentrate on the giddy high instead. "It was," I agreed softly, and when our hands found each other again, when our fingers laced together easily, I let myself sink into that sensation. We sat there for a few moments, Brady's arm around me, our hands clasped tightly, listening to the rain.

Into the stillness came a low, inquisitive rumble, a chirping hello, and then twenty pounds of pure fluff and disgruntled sass sashayed his way into the room. Winston, my odd, huge, squished-face cat, had decided to see what was keeping me from turning into his bed warmer.

Before I had a chance to warn Brady, Winston made a beeline for his feet, nudging his face happily into the arches before he wound his way around Brady's legs. Then, with one last happy exhale, Winston collapsed, engulfing Brady's feet in a gigantic pile of contented feline.

"He likes feet" was my weak explanation. Brady was laughing too hard to really care, it seemed, bending over to pet Winston, baby talking him as the cat rolled over to show his belly for even more pats. The boy was shameless.

"Who's a gigantic fluffy fatty?" Brady crooned while Winston's stubby legs kneaded the air in bliss. His squished face made him look constantly displeased with the world around him, but there was nothing the cat loved more than attention. That or tuna.

"That's Winston Churchill," I explained. Off of Brady's amused look, I shrugged, reaching down to give Winston a scratch behind his ear. "My partner—my ex-partner—uh, he was a political history professor. When he found Winston, someone had abandoned him behind the university along with the rest of the litter. Winston was the only one who survived, so Aaron, um, he said the cat deserved a fighting name."

Brady absorbed that information, stroking the thick hair of Winston's side. I really did need to take the poor cat to be groomed. It'd just been something we'd always done together, Aaron and I. The last time I'd broken down into tears in the parking lot. I really didn't need to embarrass myself like that again.

"So, political history, huh?" Brady gave me a quick smile. "You have a thing for smart guys?"

I snorted out a laugh, shrugging. "Aaron was… yeah, Aaron was kind of beyond description. But sure, I like smart guys. Why, are you not smart?" I was trying to tease, trying to ignore the horrible ache in my throat talking about him was creating.

"Well, I'm not a professor," Brady returned, watching my expression carefully. "I'm an event planner. That's how I met Tracy. I did a charity event for her firm."

"Oh." I thought I did a pretty good job of keeping my expression neutral, but Brady grinned at me, nudging my leg with his elbow.

"You totally just dismissed me!" he said with a laugh, not appearing offended so much as amused. "My God, as soon as you heard the words *event planner* you completely dismissed me."

"No, I didn't," I protested, but Brady simply grinned impishly, waving me off.

"You did. You think all I do is swan around and plan parties for the über-wealthy."

After hesitating a moment, I ventured, "Is that not what you do?"

Brady smirked. "I like to think I don't *swan* so much as *sway*."

He was teasing me. I got that after a moment and sighed, rolling my eyes at his laugh. I turned back toward him, though, when his hand found mine.

"You're going to re-evaluate your ideas of event planners," he told me, confident and somehow astoundingly sexy as he held my gaze. "Because you, Quinn O'Malley, are smitten."

"Excuse me?" I asked, sputtering, but Brady laughed at me, leaning in to kiss away the protests.

"You are smitten with me," he repeated with a little grin. "Tomorrow, you're not going to be able to stop thinking about me. And you are going to rethink this whole 'event planners are beneath me' thing. After all, that professor is your ex for a reason."

I paused. It was too long a pause; it turned teasing into dreadful silence. The air practically burned with my stillness, with that horrified nothing. The smile slid away from Brady's face as my hands, shaking, dropped from his. "Quinn?" he asked, but I shook my head, swallowing hard.

Smile. I had to smile while I said it. I had to make it sound light. Casual. No one wanted to hear about this: it was too awkward, too terrible, too real. Tracy told me I needed to not dominate every conversation with this, that I needed to learn to let go. That Aaron would have wanted me to let go.

"He died," I explained with that horrific smile on my face, my voice cracking at the edges as I strove for lightness. "So, uh, that's why he's an ex."

Brady went pale; his mouth dropped open. "Shit. Shit, Quinn, I'm so sorry. I had no idea. Tracy…. Fuck, Tracy just told me you were getting over someone."

I shook my head, drawing back, feeling like the room was spinning. Like there was a white, rushing noise in my ears that made it hard to hear anything else. "It's fine," I was saying, still smiling, still desperately smiling. "I asked her not to tell anyone a while back. I was tired of the way people looked at me when they knew."

His hands were on me again, pulling me close, and it took me a moment to realize he was hugging me. Tightly, he held on, and after a few beats of not being sure how to react, I sagged into him. I rested my head against his shoulder and closed my eyes, wishing I didn't feel exactly the same every time I said his name.

Guilt followed that thought promptly, an overwhelming wave of it. Why shouldn't I feel this? He was gone. If I let go of that grief, if I had a moment of not missing him, how could I ever say I'd loved him?

"How did it happen?" Brady was asking, distantly, and it took me a while to struggle through the answer.

"Cancer." Such a stupid little word. It was far too little, too simple, to explain what had happened. To fully encapsulate the horror of watching that big, booming man with wild red hair and a grin that lit up the sky turn into a skeleton. That the person who'd once taken up a broadsword in class, swinging it around with a manic grin while he told his students of the War of the Roses, who'd tramped across hiking trails like there was no time at all between himself and his Viking ancestors, or who'd held this tiny, mewling, starving kitten in his hands so gently, that *that* person had been slowly killed off, piece by piece. That he'd died in stages, in starvation and sores and sickness. That the man who'd kissed me so passionately, who'd touched me and made me come alive, who could turn me on with a look, the man who I was supposed to grow old with, had been stolen.

Cancer was an ugly word. But one word could never fully encompass the soul-sucking terror of living through it. And I'd do it all again, every heartbreaking moment, because it would mean that for a little while, I'd have Aaron back again. I'd have my soul in one piece.

"I'm so sorry." The most useless phrase in the world. Brady was patting my back, was trying to say something that would mean anything. There wasn't, though. I knew that. He was trying, and that was the point. "When did you lose him?"

"Almost two years ago," I said lowly, fighting off the urge to cry. I certainly didn't know this man well enough to start bawling in his arms over my dead partner.

Brady drew back, studying my face. "I really am so sorry," he whispered. I'd heard those words over and over, so much they all blurred together. But I could tell he meant them, so I gave him a sickly smile and shrugged, eyes dropping away from his.

"It's okay," I told him, voice nearly steady again. Then, taking a slow breath, I tried for some levity. "Man, this has got to be the worst first date in history."

Brady snorted inelegantly, glancing at me before he let himself smile. "Oh, honey, you clearly haven't had many bad dates. Trust me, this is nowhere near the worst. In fact—" He reached out, lightly laying his fingertips on the back of my hand. "—I kind of think it was pretty great."

He stood, carefully folded my towel, dislodged a grumbling cat with one last pat goodbye, and gathered his shoes and his sweater. I walked with him to the door, feeling wrung out and unsure. Brady smiled at me, leaning in to brush a kiss across my cheek. "I really do think you're smitten," he told me, and I found myself smiling, just barely, back at him.

Then he was gone and my apartment was empty again. Just me and a fat, now snoring cat, and the ghosts of what once was.

Chapter 2

"COME on, admit it. You loved him." Tracy's words were practically tumbling over themselves, my enthusiastic friend foregoing any normal greeting in favor of pressing for information about my date. She hugged me, grinning impishly, wild red hair a haze of curls around her head. "Spill it, Quinn. Tell me how good I am."

"You're a terrible person," I replied dryly, hugging Tracy's wife, Annabeth, as we both rolled our eyes indulgently at Tracy's exuberance. Annabeth was nearly as tall as me, slim and graceful with dark hair and blue eyes, the polar opposite of the firecracker who was my best friend. And yet they fit so wonderfully. I'd bawled like a little girl at their wedding, standing up front in my tux, clutching Tracy's bouquet and watching them exchange vows in dresses that made the whole thing look like a fairy tale. "I'm going to go order our coffee. Still take it black, Anna?"

"Quinn!" Tracy's voice rose in that impatient plea I remembered so well from childhood. It was why she always won at Monopoly, even when I had both Park Place *and* Boardwalk. "Do not walk away from me. I want to hear details."

I ignored her. Not for long, I knew. No one got away from Tracy's inquisitions for long. That was why she made an excellent attorney. But for the moment, I escaped into the line for the barista, ordering three coffees—one black, two with extra sugar and cream—

when my turn came. Standing there, blankly staring straight ahead, gave me time to get my head on straight. Last night had been…. Well, I still wasn't sure what last night was. How I felt about everything. Brady had been wonderful, sweet and perfect and gorgeous. And those kisses had definitely resurrected certain areas I thought had been packed up in mothballs and forgotten.

But last night, I'd dreamed about Aaron. I'd woken up with a smile hovering on my lips, reaching out to a side of the bed that was cold and empty. How was I supposed to kiss someone else, to even *think* about someone else, when Aaron's pillow was still there? When his clothes hung in my closet? When I slept sometimes wrapped in one of his old cardigans, desperate for even the smallest scent of his cologne? There was no point in talking about last night, because the man I loved, the only man I *should* be thinking about, wasn't ever coming back. What on earth was I supposed to say?

"Quinn?" That low voice, a soft drawl, caught my attention as I was nodding thanks to the café worker handing me the drink tray with three steaming mugs. Startled, I jumped, sloshing coffee everywhere. I definitely would have gotten burned in a fantastic display of my own carelessness if someone hadn't reached out to steady the tray, to gently take it from me when I couldn't stop staring.

Brady. Here. In my little sanctuary of a café with its nearly too pretentious local art on the wall, the piped-in sounds of some wailing folk singer, and the cheerfully mismatched ceramic cups.

"Hey," I finally managed, blinking, absently drawing my scarf tighter around my neck. My voice sounded all weird and strangled, and I cleared my throat, staring at him. The corners of his eyes were crinkled in an amused smile as he watched me, all poise and grace and skinny jeans.

"Hey." His reply came with a gentle squeeze of my arm, with a quick scent of oranges and spice that seemed to follow him. So different from Aaron's cologne of choice—he'd favored something with sandalwood. In that moment, I couldn't have said which I preferred, although Brady's was heady: completely masculine, sweet, and totally him.

I was the worst person in existence. I was comparing my blind date's choice of scents with my dead partner. Not enough therapy in the world.

"So...." Brady's voice trailed off into a smile. Drinks still in hand, he looked at me expectantly. While I'd been having my little moment, apparently the world hadn't stopped to wait for me. The world at large was unbearably rude sometimes.

"So," I breathed out with a little laugh, embarrassed and quick, and rubbed a hand through the short spikes of my hair. "Sorry. I'm just surprised to see you."

"I'd ask if it was a good surprise, but I promised myself I wouldn't use cheesy lines on you," Brady teased, taking my elbow easily and leading me away from the counter. "So I'll just assume it is." His grip was strong, confident, not assuming anything but just reassuringly *there*. His deep brown eyes went to the tray and the three cups. "I take it you're busy, though."

"Just Tracy and Anna," I said, renewing my claim on the tray. "We had a brunch date." There was an awkward pause as he looked at me and I realized I should invite him. God, I didn't know if I could. If my scrambled brain could handle all of Brady Banner this early in the morning.

"Well, don't let me keep you," he finally said, all smiles, not a trace of censure for my stunning lack of manners.

"It's not...." Christ, I was fumbling over my words like a goddamn teenager, tongue too thick in my mouth to let me speak properly. "I just was...." Waving my hand helplessly back at the table, I let out a long sigh. "We're going to talk about you."

After a beat, Brady's polite smile slipped into a grin and he started to laugh, teeth flashing as he reached out to grip my hand. "Well, now I *insist* on staying, sweetheart." He gave me a wink and bundled us over to the table, ignoring my blush to rest a hand on the small of my back. Greeting Tracy and Annabeth with kisses brushed against cheeks, he pulled out my chair and fussed over the coffee before slinging himself back, legs folded, hands clasped properly in his lap.

"I hear we're gossiping," he said with relish, eyes sparkling. "And Quinn looks *so* disturbed about my presence I just couldn't resist."

"We have to have the post-date debriefing," Tracy smirked, taking a sip of her coffee. I was too busy gaping at everyone, which was probably why Brady stole mine and took a sip, our shoulders resting comfortably together. I wasn't going to think about how achingly domestic this all was. "I was going to call you later."

"He's smitten with me." Brady nodded seriously at both women, dimples showing as he grinned at Annabeth's snort.

I wanted to die. I wanted to crawl under the table and die. My friends seemed to be having far too much fun teasing me, though. I was aware this was one of the first times I'd been out in public doing anything but grieving. I was…. Well, I *laughed* at Brady's exaggerated smirk, at Annabeth's teasing glance, at the way Tracy was crowing about how she should be a professional matchmaker.

"I think that's called a pimp, dear," Annabeth told her dryly, a smile hidden in her eyes as Tracy stuck out her tongue. They kissed lightly, their hands laced together on the table, and I let the chatter wash over me as I watched that simple sight. Just the gentle, chaste touch of two people together, two people in love. Something I'd taken for granted so many times. I'd give up the world, I'd let it all burn down around me, for one more chance at something that wonderful. That simple.

"Hey." Blinking, drawn from my thoughts, I turned my head to find Brady right there, smiling at me softly. There was a hint of concern in his eyes as he studied mine. "Want to get out of here?"

Warmth flushed my cheeks, and I immediately started to stammer out an excuse, only to have his quick, breathless laugh stop me.

"Not like that, horndog," he murmured, teasing. "I meant a walk. You look like you could use some air."

Oh. Right. Not a lewd invitation to further what we'd done last night. Not lips meeting in a clash and a soundless whimper, or hands sliding along aching, warmed skin. Just a walk. Which was totally all I wanted to do anyway.

God, I was so messed up.

"Get out of here, you two," Tracy said, grinning at us, leaning her shoulder against Annabeth's.

Her wife smiled as well, long fingers cradling her coffee mug. "We're going to hit the market anyway. Brady, are you still coming for dinner tomorrow? I'm making squash ravioli."

"Like I can resist your cooking," Brady said, standing and leaning across the table to bus a kiss across both women's cheeks. "Besides, I'm in charge of dessert." With a glance at Tracy, he turned to me, smile turning slightly more hopeful. "I make a mean flan, Quinn. You could join us? Make it a foursome? You know how these two can gang up on you." Clasping my hand to his chest, he fluttered his eyelashes, overly dramatic. "Help me, darling. You're my only hope."

I couldn't help it. He was just so ridiculous with the messy blond waves and the brown eyes and how he'd swooned just to make me smile. I laughed, loudly, the sound startling me a bit. Twice in a short period of time, when it felt it'd been... God, *forever* since I'd just *laughed*.

"Oh, fine," I grumped, but I was grinning as Brady tucked my hand in his elbow, and Tracy gave us a look like she'd single-handedly invented human emotions and tight pants and sweaters that set off deep, chocolate brown eyes.

IT WAS chilly by the river this time of year, but I just wrapped myself further in my corduroy jacket and long scarf, tugged on knitted gloves as my fingers got too cold. Brady walked next to me, silent most of the time, our breaths twin ghosts against the still air.

"I love autumn," he said, grinning as he reached up to pluck a just-turning leaf from a maple tree. He twirled the scarlet-trimmed green in his fingers before tucking it into the buttonhole of my jacket pocket. "Just the way the air smells and everything crackles. Also, I look damn good in boots."

Barking out a quick laugh, I cut a sideways glance at him. "You're...."

As I trailed off, he filled in for me with a mischievous grin. "Charming? Irresistible? Cute as a button?"

"Surprising."

Completely the opposite of Aaron. Of the tall, booming man who'd moved through life like it was a river to ford, like it was a battle he'd already won. He laughed and the whole world lit up; he smiled and it'd been like the sun rose just to see it. I'd lived in his arms, in his eyes, in the breadth and span of his passion, of his wit and gentleness, for so long that when it'd been taken from me, I'd felt like I was only part of a person. All the goodness in me, all the possibilities, they'd been put in the casket with Aaron, buried in dark earth and hidden under a stone marker.

Brady was nothing like my Aaron. He was slim and golden—instead of a lion, he was a prince. The only cardigans he owned were probably bought ironically, and I doubted he owned a single broadsword or cared at all about the War of the Roses. He was so utterly *separate* from Aaron, so unlike, it was nearly impossible for me to reconcile myself with either of them. Like night and day, I wasn't sure how I could thrive in one when I'd learned to crave the other.

"That seems to be our particular theme." Brady smoothed his fingers along my cheek, and I shuddered out a breath, eyes closing briefly. How long had it been? Not just since *this*—not just since the soft slide of skin along my own, since the hot exhale of someone's breath stirred across my face—but since the closeness that had nothing to do with our bodies. It was Brady pressing inside that quiet bubble I called my own, inside the walls everyone kept up around themselves. He was looking at me, *seeing* me, and for a moment I couldn't breathe for how incredibly long it had been.

"I can't." The words came out of me like they were pulled, like I'd ripped them off of the scars I'd thought were so well hidden. "Brady, it's not that I don't want to." Scared and lost, my eyes blinked open and found his, those ridiculously kind brown depths holding my gaze. "I do, I just... I don't think I'm ready. I don't think I *can*. It's everything, all at once, and I feel like I can't breathe."

"You keep jumping to the end." The tone was slightly scolding, though the sympathetic twist to his lips eased the shot of prickle-sick guilt I got at the recrimination. "Which I get, Quinn. I mean, shit, you lost your whole life all at once, didn't you? You're still in that headspace of twin rockers on a porch, his-and-his towels, *forever* kind of stuff. But when I look at you?" He rubbed his thumb lightly along my cheek. "I see an interesting guy I just met. Someone I'd really like to get to know. Just because I kissed you, doesn't mean we're at the big, grand declarations stage. Okay? We'll go slow. Iceberg slow." Brady's smile spread into a teasing grin. "An afternoon watching *golf* slow. We're not at the end yet. We're at the walks in the park, meeting for coffee part. You can enjoy that. It's okay."

Taking a breath, I nodded, the twisting fear in my stomach easing a bit. This was big—sure, it was. Moving on, those dreaded two words, was never going to be easy. But Brady was right—rushing ahead, second guessing myself, *assuming*; that was just going to give me an ulcer. Or drive me to drink. Maybe both. A drinking ulcer.

"So," I said, lifting my hand to gently curl my fingers around his, letting our joined hands drop between us as we resumed walking. "Are we at the movie stage? Because there's a new one out I thought sounded interesting, but I hate going alone."

The breeze from the river ruffled his hair, the artful waves becoming something more unruly. I liked it like that, I thought, watching as he wrinkled his nose at the sharp wind. I liked the look of him, less refined than the perfect aura he projected with his skinny jeans tucked into his boots, his cashmere scarf, and his manicured hands. One of those hands was now easily holding mine; the fingers were laced with my own as we walked, as his hair turned messy and his cheeks turned red from the cold. All in all, he looked more like the kind of guy who'd go see a thoroughly irredeemable action movie with me just because it was fun.

"You don't strike me as the type to care about soloing it," he admitted, cutting me a glance.

I shrugged and shivered a little in my coat, free hand wrapping my scarf more tightly around my neck. "It's not the actual movie-watching part I don't like," I tried to explain. "It's the after. I always want to talk about it with someone, to discuss what I liked, what I didn't, to make fun of the bad parts. To, you know, cry over the really sad bits or laugh so hard it hurts. If I can't mull it over with someone else, it's kind of a letdown. It's so unsatisfying, after, if I'm by myself. No one to share the experience with."

He was smiling at me. Brady was smiling, not just in general, but *at me*, and for some reason that one simple expression took my whole heart and made it ache. Casually, he tugged off his scarf and wrapped it around me, adding another layer. Then his arm followed suit, curving around my shoulders, tugging me into his side. "The movies," he agreed. "Coffee and pie after. We'll mull over peach pie à la mode and you can pretend not to notice when I eat all the crust and leave the peaches."

"That's okay," I assured him, a little bewildered by how warm and, as stupid as it sounded, *safe* I felt walking so close to him. Hesitantly, I stole my own arm around his waist in turn. "I leave the crust behind every time. The filling's my favorite."

"Well, who says opposites don't attract?" He was teasing me, but there was something good in his eyes, something more solid than mere talk of pie and movies. I liked that look, even as some distant part of me was afraid of what it meant.

Aaron had been my *solid*. My *good*. My future and my past and the person who ate the crusts of my pie. It was strange and terrifying to think of anyone else filling that role, even casually. Even as just a nice guy who was going with me to a movie. In mute horror, I wanted to scream, to throw myself away from Brady, because Aaron was *gone*. Because the only reason I was there, walking with Brady, talking about *pie* was because Aaron wasn't ever coming home. How could I possibly have something good if Aaron wasn't there to share it?

Maybe Brady read my mood shift, maybe he was just cold, but either way, he was guiding us back to the café, to our separate paths, to the rest of our day. "Tonight?" he said and I nodded, giving him a slight smile. I did want to go. I just hated myself, a little, for that want.

Our hands clasped and Brady leaned in, brushing a kiss across my cheek. Then he was gone and I was stumbling the two blocks home. I was fumbling for my keys, shoulders beginning to shake, a sick, bitter retch in my throat. I barely made it inside, shoving my door closed to collapse in front of it, before I was heaving sobs, before the acrid taste of grief was cloying in the back of my mouth.

It had hit me all over, just then, with a stunning clarity, that Aaron would never see another movie with me. Never tease me for my terrible taste in them. Never sigh and fuss as I stole all the gummy bears or pretend I put too much butter in the popcorn only to eat most of it himself. Never would we walk out the door after, laughing or crying or somber or over the moon at how wonderful it was. Never would he listen to me babble about my favorites.

He'd never again. Never *anything*.

God, I missed him.

HOW many times, over the course of the day, my fingers stole up to touch the leaf, still tucked into my buttonhole, or the extra scarf wound around my neck, I couldn't have said. But every time, a little thrill of warmth curled into my gut. Every time, I felt that on-the-balls-of-your-feet anticipation about that evening. Even though Aaron hung over my shoulder, a specter that dug guilt and hesitance into every thought, I still wanted to go. I still wanted to see Brady. I just wished, sometimes, I'd never had to meet him.

Maybe I needed therapy. Or more alcohol on a more regular basis. Either way, I was going to the movies for the first time since Aaron had gotten too ill to leave the house. That had to mean something, or nothing, or *everything*. Really, I was just trying to focus on which shirt to wear and forget the rest.

My day passed in a blur of working the books, making phone calls to suppliers, and arranging a few signing events. Running my own comic book store maybe seemed a bit Peter Pan, but I enjoyed it. Before, when I'd still had all the pieces of my life in a neat, ordered row, there'd been more to me than just someone who kept shop. Still, I made my own hours, and I got to spend time with enthusiasts and artists alike, so I couldn't really complain. Aaron had loved this shop. Graphic novelists, he'd told me somberly but with that dry twinkle in his eye, were the modern historians. The tale-tellers and the cave painters. We were the ones who recorded modern myths for the next thousand years to read. I wasn't sure how much of that was an old romantic notion and how much was truth, but it did give my quiet life a rather grand façade.

Once upon a time, I'd been one of the cave painters. Now, though, I'd lost whatever spark was necessary to make ink and color more than flat blobs on a page. There was no romance left in my work, no soul. Instead of telling the tales, I sold them. It was a good life, though. A good existence. This store had been part of my salvation, afterward. It was distinctly difficult to drown yourself in grief and sorrow when there were bills to pay, when people depended on you to open the doors. When your day was spent discussing superheroes and archvillains and radioactive insects.

Finally, though, I slipped away and walked the few blocks to my apartment, absently trying to make a list of the number of times I'd been more nervous. It was a short list. I tugged my phone out of my pocket and listened to it ring as I fumbled with my keys and shoved open the creaky old door.

"Quinn? Everything okay?"

Annabeth's voice did nothing to calm me, even though the woman probably made monks feel inadequate. She was Zen personified. I could use a little Zen. "I don't know what to wear." There was not enough money in the world to make me admit how much my voice cracked.

To Annabeth's credit, there was only a moment of hesitation, a very quiet hum as I heard the rustle of her sitting down. "Start at the beginning."

"Brady. Movies. Me and Brady and movies, and Anna, I don't know if I'm *ready* for this and who goes to the *movies* on a date anymore?" I spun in a circle, looking around the cramped studio apartment and glaring at every corner, as if the fault for this current predicament resided somewhere within. "Oh, my God. I'm going on a *date*. Like, a *date* date. Not a date I go on to make Tracy stop bothering me about my cat eating my face."

"Breathe," Anna advised me. "It's okay, Quinn. It's just the movies. People go to the movies all the time. It doesn't have to be anything more than that, right?"

I nodded, closing my eyes and pinching the bridge of my nose. "Right. Just a movie. And pie and coffee after. That's… that's not a big deal."

"Absolutely not," she agreed, voice dryly patient. "Wear that blue sweater and your nice jeans."

Okay. Okay, I could do that. "Anna…," I started. But she seemed to understand, sighing softly.

"I know, Quinn. Just take it as slow as you need to. Brady's a good guy. At the very least, it's nice to have a friend."

Friends. Yeah. We were friends. We were getting to know one another. That was all. Never mind that my hand was clutching the scarf he'd wrapped around my neck, that I hadn't taken that stupid leaf out of my jacket all day. Brady and I were friends. Not even dating.

Oddly, that made the nervous knots in my stomach ease even while an ache settled in my throat. It was a good thing, to go slow. I *needed* to go slow. I needed to not overthink every damn thing I did.

But he'd given me his scarf.

I got ready. I even gave into an extremely silly urge and put the leaf in a bud vase on my coffee table. I lived in a small apartment now. Most of my things were in storage. After Aaron, I couldn't go home anymore. I couldn't bear to walk into the house we'd bought, the rooms we'd decorated, the bedroom we'd painted together and loved in and *lived in* so completely. Aaron was in the bones of that house, in the breath of each room, in the dings and the odd creaks of the floor, the way the rain sounded on the roof. He haunted it, just like he haunted me. So I'd left, in some desperate attempt to try and become whole again.

All that had happened was I now lived in one room and my furniture was hidden in a storage unit. I couldn't leave him behind so easily.

So. On to the movies. The streets were filled, the chill in the air not deterring the flitter of people pressing around me. There were lights and smells spilling out onto the sidewalks from restaurants, music seeping from under the doors of clubs and bars, and the movie theater beckoned me, marquee ablaze. Like a moth, I followed the glow.

Brady was waiting for me. His easy grin warmed me more than a thousand scarves, and he reached out to take my mitten-clad hands, drawing me in to brush a kiss against my cheek. "Hey," he murmured, squeezing my fingers gently before letting me go. "You look great."

"You too." We got in line, bought tickets, and negotiated popcorn—Brady insisted we get the large bucket with extra butter and I was easily persuaded—and then we were in the theater. I stripped off my layers, hesitating before I unwound the borrowed scarf and offered it back to him.

"You look better in it," he told me with a smile, reaching out to touch his fingertips to the back of my hand. "Why don't you hang onto it for a while? It gives me an excuse to keep seeing you if you have it."

It was impossibly cheesy, yes, but I found myself smiling a bit in return. "How very Jane Austen of you," I murmured, but I'd admit to a bit of contentment as I tucked the scarf back around my neck.

"It's no glove left behind, but I do what I can." The previews were starting, but he didn't settle back right away. Instead he reached down and took my hand in his own. Achingly slowly, our fingers slid together, the warm press of his palm against my own making something tight clench in my gut.

"Is this okay?" he asked me in a whisper. I nodded, heat pricking the backs of my eyes, but I squeezed his hand tight.

It was. It really was okay. I liked the feel of him holding my hand. I liked the strength of his shoulder next to mine. And not just, I thought, because it was *someone* there where now I had no one. It was Brady, who was turning out to be kind and gentle and sweet. I might not know him well, yet, but yeah, him holding my hand was okay.

And I felt guilty as hell that it was.

The movie was good. Well, no, the movie was terrible, in that wonderful kind of way. There were explosions and aliens and overly buff men who went shirtless for no reason other than our enjoyment. In the end, right prevailed, as it always did, and no one important died. Even the dog lived. It was good. We walked out of the theater, still hand in hand, laughing over how awful the acting was. I was smiling, he was smiling, and for a moment, everything was perfect.

"Pie?" Brady asked, tugging my hand lightly. "Come on, I know this great diner. The coffee is strong enough to hold up a spoon."

"Sounds like my kind of place." Our steps matched as we wound our way through the evening crowd. "So, this is kind of embarrassing, but other than the fact you're a party planner who hates overly fussy cocktails and enjoys fried cheese—"

"Which, by the way, is what makes America great," he interjected with an impish grin.

I huffed out a laugh and nudged his shoulder with my own. "Fine. *Besides* the fact you're a good American cheese-loving man, I don't know much about you."

He opened the door for me, a bell chiming lightly to announce our entrance. There were tables scattered around a long counter, the clank of dishes and hum of quiet conversation, and the delicious aroma of coffee. We got seated, and I ordered the promised peach pie, Brady adding a scoop of ice cream to his order.

"Well," Brady said, sprawled out on his side of the booth, looking good in his tight black sweater. Not that he wasn't perfectly aware of how he looked. His deep brown eyes crinkled at the corners as he smiled at me, and he drummed his fingers on the back of his seat. "I'm a middle child. I went to school for biology for three semesters before I realized I couldn't stand it, dropped out, and started working catering."

"Wait." A smile curled up my lips. "You were a science geek?"

"A very handsome science geek," Brady shot back, poking a finger at me with a haughty look that only lasted through the beginnings of his laugh. Rubbing a hand through his hair, he shrugged. "I like knowing what makes people work. But now I use that knowledge for creating beautiful moments instead of cutting open frogs."

Our coffee and pie came out and I dug into the sweet fruit. As promised, Brady reached over to steal my crust. I batted at his fork with mine, but he triumphed, grinning. I didn't mind at all.

"How about you? Tracy mentioned something about a store?"

Shifting a bit, I fussed with my coffee, adding cream, keeping my eyes down. "Uh, yeah. I own a comic book store."

People had different reactions to that. Mostly, I got laughed at. Yes, the grown man still spent his days talking about comic books. And Brady did laugh, yeah, but it wasn't an unkind sound.

"Really? That's kind of adorable."

My eyes lifted to find him smiling at me. Something tight lifted in my stomach, a soaring kind of lurch, and I fiddled with my fork. "Adorable?" I murmured, quirking up an eyebrow.

"Yeah." His hand stole across the table to find mine, that smile still doing weird flippy things in my chest. "Cool. Adorable. Kind of awesome. Take your pick of adjectives."

"You really shouldn't be this sweet," I managed, kind of abruptly, though maybe it just felt that way because my cheeks were all red and I was barely able to keep from stuttering. "I just.... You're the first person I've done this with in a really long time. And Aaron...."

And Aaron. Wasn't that always the coda in everything? The start and the end and the fucking middle. *And Aaron.* Only there wasn't any *and* anymore.

But instead of pulling away, instead of recognizing the whole Titanic-sized crater of mess I was carrying around with me, Brady just tightened his grip on my hand. Hanging on past what I thought any sane person would. "Tell me about Aaron," he said, so softly, so *kindly*, that I really did start to cry then. Right in the middle of some stupid diner, over my plate of peach pie with no crust, I cried.

Just like that, Brady was sitting next to me, arm around my shoulders as he pulled me in close. "It's okay," he hushed, lips pressed against my hair. "It's okay. I'm sorry. Shit. I'm sorry, Quinn."

Making some terrible snorting sob, I shook my head. I rubbed the heels of my hands against my eyes, trying desperately to suck in air, to compose myself. "No. God, no, it's not you. Jesus, I'm just a fucking mess." I attempted a smile, shaky and blurry eyed looking up into Brady's concerned face.

"Not a mess." The backs of his fingers traced across my cheeks. It was like he didn't even care we were in public, he was so focused on me. On us. "Just a guy who's been hurting for a while."

Another terrible snotty sound and I forced myself to pull back, to not use his shirt like a place to deposit all my tears. This was only a really nice guy I'd just met. He did not need me losing my mind all over him in the middle of a diner. "Yeah, well," I mumbled, wiping my eyes on my sleeve. "Do, uh, do you want to get out of here?"

"Sure." Smoothly, Brady paid the bill, grabbed his coat, and held mine out to help me into it. He was so damn graceful about everything, like it didn't even faze him that I was blubbering everywhere in the middle of a whole bunch of people. It wasn't until we got out onto the street, his hand firmly at the small of my back, that the mortification hit.

My God. I'd turned into a Regency romance heroine.

"I can't believe I just did that," I admitted, the cold air stinging against the wetness of my cheeks. I scrubbed them more vigorously, as if that could erase my embarrassment.

"What?" Brady asked, voice a low rumble as he let his hand slide more firmly around my waist, pulling me gently into him. "Had a little moment? It's okay, Quinn." He looked over at me, expression serious behind the soft smile. "I mean that. It really is okay. You can stop apologizing to me for grieving."

Frowning slightly, I just leaned into him, letting the streets wash past me, the people, the noises, all of it. It faded away.

"I met Aaron while I was taking a shortcut across the college campus. I, uh, I was doing a presentation for their graphic arts classes.

Aaron was out on the lawn with this giant broadsword." A smile quirked up my lips and I breathed out a laugh. "He was waving it around and I just…. How do you walk away from that? This giant man with red hair and a sword, bellowing about the class system and the political structure of Rome. And he looked over at me where I was standing in this group of people who'd stopped to watch, and he smiled. And that was it, you know?"

Brady's arm tightened around me slightly. "Yeah," he murmured, thumb rubbing along my side. "Yeah, I kinda do."

Feeling a bit worn out, I let my feet follow his until we were standing outside my place. "We didn't really get coffee," I offered, quiet, eyes darting up to him and back down again as I struggled to get my key to work. "If you want to come in, uh, maybe we can make some? I don't have pie, but…."

As my voice trailed off, Brady just gave me a sad little smile. He reached out, gently tucking a strand of my hair back, fingers dropping to straighten the scarf he'd loaned me. "I'd really love to, Quinn," he said. "But we're icebergs, remember? Super glacial slow. And if I come in, I'm going to want to kiss you."

A surge of heat hit me at that, at the way he was looking at me, at how close and gorgeous he was. Following it, though, was a twist of guilt, souring the anticipation and making my eyes drop. He was right there, gently nudging my head back up with two fingers under my chin. "I had a great time tonight," he told me earnestly, gaze searching mine. "Look, you're someone who's still trying to figure everything out. I respect that. And I get that until you do, I'm going to be living with the ghost of your ex for a while. But I like you. We click. So I'm okay with just being your movie buddy for the time being."

Taking a deep breath, I nodded. "I had a good time too, Brady," I assured him. I reached out to fuss with his jacket, trying to laugh at my own stupidity. "Even if I was a total spaz."

"Yeah, well, I like spazzes sometimes," he rumbled, hands covering mine. We stood like that for a few beats, just warmth and closeness and the depths of his eyes.

I leaned in and kissed his cheek, softly, a bare brush of my lips against his skin. I felt him shudder in a breath under my hands, and he tilted his head to return the touch.

"Tomorrow?" he asked quietly, voice a breath against my ear. "Tracy's dinner looms."

I nodded, pulling back with reluctance and a strange, sick twist of relief at the distance. "Wouldn't miss it."

With one last smile, one last trail of his fingers against mine, he was gone. And I was alone again.

Chapter 3

THE cat got sick on the carpet.

I'd dreamed of Aaron. Nothing earth-shattering—but then again, when the world itself had ended around you, you didn't long for the grand anymore. I dreamed of his weight in the bed beside me, of the warmth of his legs under the sheets next to mind. I dreamed I wasn't alone.

And then the goddamn cat got sick on the carpet.

I woke from bliss to the cacophonous retching sounds of Winston deciding the best way to wake me up was to redeposit his previous dinner on the floor next to my bed. For a moment I just lay there, staring at the ceiling, at the lazy turn of the ceiling fan. Just for a moment, I let myself miss Aaron so much it hurt to breathe.

Winston's substantial weight landed on my stomach, sharp claws kneading me through the blanket. "Yeah, yeah," I sighed, rubbing a hand through his fur. Winston arched up into it, a rumbling, rusty purr resonating through him. After a moment, with a head nudge against my arm, he padded over to the empty pillow next to me and collapsed into a furry circle.

So we lay there. Him and me, in a bed that was too big, me staring blankly at the ceiling and watching the fan turn. It wasn't Aaron's pillow any longer. Just an empty spot for the cat to nap.

Eventually, I had to move. I cleaned up after Winston, I made coffee, I lived. I went about my life. And the dream of Aaron faded, as they always did, because he wasn't real. All that personality, that giant, beautiful man, had been reduced to a ghost.

Shuffling into the living room, I looked around, a bit at a loss. I had my coffee in my hand, the sun was peering through the windows, the couch was empty. It seemed a simple equation. But what did I *do*, really? What was the point of sitting? Of drinking the damn coffee, of staring out the window, of doing *anything*? Aaron couldn't. Instead of warmth and love and laughter, instead of planning our weekend or reading the paper in cozy silence, it would just be me.

I did manage to sit at some point. The coffee was cold by then. It didn't matter; honestly, I didn't want to drink it. I wasn't sure how long I sat curled up on *our* couch that was now *my* couch, but it was long enough that Winston decided to come and check why I wasn't attending to his every whim. My bare feet were requisitioned as his new nap spot, and he blinked happily at me as his paws made biscuits with the air.

Finally, though, I pulled myself out of the world of shadows and half-seen ghosts. I went to the front door and pulled it open, expecting to find my paper curled up on the front welcome mat. And it was; my paper guy was very meticulous. No paper in the bushes for me. Then again, I didn't have bushes, so that probably helped.

But next to the paper was a white bakery box.

Frowning, glancing around, I hesitantly picked both up, juggling them as I nudged Winston away from the open door and headed back inside. I wasn't expecting a package, not that there was a label or anything to give me a hint what it might be. Probably not a bomb. I wasn't exactly bomb material. Was anthrax still a thing?

After putting the box down on the kitchen table, I pulled a chair over and sat, chin resting on my folded arms, studying it. It didn't appear to be ticking. And it was too small to hold a head of some kind. Maybe a hand. A smaller body part would definitely fit.

I really needed to stop watching crime television.

"Okay, O'Malley," I muttered, rolling my shoulders back. "You are not afraid of a white box." Right. No Brad Pitt moments here.

After tugging open the top, I stared down inside for a long beat, completely speechless.

Inside was a delicious-looking bowl of peach pie filling. Not a crust to be seen.

BOTTLE of wine in hand, I knocked on Tracy's door. I was nervous. I was wearing a corduroy jacket over a T-shirt, I'd shaved, and I was *nervous* going to have dinner with my two best friends. Then again, it wasn't seeing them that had my stomach in knots.

"Quinn!" Tracy opened the door, her trademark smile filling the room. She bussed a kiss against my cheek, hauling me in for a hug. "I'm so glad you came."

"And he brought wine." Annabeth was next, a calm hug following Tracy's exuberance, both of them feeling more like home than anything else I had left. "My favorite. Someone's trying to spoil us."

"Just a thank you," I insisted as Anna took the wine away toward the living room with a kiss to Tracy's cheek.

"For what?" Tracy took my arm and led me into the kitchen. There was a knowing, smug glint in her eyes as we walked, the source of which I found as I looked up.

Brady was there. His sleeves were rolled up, there was flour on his cheek, his hair was mussed, and he was laughing with Anna as she searched for a corkscrew. And my heart just… stopped.

"Shut up," I muttered to her, leaving her side to go to his. Brady greeted me with a warm smile and a hug, careful not to get his mess all over me.

"Sorry," he said with another laugh, running a hand through his hair. "I'm a disaster area when I bake. But, uh, it's good to see you, Quinn."

"You too." I was smiling back. God, how could I *not* smile back? "You, um." Daringly, I reached out, an action that started as me fixing his collar but turned, somehow, into my hand just resting over his heart. His smile softened, and he took a step forward, eyes full of something that made my stomach surge, that dangerous, anticipatory lift shivering through me.

The oven timer went off and the moment ended. My hand slipped away; Brady wrinkled his nose regretfully, but he turned to save the flan from burning. Taking a deep breath, I went to the wine like a homing pigeon. Annabeth gave me a sympathetic look, gripping my upper arm for a moment before pouring me a glass.

"So, I have an opening in two months at the gallery. One of my artists just pulled out." She smiled at me as I gulped down my first drink, eyes straying back over toward the kitchen. Brady was pouring and stirring, mixing something or other, and somehow all of it looked really good while he was doing it.

Wait. Annabeth was giving me that expectant look, which meant probably she'd just said something I was supposed to respond to. I rewound the whole conversation in my mind and blinked, startled.

"Are you asking me to do a showing?" I nearly stumbled over the word. "Anna, that's really…."

She was just looking at me with those totally accepting, infinitely patient eyes. Kind of like Mother Theresa crossed with a bulldog. She wasn't going to let me stammer my way out of this. Tracy would push obviously, would take you by the damn hand and lead you to the water and shove your face down and give you a ten-page list on why you should drink. Anna, though, would walk beside you until you didn't even realize she'd directed where you were going and then would sit there and wait for you to drink on your own. They were a diabolical team. I expected them to take over the world any day now.

"It's been more than two years, Quinn," Anna reminded me softly, rubbing her hand along my arm, steel behind her eyes. "That's a long time to not be happy."

"A show, though, Anna?"

"A show about what?" Brady had joined us with a grin, his fingertips resting lightly on the small of my back as he reached over to take a glass of wine. I couldn't help but give him a little smile, nudging my shoulder against his.

"Quinn is an artist. Quite a good one, actually. I'm trying to entice him to save me from having bare walls for two weeks." Annabeth gave me a look over the top of her glass, what I could only categorize as a smirk in her gaze.

Brady pulled back enough to give me a look, eyebrows winging up. "Really? I didn't know that."

Shuffling my feet, I sighed, narrowing my eyes at Anna, who suddenly announced, tone an overt attempt at casual, "I think I need to go check on Tracy and the pasta. Excuse me, boys."

Evil woman.

"Yeah." I shrugged once she was swaying her way back to the kitchen. Was it possible for a *walk* to be smug? Because hers was.

Okay. Well, this was a fun party story. Refilling my glass, I glanced up at him, at those wicked brown eyes under the now messy curls, at the flour he probably didn't even realize was still brushed across his forehead. I reached out to smooth it off his skin, feeling my expression softening, the tense defensiveness I had when broaching this subject fading a bit. Brady had never done anything to make me think he was going to pry or push. He just wanted to know.

"I used to draw and ink my own graphic novel," I explained with a wry little twist of my lips. "I did some shows with the artwork. It was just something I used to do, you know? But once Aaron got really sick, I couldn't.... None of the colors made sense anymore." I didn't know if he'd understand that—hell, some days it didn't make sense to me either. But Brady nodded, wrapping an arm around my shoulders and kissing my temple.

"Well, if you decide you want to grace Anna with your brilliance—" He laughed at that and I did too. It was a quiet choked sound, but I laughed. And I didn't cry. Which was a first for me with Brady, embarrassingly enough. "—I will be the first one in line at the gallery to see your work."

Rolling my eyes at his teasing, I took his hand and led him back into the kitchen. Back into the circle of warmth, into the hearth where two of my favorite women in the world were busy cooking and trying not to stare at us. "Since no one will let me cook—" I started, and Tracy laughed, shaking her head as she busily stirred sauce bubbling on the stove.

"You mean because no one here is suicidal," she poked fun at me, sticking her tongue out when I glared.

"*Anyway,*" I said, accidentally on purpose tugging her hair out of its ponytail, "how about I set the table?"

"I'll help." Brady smoothly followed me, grabbing the plates when I went for the silverware. "Dessert's done. I'm officially out of things to do."

We went into the dining room, the sound of the clatter of pans and the women's voices fading as the door swung shut behind us. Moving around the table, I carefully arranged the forks and knives in their appropriate spots. Brady was opposite me, setting the plates onto the linen tablecloth. My eyes kept going to his, over and over, our gazes meeting in a spark of heat before I forced my head back down. The clatter of a plate on the table made me glance up again and there he was, *looking* at me.

We danced, the two of us, around the table. Putting silverware down. Plates. Napkins. Mundane actions and yet every one made heat surge in my gut because during each one he was silently watching me, movements graceful, hands so careful with each piece. We moved closer to one another until he was pressed against my back, arms wrapped around me to put the last plate down.

"Done," he breathed against my neck, nose nudging in behind my ear.

With a low noise, I turned, grabbed his tie, and hauled him in for a kiss. An arm braced on either side of me, Brady went willingly, leaning me back across the table. Neat place settings scattered under me, but hell if I cared. Our tongues tangled together, the warm press of Brady's lips on mine turning into a hungry gasp of need, a sharp thrill as we melted into one another.

The frantic kiss slowed into something sweet, into softness and my hand tangling into Brady's hair. We parted, heaving breaths, lips sliding along each other's as if we couldn't bear to move further away. "Hey," I finally said, a smile spreading across my face.

Brady laughed, nuzzling his nose against mine. "Hey, yourself," he murmured.

"You sent me pie."

Brady lightly nipped at my lower lip. Objectively, my first thought on that would have been *what the hell* because who *bit* someone, but the jolt of desire that hit my stomach at the little spike of pain totally shorted out any of my protests. I must have made a strangled, soft noise because Brady grinned, smooth as honey, and did it again, catching my lip between his teeth and then sucking away the sting.

"I did," he replied, voice a rumble I could feel in every inch of me.

"With no crusts." Odd how utterly hoarse my tone had gone, like all the air had gotten caught in a ball in my throat.

"None at all." Brady kissed me again, one hand sliding down my side to settle at my waist.

"Thank you," I whispered, lips moving along his jaw to his ear. I could feel his smile against my cheek and he breathed out a laugh, quiet and low.

"I'm glad you came tonight."

God, so was I.

Finally, we stood again, fingers tangling together as we straightened our clothes, as we laughed over swollen lips, as he kissed the blush on my cheek and I stood up on the balls of my feet to press my lips against the soft skin just in front of his ear. We rearranged the plates and silverware and napkins, grinning at one another. Sharing that moment between us with every look.

Slow, yeah. Glacier slow. But Christ, he just looked so good tonight.

"Ta da!" Tracy came into the room bearing a platter filled with steaming ravioli and butter sauce. Annabeth followed with bread and salad. We bustled about, helping them set everything up, Brady grabbing the wine and our glasses, and then we settled in.

Brady took a deep breath, grinning and raising his glass to Tracy and Anna. "This smells delicious. Much better than the frozen pizza I had planned."

"Agreed." I toasted them both, but my gaze kept being drawn to Brady, sitting across from me. His hair was still mussed from where my fingers had been caught in silk-soft waves, his cheeks were flushed a bit, and I liked to think it was more than just the wine and the candles that made him smile like that. It was terrifying to feel the surge of heat again, to be caught up in someone's eyes. It was like I was waking up, bit by bit, the fog of the past two years melting in a puddle of peach pie and borrowed scarves.

After dinner, Brady and I found ourselves in the kitchen, washing dishes side by side, the gentle clink of plates and cups underscoring the soft music coming from the other room. We were silent, the two of us, bubbles caught on my arms, Brady's head bent over the drying rack.

I'd kissed him. Impulsively, sweetly, I'd kissed him. In that moment, there'd been no Aaron at all. Honestly, I wasn't sure what that meant. Ever since he'd died, ever since someone had taken my heart and laid it in cold dirt, had covered it with etched stone, people had been telling me to *move on*. To mourn him and to learn to live again.

It's what he'd want, I'd been told.

You deserve to find someone new. As if it was that simple. As if my life could be shaken like a snow globe, turned over and inside out and the view changed. It was a puzzle, missing pieces forgotten as I struggled to make a new image whole.

I wouldn't want him to move on. That was my deep, dark secret. If I'd been the one to die, if it'd been me, I wouldn't want him to find solace in someone else's arms. Those were *my* kisses, soft and gentle on his lips. My laugh that had lit up the sky. My hands that had held and stroked and made real. He'd been mine, and I was his. I still was his, wasn't I? Isn't that what love was?

Except I'd kissed Brady.

Except I wanted to do it again.

The water swirled down the drain, disappearing in a curl of velvet soapsuds. For a beat, there was nothing. Just us, Brady and I, standing and staring down at the sink.

"I miss him," I whispered, voice breaking. "Every second, like I'm screaming all the time, and I can't stop. I want to go up to people and ask them why they can't hear it. Why they can be smiling or laughing, why can people *eat* or *drink* or *live* when he'll never do any of it again. How can I be happy without him? How can anything make any fucking sense?" My eyes went to his, to those damned beautiful depths, so kind and so confused. I could see it in his expression; what could he say? What could anyone?

"But then I kiss you." I moved a step forward, a magnet on string, his iron sweet solidness drawing me in. "I kiss you and I don't miss him. I kiss you and I'm not living in that place. I'm not soaked in sickness and sadness and grief. I just... *am*. I can breathe."

With a soft noise, he reached out for me, gentle fingers trailing along my cheeks before he hooked me in close, before he did just that. He kissed me, hard enough I couldn't do anything but be right there, with him. In that moment, in that little glimmer of life, I wrapped myself in him.

"It scares me," I admitted in a whisper. "I don't know if I want to keep kissing you forever or hate you for making me forget him."

Brady's lips twisted downward in sympathy as he fussed with my hair, brushing it back from my forehead. "I don't know what to say to you," he murmured, shaking his head. "I can't imagine what you're feeling. I just...." Huffing out a sigh, he kissed my forehead and wrapped his arms around me. "I don't want you to forget him, babe. He was a part of you. He *is* a part of you. This isn't you trying to replace him. It's just where you are now, you know?"

Face pressed into his chest, I nodded. It made sense. I knew it made sense. So why did I still feel sick with guilt just standing there with him?

Eventually we pulled apart, hand in hand as we walked into the living room. There was flan and coffee, there was laughter and storytelling and conversation that went over my head. I sat in near silence, contributing a smile from time to time, a quiet laugh when it was needed. Mostly, I let myself float away on the feeling of not being alone. On the noise and the closeness that didn't allow any ghosts at all in.

"Let me walk you home." Brady took my arm, wrinkling his nose at me in a smile as he tucked my scarf tighter around my neck.

The moon was plump and full above us, hung in the crook of the buildings we passed, caught in tree branches and skylines. Our breath made smoky trails as we walked, footsteps crisp on the pavement. Brady was warm, solid next to me, hand never leaving mine.

"I meant what I said," he broke the silence, glancing over at me. "I'll go slow. No matter how many times you grab me and kiss me." He smiled, teasing, nudging my side with his elbow. "No matter how gorgeous you look tonight."

Worrying my lower lip, I tilted my head back, up toward the sky. Letting the night air surround us, I paused, taking deep breaths, eyes falling closed.

"I'm confused," I admitted.

"I know."

IT WAS raining again. Fat drops beat against the window outside my store, sliding snakelike down the glass to join the rush of water along the sidewalk. No one had come into the store in hours. I'd sent Marty, my afternoon cashier, home early. Even with all the lights on, the world looked dim and half-asleep; there was no use in both of us spending our evening staring at the empty aisles.

A sketchbook was open in front of me. White pages mocked me, smooth and open and meaningless. Every time I settled in to put pencil to it, to stroke life from the empty expanse, it was like I froze. Like any story I might coax up from lead and paper was already buried and forgotten.

Irritated with myself, with my inability to do anything useful at all, I flipped the sketchbook closed. Shoving it in a drawer brought me only the smallest bit of satisfaction. Lighting it on fire, perhaps, would have been more fulfilling, but I didn't think my insurance guy would appreciate the sentiment.

The bell above the door jangled merrily as someone took shelter from the storm. I barely glanced up; the downpour was a roar against the roof, a beast let loose on the deserted streets of the city. I doubted any true customers had braved the weather just to pick up the latest issue of crime fighting antics.

"So, what would you recommend?" Two comics were laid on the counter in front of me as that silk-smooth voice wound its way around me, tugging my stomach into flip-flops. "Bug-bitten superheroes or the gritty antihero with a chip on his shoulder?"

Brady was smiling at me, umbrella dripping on the floor, blond hair in messy waves from the wind. For all his knee-high boots and perfectly fitted leather jacket, he looked strangely at home in my store. Maybe it was just the way he was looking at me, corners of his eyes crinkled, whole expression open, like he'd come out in the sopping rain just for a chance at seeing me. Like that, somehow, would have been worth the trouble.

"What are you doing here?" God, I was an idiot. The words were out before I could catch them and haul them back. It was a valid question, sure, but I definitely hadn't meant to sound so blunt. Wincing, I reached out, fingers snagging the cuff of his jacket. "Not that it's, you know, *entirely* unfortunate you stopped by," I said softly, studying his face. "I just wasn't expecting you."

"I thought you needed soup." He held out a brown paper bag, tightly rolled against the cold outside. "Actually, *I* needed soup. It's my morning off, so I made up a huge pot of vegetable stew. Only thing to do, really, with it raining cats and oversized dogs out." While he talked, he pulled out two containers, unscrewing the lids and fishing out spoons from the bag as well. Next followed bread, crusty and still steaming with warmth. My eyes must have gone huge because Brady's grin turned absolutely smug.

"Oh, yeah. I made bread too. Since I had a little time."

"You *made* all of this?" I took the offered spoon, leaning over the food to take in a deep breath. A happy little noise escaped me as I closed my eyes, drowning in the spice and the smoky undertone of tomatoes, the yeasty goodness of fresh bread. "This is amazing. You are amazing."

Brady waved his spoon, dismissing my praise, but he did look extremely satisfied. "After everything was done, I realized the only thing missing was good company. Hence"—he gestured at himself with a slight bow—"me. Here. With you."

Laughing, I returned the bow, head inclining as I strove to maintain my serious expression. "Well, then. So long as you brought soup, I guess that's okay, then."

"*And* bread," Brady pointed out. "And my fantastic company."

"That is quite a deal I'm getting. Good thing I didn't have lunch plans already. I can't think of anything better." Picking up the soup, my smile just a little shy, I nodded toward the back room. "Come on. I've got just the spot."

Through the swinging door, through the stockroom, I led Brady back into what had been, once upon a time, my sanctuary. Huge skylights covered the ceiling, the rain here more like a bass drum that pounded an underscore to our movements. There were long wooden tables scored with chalk and paint, white sheets covering canvasses, sketchbooks laid around like scattered leaves. Setting down the soup on a low table, I tugged a dusty sheet off the couch.

"Sorry," I murmured, wincing a bit. "I, uh, I don't come in here often."

The couch wasn't so bad, though, and Brady sprawled out onto it, that beautiful, calm smile easing the tense knot in my stomach. "It's perfect." He wasn't poking around, wasn't asking me questions. His gaze had gone over everything, brilliant and quick, much more intelligent than he'd ever say. It wasn't exactly the Orient Express or anything—the mystery was only as deep as two years' worth of dust, as charcoal and paints lying abandoned. But he didn't pry. He just arranged our food and dug around in the bag for more napkins.

"Let me just lock up," I told him, nervously pleating my T-shirt hem in my fingers. He was just so *there*, so gorgeous and unassuming while taking up far more room on that couch than I'd ever imagined him capable of. Aaron had watched me from there, had sat reading his books or grading papers, sprawled out, green eyes darting to me again and again with so much tenderness it still made me ache. After, in that terrible desert of *after,* the couch had sat empty, waiting.

And now Brady was there.

I bustled to the front of the store again and glanced out the windows at the river of water rushing along the sidewalk to the storm drain. I couldn't see anyone else around. Brady's car was parked on the street in front; for all it appeared, he might be the last man left in the city. The streets were nothing more than pounding rain and scattered, drowned spots of color from the leaves.

After locking the door, I grabbed two bottles of water from the small fridge in the stockroom. "Sorry I don't have anything stronger," I apologized as I walked back into the studio. "For some reason, drinking on the job is frowned on."

Brady was standing next to a canvas. The sheet was off, and he was staring at it, head cocked to the side. For a moment, a cold, sour feeling flashed through me, making me quite sure I was going to be sick. In three steps I was at his side, shaking hands tugging the covering back over the paint, hiding it away again.

"Sorry," he murmured. "I was getting rags to wipe off the table, and I bumped it and…." He rubbed a hand through his hair, expression torn between apology and something I couldn't quite identify. Said rags were in his hand, and the paintbrush that had been sitting on the easel was on the floor. I didn't doubt him. It was just that no one had seen my work since Aaron.

"I am sorry, Quinn." Brady was right there, hands on my shoulders, thumbs rubbing against my arms. I realized I'd gone utterly still, gaze caught on the white sheet draped over the picture. "It was beautiful, though. I'm sorry I saw something you weren't ready for me to, but I have to say, it was amazing."

Dragging in a breath, I huffed out a sound that was probably supposed to be a laugh. I rubbed my hand across my face and jerked my chin in a nod, eyes still distant. I looked up at him after another beat and nodded once more, surer this time. "It's okay," I said. "It's just a painting."

It was. It was just my work, just a part of me that had been frozen and forgotten for so long it hurt to acknowledge it. Like pins and needles when your arm fell asleep. Slowly, heart thundering louder than the rain, I reached out to tug the sheet away again.

The painting was nothing special, I thought. A knight, standing on the roof of a modern building, armor tarnished and bloodstained, sword in hand as the lights of the city winked out around him. It was a piece I'd been preparing for a gallery show, before Aaron had taken a turn for the worse. Before my days had become the sterile, antiseptic scent of the hospital, before my nights had been clinging to his hand, paper-thin skin almost translucent under my touch.

"What is it?" Brady asked, standing next to me, his shoulder warm and solid beside my own.

Sighing, I put the bottles of water down and wrapped my arms around myself. "It's a panel from one of my graphic novels. I had this character. The Knight. He was displaced from his own time, dropped into modern-day New York, and he became a crime fighter of a sort. The cynicism and horrors he saw gradually wore him down, all the idealism and innocence and purity he'd had before."

I moved to another canvas, this one propped against a wall. Turning it around, I revealed the Knight with another man, curly haired and bright eyed, their hands clasped, standing trembling on the edge of a kiss. "This was his partner, a mortician named Stuart. They fell in love. Stuart was the Knight's humanity."

"What happened to them?" Brady was beside me, crouching down to examine the painting.

"I couldn't draw them anymore." I shrugged, eyes dropping. The Knight was red haired and so *alive*, so achingly real. It wasn't Aaron's face, no, but he'd been my muse. In all things, but especially in this, he was my muse. "The Knight lost his last flicker of hope and there was nothing more to tell."

Brady was silent for a moment. He stood, holding the painting up to the light. Strong hands clasped the edges of the canvas so gently. His gaze was intent as he studied my work. "Is this what Annabeth wanted you to show? This series?"

"The Knight's Heart," I murmured, lips twisting wryly. "I suppose so. It's what I was working on, before."

"And you don't want to put it up." He nodded, carefully laying the painting down on one of the long worktables.

"It's not finished." I found another one, placing it next to the other two. The Knight fighting, his sword a blur of motion, blood and dirt clinging to him. Stuart was beside him, glory and love. "The series. It's not done. And I can't...." I shook my head, hands in my pockets, staring down at the paintings. "I don't know the person who painted these. I can't feel the story anymore. Every time I try to draw, it ends up as nothing. Meaningless."

After a moment, Brady reached out, drawing me into his embrace. I hadn't realized how tensely I was holding myself until his arms circled me, until I sagged into him. "Then you need to find a new story to tell," he murmured, rubbing his hand gently up and down my back.

I tried to laugh because he made it sound so easy. Instead I just wound up tucking my head in under his chin, reaching slowly, so achingly slowly, up to cling to his jacket. "Maybe," I agreed, softly. It wasn't easy. I knew that. But somehow, the gentle faith he seemed to have in me made it sound possible.

After a few moments, Brady tutted over the dust on my shirt. He fussed with my hair and led me back to the couch. We sat, knees pressed together, and Brady handed me my soup.

It was utterly delicious. Just enough tang and bite to chase away the chill, rich with vegetables and little pops of soft pasta. "Brady," I murmured, surprised, spoon dipping in again and again. "This is incredible. I can't believe you *made* this."

"Try the bread" was his only response as he nudged a piece closer to me, but there was a pleased curve to his lips that warmed me more than even the soup.

The bread was light, chewy, and fantastic. I actually made an obscene little noise as I swallowed, melted butter leaving behind a salty sweet tang against my tongue. "My God," I muttered, eagerly taking another bite. "This is the best thing I've had in my mouth in, like, ever."

The sound of Brady's laugh was a thrilling baritone, bouncing off the walls, dancing with the patter of the rain. "Normally, I'd take that as a challenge," he teased me, eyes crinkling at the corners mischievously. "But since it's a compliment to the chef, I'll just say thank you."

I rolled my eyes, too busy stuffing my face to quip back. "Where did you learn this?" Perhaps soup was dreadfully easy, and perhaps the bread was child's play to him, but to someone who lived out of cans and knew the corner deli staff on a first-name basis, it was wizardry.

"Catering," he shrugged. "And I've always liked to cook. Middle kid of three sisters, I spent a lot of time in the kitchen. My mom was from a big Italian family, my dad was Swedish, so food is pretty much how we show emotions. No matter what's going on, if you're happy or sad or in love, you cook. There's a meal for all occasions."

He was watching me with a strange intensity, a seriousness behind the smile that made my stomach go into knots. I didn't know what it meant, but I felt like I should. Like if I'd just turn my head, I'd catch the whole of it from the corner of my eye. "What's this meal mean?" I asked, searching his face. Wondering what it was I was missing.

But just like that, the moment was gone. Brady smiled at me and leaned back in the couch, legs akimbo, soup finished. "It's raining outside and I wanted to see you," he said with an elegant lift of his shoulders. "Soup is very good for that."

I agreed with a happy murmur, chasing the last green bean around the bottom of my bowl before I joined him in a sprawl. His arm stole around me, my head listed toward his shoulder, and the rain kept up its symphony above us. It was warm there, with him, side to side. I laid my hand on his leg and he found my fingers with his own. "Thank you," I murmured, rubbing my cheek absently against him.

"For the food?" he asked, so softly, so *tenderly,* it made me ache to hear it.

"Not just for the food," I admitted, tilting my head back to look at him. He smiled at me, and my lips curved upward in reply.

For a long time, we just sat like that. On the couch that was no longer Aaron's, in the room that was no longer my haven. For the first time, though, new memories seemed to overtake the ghosts. Instead of only picturing Aaron there, I now thought of the sweet tang of the tomatoes, the salty chewiness of the buttered bread, the way my body seemed to melt into Brady's side, the warmth of his smile. Instead of canvases telling a story I no longer knew, there was the hesitant sprout of something different. Of the idea of an idea. Of the hope of something new.

Aaron was there, yes. But right then, so was Brady.

"So, hey, I was going to ask." Brady's fingers were painting soft trails up and down my arm, leaving goose bumps in their wake. "I have this event next week. A fund-raiser ball, masquerade themed. Lots of formalwear and masks and fancy food. No soup"—I could hear the quick smile in his voice—"but I do make a pretty tasty caviar quiche."

It took me a moment to understand what was going on. To be fair, it'd been years since I'd felt this relaxed, this utterly content. I wasn't sure if that was a good thing or not, to let myself be so at peace with Brady, but God, it felt good.

"You're asking me to attend?" I blinked, a little surprised. "Uh. Well, I'm not really the fund-raiser type, and I definitely don't go to, um, balls or whatever. I guess I can make a donation? What's the cause?"

After a beat, Brady breathed out a laugh, pulling back just enough to see my face. "No, God, that's... I mean, yes, I want you to go. As my date." He gave me a smile, much more uncertain than his usual ones. "I'm the event planner, so it's a working date for me, but I thought, you know, we could dance a bit, have some good wine, you could eat my food...." He trailed off, already waving off the suggestion. "It's not a big deal. Probably be really boring, actually. I'm sure you have better things to do."

I didn't dance. Hell, I wasn't even sure I knew how. Aaron had owned exactly one suit, which he'd bought for our commitment ceremony and I'd torn off of him that night. He'd never worn it again. He didn't like pageantry or dress clothes that weren't from the pages of a history book. I'd been content in his casual lifestyle. To be honest, I'd never thought about anything different. I only had one suit too. I'd worn it to our ceremony and then again to Aaron's funeral.

"I don't own a tux," I said, but to my surprise, I'd started to smile. It was unsure, held mostly in my eyes as I looked up at him, but it was reflected back tenfold by the beaming grin Brady gave me. "And I don't know how to dance."

"I know a place we can get you one." Brady looked positively gleeful at the thought. "We'll go shopping this weekend. And I"—he took my hand, feathering a kiss to my knuckles—"will teach you to dance. I promise not to make a peep if you step on my toes."

We sank back into the couch, Brady still holding my hand, and I was smiling. We were going to a ball. It sounded completely unlike me. I was quite sure no matter how many promises Brady made, he'd regret trying to get my clumsy self out onto any kind of dance floor. But there was going to be a ball and tuxes and apparently some form of quiche. And I'd admit a part of me was looking forward to it.

"It's for the Children's Literacy Fund," Brady told me, absently playing his fingers through my hair. My eyes immediately fell half-shut as I arched up into his hand. I was such a sucker for that. "The theme is Unmasking the Imagination. Very fantasy driven. Very posh." He grinned, dropping a kiss lightly onto my head. "You are going to have fun. I promise."

He seemed to enjoy my reaction to him sliding his hand through my hair, because he didn't stop. I was practically melted all over him, embarrassingly so, but I'd be ashamed of myself later. Right then, I rumbled a soft, contented noise, happily leaning my head against him. "Weirdly, I believe you. Even if I have to put on a penguin suit."

"You'll look adorable." Brady's voice was warm, hot chocolate in the dead of winter, curling around me.

"Flatterer." The word was mumbled. I turned to sling my arm across his waist, the thrum of the rain on the skylights making it seem as though the entire world had been washed away. There were only the two of us.

"It's part of my charm." He sprawled down further, taking me with him. We rested together, his fingers through my hair soothing me into the twilight haze of the half awake.

"I'm going to fall asleep on you," I announced.

His lips were dry and sweet against my forehead. "Good. My evil plan is complete."

With a rumbled sigh of a laugh, I tipped my head up just enough to brush a kiss to his jaw. "You're ridiculous. I'm glad you came in out of the rain."

As I drifted off, I heard him say, so quiet I wasn't even sure if I was meant to hear, "I'm glad you let me in."

Chapter 4

"I REALLY don't think *tails* are necessary." No matter what kind of torture I was put through, no matter how much money was offered for the information, I would never admit to how high-pitched my voice had gotten with that sentence. "Or a top hat." Spinning around on the raised platform in front of the three mirrors, I scanned the shop for Brady. The fluttering woman next to me was busy measuring various body parts for God knew what. She ignored my increasing panic in favor of handing me a swath of ruby red fabric.

"It's a cummerbund," she explained off of my bewildered look. "It goes around your waist. Go on, put it on."

I did so dutifully, looking back at myself in the mirrors. The tux was pinned in places, the coat had buttons and tails, and there was a hat on my head that seemed like it was desperately missing Abraham Lincoln. In short, I looked like an idiot.

"Excuse me," I asked the woman who was gathering up her pins and tape measure. "Have you seen my, er…." I trailed off, because yeah, having a little relationship-status crisis in front of the no-nonsense head of alterations was not high on my to-do list. "Brady. The man who came in with me. Have you seen him?"

She just gave me a look, eyebrow arched, and jutted her chin behind me. Turning, I saw Brady speaking with one of the salesmen. They were discussing ties in deep royal blue, Brady laughing as they were held up one by one. He was in a suit similar to mine, but where I just made it all seem so ridiculous, Brady was absolutely breathtaking.

He seemed regal, somehow, moving with an unerring grace, charm in every step. I watched him, drinking in the absent wave of his hand, the waterfall of blond curls against his forehead, the strong arch of his nose. Little things, pieces of a whole, but even taken separately they were utterly beguiling.

"Damn," I muttered, continuing to stare.

"No kidding," the alterations woman beside me said dryly. When I gave her an amused look, she shrugged. "What? I can't look?"

Biting back a laugh, I shook my head. "I guess I can't blame you for that." He did look *very* good. She helped me take off the cummerbund and the jacket, shaking out the fine material as if to make sure I hadn't harmed it.

"Now that's disappointing." Brady's voice curled around me, tugging honey-warm curls into my gut as I caught sight of his smile in the mirror. "I rather liked the tails."

"I looked like a penguin," I informed him, but my lips were turning upward despite my misgivings about my aptitude for formalwear. "All I needed was a cane and I could have started to make evil plots to take down superheroes."

"You are such a geek," Brady teased, taking a step up onto the platform so he was pressed in behind me. My breath caught as he gently reached around, looping a tie around my neck and doing up the knot. His chin was resting on my shoulder, his body warm and solid against my back. I honestly might have made some kind of strangled, muffled sound, eyes flying wide as I met his in the mirror.

"It'll bring out your eyes" was all he said, but the heat in his gaze made everything else seem unimportant. His arms were wrapped around me and I found myself leaning back against him, the curve of his body welcoming me in. How he was looking at me sent little pops of anticipation all along my skin, like I'd suddenly woken up, like every place he was touching me was the center of all my focus.

"Eyes are good," I managed and he grinned slowly. He knew what he was doing, and I was hardly innocent. Pressing back into him, I was rewarded by how his arms tightened around my waist.

His lips brushed my ear. "We're in public, Mr. O'Malley," Brady murmured, and I huffed in a quiet little laugh.

"You're the one who decided to tie my tie like this," I pointed out, a blush heating up my cheeks. He looked just as flushed, but I could see the pleased smile, hidden as he bowed his head to kiss my shoulder. I was flirting. Not very well, maybe, but I'd never claimed to be Casanova.

In that moment, though, we were just two guys. It was only a moment, only our gazes meeting in a mirror before Brady stepped away, before I was fiddling with the tie, before the moment after that one took over. But God, just for that second, it'd been amazing.

Brady stood next to me, nudging my shoulder with his. "I just wanted to make sure it was on right," he murmured, giving me a wink as he straightened his jacket, turning to check the view from the side as well. I could verify that all angles seemed to be working for him.

"Whatever would I do without you?" My lips barely moved upward, but the corners of my eyes crinkled at him, a playful tone to my voice.

"Suffer greatly," Brady sighed overdramatically.

He wandered over to a rack, paging through the jackets until he found one to his liking. This one was without tails, thank God, soft and fitted. It came with a matching waistcoat, which Brady promptly set out to try on me. I tried to protest, but one elegant eyebrow arched at me and I swallowed my words back.

When he stepped back, I had to admit I was a little surprised. I wouldn't be winning any awards, but at least I looked less like I was wearing a *Masterpiece Theatre* character's castoffs.

"Not bad," he murmured. There was appreciation in his eyes that made my whole body shiver. "I think you are ready for a ball, sweetheart."

"I meet with your approval, Mr. Banner?"

Brady reached out, catching my hand and drawing me down from the platform to stand on the floor next to him. His fingers gentled through my hair and he smiled, so soft and brilliant I wished I had a rainbow of paints right then to try and capture a tenth of it. "Always, Mr. O'Malley," he murmured, and I found I wouldn't have cared at all if this suit had ten tails and a hat that scraped the ceiling if it meant he looked at me like that even once more.

"AT LEAST let me buy you lunch," I insisted. There was a garment bag over my arm, Brady carrying one of his own as well. The tuxes had been purchased, I'd promised to get my dress shoes shined, and with one last regretful look at the top hat, Brady had pronounced me finished.

Whistling for a cab, Brady gave me a considering look. "Do you trust me?"

"What, are we jumping off buildings?" I asked, a smile flickering across my lips.

Brady just laughed, a little thrill of a sound, and took my hand. "Something like that." We bustled into a cab, Brady sitting close, our hips bumping together comfortably. As he gave the taxi driver an address, I tried to guess where we were going. There were several delis on that street I knew of, and one decent Indian place. Any of those would do for a lunch.

Ten minutes later, though, we were pulling up in front of a wide alleyway filled with stalls, brilliantly colored awnings covering some, baskets and counters filled with food. It was a little farmer's market in the middle of the city, produce making a kaleidoscope background for the people leisurely shopping and tasting and talking. Brady led me out, grinning at my confused look.

"My apartment is about a block away," he explained. "I like to stop here on my nights off and see what looks good. I'm going to make you lunch."

Immediately, I protested, feeling guilty. "No, really, that's so much trouble. We can just go to a restaurant."

Brady simply took my hand in his, lifting one shoulder in an elegant, careless shrug. "I want to cook for you," he said. His lips curved upward slowly into a charming grin as he backed up toward the market, drawing me with him. "Italian mother, remember? I always want to cook for people I care about."

It was there, in those words, that little heart-stopping declaration. All the looks I couldn't quite figure out, the way he held my hand, the soft smiles that seemed to warm me from the inside, they had their birth in those few precious words. He cared about me.

It was utterly terrifying.

It was everything I wanted to hear.

Conflicted, I let myself be tugged in. It was only lunch. There wasn't any reason to be worried about a meal spent together. Friends did this all the time. And even if he did cook for me, I'd simply return the favor with a nice meal out the next time around. I couldn't let that sudden jump of guilt sour something good.

Arm in arm, we wandered around, smelling the fresh, earthy aroma of fruits and vegetables that had been tucked away in loamy soil just hours ago. The people who passed looked more relaxed than my usual supermarket crowd; a couple was taking time to taste some gorgeous late-season melon, and a mom and her kids were carefully looking through the peppers at another stall, talking with the merchant about what would be best for her recipe. It was a huge, vibrant community, flanked by two closed stalls displaying gorgeous cuts of meat and tempting sausages. Everything you could think you might want was right there, fresher than anything. Hell, the eggs guy had a few chickens behind him, contentedly milling about in a large pen.

"Brady!" A woman in a vivid blue skirt, like she'd wrapped the sky around her hips to fall gently to her ankles, was grabbing Brady in a huge hug. Her head barely reached his chin, dark hair in a loose braid. A grin that lit up the whole city beamed over to me next. "And you brought a friend? Look at you, getting out there. It's about time."

Brady rolled his eyes, flushing a bit, but his arm was wrapped around the woman's shoulders as he introduced us. "Maya, this is Quinn, a friend of mine. Quinn, Maya runs the place."

"You sell the produce here?" I asked, impressed. The stall next to us was overflowing with fall root vegetables, vivid oranges and purples and browns, a checkered quilt of them spread out over the rough wooden table. "It's really beautiful-looking. I'm not much of a cook, but even I can tell it's amazing."

Maya laughed lightly, and Brady just grinned wider. "I meant *the place*. As in all of it. Maya organizes the entire Farmer's Market."

Oh. Well, that was something quite a bit bigger than turnips. "Then *you're* kind of amazing," I told her honestly, and she squeezed my arm, eyes dancing as she looked up at Brady.

"Oh, I like him. You should keep him around. Smart ones are always worth a little extra effort." She gave Brady another hug before turning to me, kissing both of my cheeks in welcome. She smelled like growing things, like oranges and dirt and sunshine. I liked her. She was solid and warm and had freckles across dark skin. I thought Annabeth and Tracy would love her and her market, the way she had of laughing.

"Brady is making me lunch," I informed her with a slight smile, one that only grew when I felt Brady's hand finding mine, our fingers tangling together once more. "I think that's more than enough effort. I'm not that smart."

"Romantic lunch, eh?" Maya took my arm and led us through the bustle of the market. "Brady, have you seen Lawrence's peas? And Gerald's sons brought in the most beautiful pancetta with their sausages this morning."

I would have argued the *romantic* adjective, but I was being drawn along, meeting stall owners—Lawrence, Gerald, and Gerald's three sons included. We were discussing peas and pasta and a rich, creamy parmesan sauce; I was holding the bag while Brady smiled at me and shared a taste of the pancetta. It was kind of perfect. The peas, too, the market and the people, but mostly just us. Just the way Brady's hand fit with mine, warm against the chill in the air, how our shoulders bumped together and how his eyes would find me over and over again. Like no matter how many people he was talking to, laughing with, or seriously discussing the varied uses of kale beside, I mattered. He drew me in every time, an arm around my shoulders, a smile, the looks he gave me, and I felt like I belonged. In this hodgepodge little world, I belonged because he did, and I was with him.

Aaron had done the same thing. With his dusty books, he'd never been so absorbed that I wasn't given a smile or a small touch, a simple gesture to make me a part of whatever he was experiencing. We could be working side by side, both lost in our own thoughts, but Aaron's shoulder had been against mine, his eyes had found my own from across the room, and I'd *belonged*. Just that simple, just that easy, I'd been his and he'd been utterly mine.

Strangely, though, the memory didn't make me pull away from Brady. Contrasting the two wasn't an exercise in guilt or self-condemnation. It just made me feel warm. Like this part, the belonging, was simply the other side of that word. *Care*. If you cared for someone, however much, however little, this was what happened. You brought them into your circle. You held their hand and read about Charlemagne.

Or you wrapped your arm around them while you discussed the merits of early fall peas.

We left the market with more hugs from Maya and a bag fairly brimming with delicious fare. Brady hadn't been lying—his apartment was only a short walk away, a large studio with lofty ceilings and a huge kitchen. His bed was in the corner, half-hidden behind wooden screens I suddenly itched to cover in paint. Maybe, someday, which was a thought that both terrified me and felt just as right as the rest of the day. Planning for something more than lunch, for other afternoons spent here, for Brady more solid in my life filled with ghosts: that was scary. It was bottom-of-your-gut-dropping-out horrifying, and yet as we unwound scarves, mine still-borrowed cashmere, his catching on his hair as we laughed, and as we hung up jackets, I held onto it. That terrifying, exhilarating, hopeful thought of more. I held it between chilly fingers, and I let it stay.

THE sound of the knife slicing through the vegetables leant a comforting, steady beat to our conversation. "I don't care," Brady told me, one perfect eyebrow arching. "There's no way you will ever convince me."

"You're just being stubborn." With a quick grin, I stole a taste of the cheese he'd grated. It was salty, rich, and absolutely wonderful.

"No, I refuse to admit that getting a manicure is a waste of time for *anyone*." With a mock-horrified look, Brady dumped the peas and garlic into the pan where the pancetta had been crisping. The apartment was immediately filled with the most glorious smell, and I took a deep, appreciative breath.

Brady was kind of amazing as he worked. Every movement was graceful, like he'd planned every step in advance, none of them wasted. He chopped and stirred and tasted everything, adding a bit more of this, a little of that, all of it in the time it would have taken me to figure out how to open the bag of pasta. He was a bit messy, though, mostly because he kept rubbing his arm across his forehead without realizing he'd gotten sauce on his shirt. I'd now wiped off a smudge from his nose twice, laughing at him. It was a surprising dichotomy, the grace with the chaos. Then again, that was what I was coming to expect from Brady.

"Here," he said, leaning over with a steaming spoon holding a bit of the sauce, his hand cupped under it to catch any drips. "Taste this. Too much nutmeg?"

"Nutmeg?" I repeated, all but wrinkling my nose. But on his expectant look, I did as I was told, swallowing dutifully. It was incredible. Though the spice had conjured up images of Christmas cookies—not exactly what you wanted from your creamy pasta dish—instead it was a light note in the back of the sharp salt of the cheese, the cream almost light despite its richness. I hummed lightly in appreciation as Brady grinned at me.

"Don't doubt me, grasshopper," he teased, bopping my shoulder with a towel as he wiped down the countertop. "About cooking, nail care, or where to find the best coffee this side of 32nd."

"I still think it'd be a waste," I countered, going to his side to help him clean up. He tried to protest, but I just ducked under his waving arm and began loading the dishwasher with his cooking bowls and spoons. After a moment, he moved in alongside me, both of us fitting so well, moving together simply. "Artists can't keep nice nails, we're always chipping or getting paint thinner on them, or what have you. It wouldn't last ten minutes."

Except I wasn't really an artist anymore, was I? I was a washed-up comic book store owner who pretended he could doodle. Pausing, eyebrows beetling together, I tried to hide my sudden discomfort.

Brady's hip nudged against mine and I looked up to find him standing there, utterly still after his whirlwind of cooking, watching me. Leaning in very gently, he kissed me. It was barely more than a brush of a promise, our lips ghosting together and then separated with a longing exhale. But he followed it up with a slow smile, one that twisted heat into my gut and sent it soaring, a kite on a string.

"You are an artist," he assured me in a murmur, tucking a strand of hair back behind my ear. Reading my mind, perhaps, or just the expression on my face. Aaron had always said I was a book, easily read by anyone who cared enough to pay attention. "Paints and canvases don't make you one. It's how you see the world, and that hasn't changed. You're an artist." His soft smile broadened and he playfully clucked his tongue at me. "An artist with *horribly* neglected nails. Seriously, it's a tragedy. Anyone with hands as gorgeous as yours should be pampering them."

I hardly resisted rolling my eyes at the compliment, because seriously, who looked at *hands*? Instead I just prodded his shoulder with said neglected fingers and gave him a grateful little smile as I went hunting for the plates. Finding a nice-looking bottle of wine, I uncorked it to let it breathe while I bustled about, setting two places for us at the small table Brady had set against a window.

With a few deft movements, Brady dumped the pasta into the sauce and stirred it all together. He plated it while I poured the wine, and we took our seats together. The first bite had my eyebrows winging upward in surprise, fingertips touching my lips. "Oh my God, this is fantastic," I mumbled around another huge bite, far too concerned with eating to worry about manners. "Did you seriously just make this? I sat here and watched you and it looked so *easy*, but this is amazing."

Brady's laugh was a low, throaty chuckle, and he nudged his foot against my ankle under the table. "See? Cooking isn't hard. You could do this."

"I can make oddly shaped pancakes and scrambled eggs," I told him, taking a sip of the wine. "That's my entire repertoire."

His smile was slow and warm, slipping across his face like dawn. "I love breakfast foods," he rumbled, and all at once heat touched my cheeks. I liked the idea of *breakfast*, of lazy mornings and coffee and lopsided pancakes. For a moment, I let myself try to picture him in my kitchen, sleep tousled and barefoot.

It hurt. Just the idea of someone else there, in the space that'd been *his*. The ache of a muscle that hadn't been stretched, the sharp twinge of something waking up that I'd left alone for far too long. Aaron had eaten my eggs, had put far too much syrup on my pancakes, had teased me into wakefulness, and now he wasn't there. Instead my mind offered an image of Brady, of perfect golden curls mussed, of eyes dancing as he laughed, as we started the morning in the same space.

It hurt, yes. But like growing pains, like shaking off the ghosts and daring to breathe again. I didn't know if I *could* have any of this. If I should. If loving Aaron would leave me room for anything else. But the possibility was there, the still, small hope, and I couldn't help but wonder at its warmth.

Hesitating, I offered, eyes on my plate as my fork made meandering paths through the cream sauce, "Maybe I'll have to return the favor. Though nothing I make is going to equal this."

Brady paused, taking a drink, stirring his pasta on his plate. Searching for words. I was beginning to know him, coming to be able to read the little crinkles at the corners of his eyes, how he'd fidget with long fingers when he was deciding what to say. "I think perfectly round pancakes are highly overrated," he murmured, deep brown depths flicking up to find me.

There was a want in his gaze that scared me, but I didn't look away. The quick clench in my stomach, the way my whole body shivered—I let it happen. I embraced the scary *what if*, because what happened after had so many possibilities.

"I loved Aaron," I said after a long moment.

Brady's expression softened, his hand coming over to cover mine. "I know," he whispered. "I love how much you love him. I think it means something, that you and he had such a great relationship."

I laced my fingers with his, trying so hard to mirror his smile though my own felt shaky.

"But...." He stopped himself, feeling out the words, so different from his usual confidence. "But I don't think loving him and losing him means you should die too, Quinn. I'm not going to pretend I understand what that's like, what you're feeling, and I'm not going to give you some stupid shit about what he'd want. Truth is, I don't know. All I can say—" He ducked his head a little, finding my gaze and holding it, so sweetly and intently I immediately wanted to look away again. "—is that I think you're worth it. I think you're worth lopsided pancakes and soup in the rain and borrowed scarves. Okay?"

The table was in between us, plates of half-eaten pasta forgotten. I managed to get to him without knocking anything over, which was a slight miracle, and leaned in to kiss him. Our lips met softly at first, a gentle push and pull. But then, with a strangled little noise, I claimed his mouth, shoving myself into his lap so I could get closer.

Brady's hands slid up my arms to bury themselves in my hair, and I moaned deeply at the tug of him pulling me closer. We moved together, my fingers curled around his shoulders, our bodies pressing together so close there wasn't any space at all between us.

Tongue tangled urgently with his, I gasped when Brady bit my lip, then shivered as I returned the favor. He laughed into my mouth when I hauled him back in again, our breaths heaving into the pauses between. Electric heat stroked under my skin, racing through me, insistent and absolute.

There were calluses on his fingertips, and they painted a trail up my spine as Brady's hands pushed under my shirt. My own fingers shook as I tried to get his buttons undone. When I succeeded, I ducked my head to trace kisses along newly exposed skin. It was like I was on fire, like something had seized me with desperate *need*. I wanted Brady; I wanted that strength and the mischievous energy. I wanted his perfectly done hair to muss under my hands, those beautiful lips to go bee-stung wonderful with my kisses, the depths of cocoa-sweet eyes to darken with his own desire. I needed that: to feel alive, to feel Brady responding to every touch. So I reached out, smoothing his shirt off his shoulders, letting him tug mine away in return.

Our next embrace was like thunder and lightning and swell, skin meeting skin. I gasped softly, and he caught the sound in a hard kiss, arms closing around me, hands spanning my back as Brady tugged me into him. Rocking down against him, sending friction-skittering pleasure in every motion, I twisted my fingers into his curls. I tugged his head back so I could suck darkening, wet kisses along his neck.

"Bed," he managed, throaty and low, the rumble of his voice setting off fireworks. "Yes? Quinn, babe, do you want to go to bed with me?"

I met his eyes, seeing the want there, knowing mine mirrored the same.

There was no Aaron here. No fire red, no deep forest green. When I reached out, it was Brady under my hand; when I kissed, it was only him I tasted on my tongue. Nodding, I slid off his lap and held out my hand. Brady took it, watching me, worry there until I drew him close.

"Bed," I agreed in a rumble, eyes sliding shut as Brady teased his lips along my throat, as he dropped to his knees to press hungry, sucking kisses to my chest, my stomach, down to bump his chin against my belt.

We stumbled backward together, him with playful pushes, and I laughed as I sprawled back across his bed. Brady lost no time in undoing my belt, mouthing my cock through my jeans as he worked the zipper down. My eyes rolled back and I hissed in a breath, stunned as arousal slammed through me.

I hadn't been turned on since Aaron, since before the end. The idea of doing this alone seemed like a betrayal of sorts. Even now, the thought rose and I shoved it away, refusing to acknowledge the sour guilt that rounded out every jolt of pleasure. Aaron was gone. He was gone and Brady was here, Brady was kissing my hips, my thighs, slipping my jeans off of me and tossing them away. Not Aaron. And I wouldn't think about the differences.

Then again, it was hard to think about *anything* when Brady ghosted his tongue down the length of me. I cried out softly, arching my hips, panting little breaths.

"You're gorgeous," he told me, moving up my body to kiss me again. "God, Quinn, you're so beautiful."

I met his gaze, touching his cheek and sliding my fingers up to explore the arc of it. "I wish I could paint you," I murmured and he smiled. I meant it. If I had paints right then to capture the way his hair fell across his forehead, golden waves framing expressive eyes, a jaw strong enough to hold every kiss, every murmured word, lips that drew me to them again and again, the way he moved with such elegance, how his skin shone, dappled with sun, I would have stopped everything. I would have drowned myself in his beauty, over and over, until my hands bled with the colors of him.

Laughing, soft and sweet, Brady sprawled between my legs. He spent time kissing my thighs, the dents of my hips, wicked tongue chasing sighs and moans from me. Restless, I ran my hands along his arms, through his hair, anywhere I could reach him. As he lowered those intoxicating lips down to purse around my cock, his fingers found mine and we clasped them together as I groaned his name to the heavens.

Slowly he dragged his mouth up to the tip, teasing against my slit until I was sure I'd come apart from wanting. Down, then, again, Brady's eyes sparking in satisfaction as he watched me, my legs akimbo around him, his lips cherry bright against the flushed length of my dick. He swallowed around me, pressure and beautiful friction dragging me up. The heat of him, the wet tightness of his mouth, was like touching God, too much glory and too much pleasure, almost painful in how much I needed him. How I wanted more.

"Please," I begged as he moved on me, as he ducked down again, twisting his tongue and sending my toes curling. "God, Brady, you're perfect. Just like that, *please*."

And God, did he. Like all he'd wanted to do, like what he'd been *born* to do, was take me deeper, was suck and twist and stroke until I was incoherent. It'd been so long, and it was like Brady knew that. Not just the number of days, but the length of them, the weary aloneness of them he was now attempting to remedy, every second, one touch at a time.

When I came, it was with a panted warning, my heels digging into the mattress as if to spread myself further for him, like in those last moments I was nothing except my pleasure, insensate to anything except Brady. It hit me like a wave, white shocking ecstasy, spinning me up until I was so tight I couldn't breathe, until every movement of Brady's mouth was like brilliant torment.

Sagging back down, heaving in breaths around stunned moans, I reached out for him. For Brady, for the only person who was there for me to touch. I reached for him and found him and drew him up to me. We kissed, words lost inside of it, my arms and legs wrapping around him until we were all but one.

"Hey," he whispered and I smiled, rubbing our noses together gently, resting my forehead against his.

"Hey," I returned, trying, still, not to think. To simply *exist* there, with him, in rumpled sheets and soft skin.

I turned us, straddling him, considering all that beautifully bared skin. There was a faint trail of freckles down his side and I followed them with my tongue, experimentally scraping my teeth along his skin. I was rewarded with a shiver and a moan, and I smiled to myself, repeating the movement until the skin was pink under my attentions, until Brady was reduced to begging little whimpers.

His body wasn't what I was expecting. In the haze of need, in the soft space under sheets, between kisses, my mind was reaching out for what I'd known, what didn't exist any longer. So I hesitated, I fumbled, but in the end Brady's skin was sweet, the noises he was making drove heat right through me, and I managed to get his pants off with a murmur of appreciation.

It was definitely a sight worthy of driving any other thoughts out of my head. Brady was thick and long, the soft nestle of deep golden curls between his legs mirroring the messy waves on his head. He watched me as I touched, as I explored, as I bowed my head to taste him with soft flicks of my tongue.

"Quinn." His hand moved along my shoulder, strong fingers slipping along my skin, restless and needy. Brady was hot and full on my tongue, velvet smooth, and I moaned around him. Christ, it'd been so long, and I'd truly forgotten how *much* I liked doing this.

Sinking down until I couldn't take him any deeper, I wrapped my fingers around the base of his cock, stroking him as I feathered my tongue along the underside of it. My cheeks hollowed, eyes flicking up to Brady's face. *God*, he was beautiful. A jolt of pounding need hit me, twisting around my gut and sinking straight south. I had no idea I could get hard again this fast, not anymore, but Brady's legs were wrapping around me, hitched up over my shoulders, little moans and pleas getting lost in every breath, and how could I *not*?

For the first time since losing Aaron, I *felt*. Like everywhere Brady was touching me was suddenly, gloriously alive, like my mouth and my lips and tongue were *everything*, because that was how I was connected to him.

Vaguely, so absorbed in him, in touching and tasting him, I barely noticed anything else, I realized Brady was moving. He had reached down to grasp my hip, my leg, manhandling me until I was sprawled out beside him, until he could turn on his side and me on mine. His mouth closed on me again and I had to pull back to gasp, loudly, lips wet and blushed and already hungry for more of him. Even that brief separation seemed too painful.

The taste of him, salty sour sweet in my mouth was heady and addicting. He smelled masculine, like sweat and heat and need, like citrus and sex. I buried my face between his legs, begging him for something concrete—more than words, because Aaron and I had had words, beautiful words, pretty words exchanged, but in the end the words had faded away. I wanted to touch him and know he was *there*, because Aaron had always been there when I could touch him. Until he wasn't anymore. But if I touched Brady, if he touched me, if we tasted and took and gave until we were undone, then he was *there*. Then so was I.

My name tumbled from Brady's lips as he jerked around me, as I felt him tighten and thrust in my mouth. I followed, exhausted and exhilarated and coming for him. For the way he moved and sounded and smelled, for how he tasted on my tongue. For the way he said my name.

Chests heaving, bodies slick with sweat, we lay there in a tangle of limbs. Brady moved first, rolling over to collapse again half on top of me, face buried in my neck. "That was incredible," he murmured, kissing my collarbone, lips sweet against my throat. "*You* are fucking incredible, sweetheart."

"It was good," I said softly, sounding more than a little stunned. I stared up at the ceiling, wondering at the tingling in my toes, my fingers, at the way my body had melted into him.

"Did you think it wouldn't be?" Brady teased me, propping his head up on one hand. My eyes tracked to him, to that lovely face, and my fingertips lightly touched his lips, his cheeks, the crinkle in his forehead. Pieces of the whole I was beginning to learn.

His hand swept idly along my side and I took a slow breath, feeling it with every part of me. "I didn't know if it could be anymore," I admitted.

Brady's expression softened and he leaned down to kiss me slowly. We lay there for a long time, Brady curled up against me, head on my shoulder.

It really had been wonderful.

And Aaron hadn't been there at all.

BRADY was asleep. I was watching his ceiling fan move in lazy, wobbly circles above us, my hand half-tangled in the curls at the nape of his neck. He was passed out on me, arm slung around my waist, breath rising and falling in a slow, steady rhythm. We'd kissed and touched and held each other until Brady's eyes had grown heavy, until, in the warm afternoon sun, he'd stretched out and dropped off to sleep. I, however, was left staring blankly, counting fan rotations and lost in the maze of my own mind.

I'd just slept with a man who wasn't Aaron.

Never in a hundred years would I have thought about cheating. It wasn't in my makeup; it wasn't something I thought I could live with. So I wasn't sure if this was what everyone felt like, after, if this was a normal thing, to have your stomach in sick knots, to have that oily roll under your skin, undulating in aching guilt.

Yes, I knew Aaron was dead. Yes, I knew it was impossible to cheat on someone who wasn't there any longer. But I'd had sex with someone who wasn't *him*, and even though I knew all of that, it didn't seem to matter.

I'd had sex with Brady.

And it had been *good*.

God, I thought I was going to be sick.

Carefully, I eased myself out from under Brady. He rolled over, arm reaching out to lightly touch me. An adorable little smile slipped across his lips as he breathed out a sigh, soothing back into sleep. I watched him for a few moments before getting out of bed and finding my pants. I buttoned my shirt with shaking fingers, and I didn't bother to tie my shoes. Grabbing my hanging bag with the tux inside, I closed his door as silently as I could and made my way out into the street.

The taxi ride passed in a total blur. Before I knew it, I was home, again, going room to room in the stillness. Winston padded behind me, tail swishing as we chased shadows, as I looked everywhere for something that didn't exist.

The apartment was empty. Of course it was. Aaron had never been here; this was the life I'd forged without him. Why, then, could I feel his ghost everywhere? Why did he linger, silent and steady, just out of the corner of my eye? It was like all that emptiness, all that *stillness*, coalesced into the memory of him. Aaron was there, except it wasn't him at all. No booming laugh jolted my heart back to beating; no strong arms soothed away the chill. It was me and a cat and nothing else at all.

I wound up in the bedroom, one of Aaron's old cardigans wrapped around me. The sleeves were too long, the buttons hanging by threads, but I buried myself in it. Only the slightest hint of Aaron's scent remained and I struggled to capture it, to remember what it felt like to be surrounded by him, vivid, alive, brilliant.

Winston at my feet, the faded sweater engulfing me, I sat in my empty room without him.

I'd slept with Brady. Maybe that was forgivable. Maybe that was what I was supposed to be doing. *Moving on*, Tracy kept calling it.

I just hadn't expected to like it so much. To *feel* so much.

So I sat, missing the scent of Aaron, catching traces of Brady's cologne on my shirt.

Tears running down my face, I sat.

Someone other than Aaron had touched me. Had made me shudder and sigh and moan. I'd felt all those things with *someone else*, and even though I kept telling myself it was all right, it was normal, it was *healthy*, even, I still felt like I'd betrayed him.

I'd wanted Brady.

How could I want anyone but Aaron? I loved him. He was the man I was supposed to spend my life with; he was the beginning and the end; he was every moment in between. We'd promised each other faithfulness and caring, and now he was gone and I wanted someone else.

Even then, choking on my sobs, head buried in the soft fabric of Aaron's cardigan, I wanted Brady. And that scared me to death.

I fumbled for my phone, jabbing at the screen until I heard the sound of Tracy's phone ringing. She answered me with a smile in her voice, the soft noise of voices in the background clueing me in that I might have caught her at work.

Normally, I'd apologize, offer to try back at a better time. All I could do then, though, was shudder in a breath and tell her, voice breaking around every word, "He's really dead."

There was a beat, the sound of a door closing, and the background noises hushed. "Quinn? Honey, what's wrong?"

"He's really gone, Trace. Aaron isn't here."

There was so much worry in her voice, every word deliberate, feeling her way over ice that was already cracking under her feet. "I know, Quinn. He's been gone for two years. What happened? Talk to me, sweetie."

Heaving in short, stuttered breaths, I couldn't seem to get enough air into my lungs. "Brady and I... I cheated on Aaron. I slept with Brady and I wanted to and it was really good, and I shouldn't have. I shouldn't be able to, not with anyone else. But I could, and he's not here, he's not *anywhere*, and oh, God, Trace, he's really gone, isn't he?"

"Yeah, Quinn," she told me, so softly I almost didn't hear her. "Yeah, he is." A pause and she sighed. "Where are you? I'm coming over."

"No." Snuffling in a horrible-sounding snorted sigh, I tried to get myself together. I must have sounded like a loon. "No, it's okay. I just want to be here alone for a while."

She didn't like that, but she finally agreed. "Okay. But call me if you change your mind." Another long moment of silence and she added, "Brady's a really good guy, Quinn. I'm glad you two are together. And I think this could be something great, if you let it. I know it's hard, but this was an important thing. You're going to be okay. And Aaron wouldn't be mad."

Of course he would be. I'd cheated on him. But I just nodded and sniffed quietly. "I'm okay. Talk to you later, Trace."

The phone went silent and I let it fall away.

Chapter 5

ONE of the major benefits of owning your own store was not having to think of a reason when you called in sick. I just texted my staff—well, the three people who helped me with the register and stocking, but *staff* made me sound like a successful businessman rather than a guy who sold comic books—and curled back up into bed. I'd fallen asleep on the floor sometime the night before, still wrapped in Aaron's old sweater. The sun and the sharp ache in my back woke me up just long enough for me to crawl under the covers and sink into my mattress.

Dreams had haunted me all night, making sleep all but impossible. The idea of getting up, though, of showering and shaving and facing the world, was like a lodestone around my neck. I couldn't even fathom the thought of it. So I crawled under the covers and hid, like I was seven years old again and afraid of the dark.

He wasn't here. Aaron. He'd never been here. Some days, though, I reached for him. Some days I let my hand slide along the coolness of his pillow, the empty side of the bed. Some days it seemed like he was only just out of reach. Like any moment I'd feel his hands on my shoulders, a soft kiss at the nape of my neck, his arms around my waist, and I'd be home. I knew Aaron wasn't in these walls and in these rooms, but some days, I would feel him.

Today, though, there was nothing. Ghosts of ghosts, a shivery ache that seemed to clench at every breath. He was further away now than he'd ever been, buried under six feet of dirt. I stayed in bed and missed him with guilty, heaving breaths.

Winston shoved me out of bed. An overweight ball of fluff and squished-face disappointment headbutted me until I gave in, rolling out from under the covers many hours past my usual morning. It was afternoon by the time I made my way to the kitchen, numb and hurting, exhausted down to my bones. Every inch of me felt battered and bruised, but Winston had decided I'd moped long enough, so I was pushed from bed out into the world.

He curled around my feet as I walked, purring that odd rusty sound as he pranced over to his food dish. I fed him and declined to do the same for myself. Instead I sat at the kitchen table and stared. There, in a silly little vase, was a single leaf. It'd gone brown by now, the vibrant red faded, but I hadn't thrown it away.

Aaron had never been here. Had never touched these floors, had never filled this space. But Brady had. The borrowed scarf hung by the door, the leaf he'd given me with careless, windblown smiles was here on the table. Sleeping with him had only been one part of the betrayal. It wasn't just that I'd had sex with Brady; it was the scarf and the movies and the crusts of my pie. That I'd given him parts of a place Aaron had never been.

A knock sounded loudly and I jumped, banging my knee on the table and cursing at the jolt of pain. Winston gave me a withering stare, prancing over to the door and rubbing against the frame, rear end wiggling in excitement. Sure enough, Tracy's voice soon sounded from the other side. "Let me in, Quinn. I brought coffee and bagels with that ridiculous raspberry cream cheese you love."

I didn't want raspberry cream cheese. I didn't want Tracy and her kindness—with those concerned looks and the way she had of making me *talk* about shit. I just wanted to go hide in bed some more and pretend burrowing under covers was a perfectly adult way of dealing with things. But sadly, Tracy kept knocking, and I figured she'd probably call some kind of intervention if I turned down free coffee.

So, reluctantly, I stumbled my way to the door in boxers and a worn gray T-shirt, wrapped in Aaron's old blue cardigan. Winston practically darted outside when I let Tracy in, vibrating his happiness.

He loved Tracy. Tracy fed him people food, let him nap on her bare feet, and rubbed that spot under his chin. Winston was a traitor and a turncoat, perfectly willing to abandon me for the promise of a nice piece of cheese and someone to feed his foot fetish.

"You look like shit," Tracy greeted me, up on her tiptoes to brush a kiss across my cheek, wrinkling her nose at the stubble.

"You know, you really should get a job in motivational speaking," I told her dryly, shoving my fat cat back inside and firmly shutting the door on the real world. "Or grief therapy. You have that touch."

She put the coffee and a brown paper bag on the table before scooping up Winston and collapsing down into a chair. "Yes, because you're such a fragile flower," she snorted, grinning as the cat happily butted against her face. "Come on, Quinn. Sit down, have some breakfast. Tell me what's going on."

"You didn't have to come over," I told her, stubbornly wrapping my arms around myself, that ache starting again in my throat at the soft pull of the sweater against my skin.

Hitching up an eyebrow, Tracy began unpacking the bagels. "Actually, I did. I left you three messages, and you never returned any of them." Her expression softened. "I was worried, Quinn."

Crap. My phone. Which was probably still in my jeans pocket. Sighing, I rubbed a hand through my hair and wandered into the bedroom to check. Sure enough, my phone was blinking urgently at me, discarded in the puddle of jeans and shirt I'd left behind last night.

Scrolling through the missed calls and messages, I frowned. Three from Tracy, two from Annabeth, and six from Brady. He'd called twice and sent four text messages, the tone going from gently teasing to worried to flat-out concerned.

Yeah. I supposed disappearing from a guy's bed after sleeping with him the first time warranted a few messages.

Sitting down at the table next to Tracy, I studied the texts.

Hey, sry I missed you. You were fantastic. Mind blowing. Pls tell me I can cook for you again? ;)

It was good, you were good, everything was rly rly good. p. much best ever. call me?

Ok, now Im worried. Just txt to let me kno you're alive?

Quinn, bb, please.

I deleted them one by one before letting the phone fall to the table. Resting my head in my hands, I ignored Tracy's patient look. Yeah, right. She was like a schnauzer with a chew toy. There wasn't a force on earth that would shake her away from whatever she'd come here to say.

"Brady call you?" she asked, all innocent, like she didn't already know.

"Where's the coffee?" I grunted, ignoring the topic. Tracy frowned at me, but she handed me my cup and I took a grateful sip, getting up to rummage around for the sugar. Tracy never put enough in. Then again, I tended to add enough to give the average person a diabetic coma.

"He called me this morning. He's worried, Quinn. According to him, you just took off." She was quiet as I fixed my coffee, as I puttered around the kitchen, delaying the conversation. "I told him that didn't sound like you," she eventually continued, voice raising slightly, forcing me to hear her even though I had decided right then was the best possible time to reorganize my canned goods.

"Quinn." It was how she said my name. Not harshly, not with frustration or anger. Just so concerned. Softly, she said my name, my best friend, my oldest friend, one half of the tattered remains of my very small family. Sighing, shoulders slumping, I stopped fussing and stalling.

"I slept with him," I said in a mumble.

"I know," Tracy told me gently. "You called me sounding worse than I've heard you in a long time. You left without saying anything to Brady, and now you're not returning his calls. What's going on?"

"I *slept* with *Brady*." Like if I could say it the right way she'd get it. "We had sex and it was really good, Trace. I liked it. I wanted it."

Sighing, she moved to stand behind me and wrapped her arms around me in a hug. "Okay," she murmured. "None of that sounds like a bad thing."

But then she got it. Her fingers tightened on the fabric of Aaron's sweater and she understood. "But he wasn't Aaron," she said softly, and I hung my head, ashamed and guilty and so confused I felt sick. It was what I'd told her last night, choking on tears and distraught. Maybe she'd thought a good night's sleep would make things seem better. "God, Quinn, do you actually believe you *cheated*?"

"I slept with someone who wasn't Aaron." The words just kept getting repeated, over and over, in my head. Saying them out loud slammed the sound of them into me, a hard and heavy ache that clawed at my throat.

"Aaron's gone, hon," Tracy reminded me. "Wearing his sweaters and living like he's not won't change that. I know it sucks, I know it's not fair, but—"

"What?" I cut her off harshly. "It's what *he'd want*?" God, I was so sick of hearing that, sick of people giving me that goddamn pitying stare and telling me, all righteous and sure, what Aaron would want. As if they knew. As if anyone could fucking *know*.

"Even if it isn't, it's what you *do*, Quinn. It's been two years."

"Is there supposed to be some kind of time limit?" Anger was easier than grief; being mad was so much *easier* than looking her in the eyes. "Seven hundred thirty days, that's all right, but seven hundred thirty-*one* and you get your ass back in the game. Never mind that it was supposed to be forever. That I shouldn't be able to *feel* this at all."

Silent for a moment, Tracy just folded her arms, fixing me with her *lawyer* stare. The one that let me know she'd just stand there and *wait* for me to be done ranting. Sagging a bit, I leaned against the counter, exhausted.

"You're right," she said, very quietly. "I don't know what Aaron would want. No one does. Because he can't *want* anything, Quinn. He's gone. You're the one that's still here, that's still living, and every second takes you further away from him. You can't stop that. Not by hiding in your room, not by wearing his sweaters, and you sure as hell can't by treating people like shit."

When I went to apologize, she held up her hand, stopping me. "Not me, you idiot. Brady. Ranting, getting mad, that's what you do when you're trying to move on. But you don't get to sleep with someone and bail without so much as a phone call. That's not grief, Quinn. That's just being a giant dick."

She was right. I just wished she wasn't.

"I don't know what to say to him," I mumbled, staring at the ground like a scolded two-year-old. "It was really nice, Trace." Tears pricked at my eyes again and I wrapped my arms around me, the weight of Aaron's cardigan not nearly as comforting as it once had been. "The stupid thing is, he was great. And I want to call him, which just makes me feel like shit, because I shouldn't."

"Why not?" she asked, going to me, hands rubbing comfortingly up and down my arms.

"Because," I answered, and I didn't know how else to explain it. Because Brady was slim and golden and wonderful and nothing like what I'd had before. Because being with him had made parts of me, places in me, wake up to a world where everything I'd counted on was gone.

Because for that little while, I hadn't hurt. Hadn't grieved, hadn't *missed him* with that tight, pervasive ache.

"Because," I started again, voice breaking, "he's not Aaron."

TRACY did leave, eventually. She hugged me, and we sat on my couch. I wrapped myself in Brady's scarf and Aaron's sweater. I sat and she sat and we watched mind-numbing television and I said, very softly, through snot and tears, "I'm sorry."

And she said, "I know," and kissed my cheek. Because Tracy was my family, was half of the two I had left. My parents had died a long time ago. I knew grief. I knew loss. Except losing Aaron was less like losing a piece of me and more like waking up to find there was nothing of me left at all. My mom and dad had taken parts of my heart. Aaron, though, had simply blown me all to hell. But there was Tracy, still, and her wife, now my other sister. So she hugged me and forgave me and didn't say a damn word when I pulled that borrowed cashmere around my neck and huddled in, chilled.

Hours later, before she left, she pressed her lips to the top of my head, hand squeezing my own. "Call him," she urged me, but I couldn't.

What would I say?

I did, however, take the coward's path and send a text. One text, after which I hid my phone away because if I didn't see the accusing blinking light, I could pretend like it didn't exist at all.

I'm okay. Can't deal.

Two things that were so diametrically opposed I was half-surprised putting them in the same text hadn't ripped apart some kind of space-time continuum. The thing was, they were also true. What we'd done had been *okay* in the best sense of the word. It'd been awakening and achingly gorgeous. When I closed my eyes, I could see tousled dark gold strands; I could taste sweet skin.

Which led to the second half. I couldn't deal. I could not fucking *deal* with a world where Brady existed next to me, where I dreamed of his lips. Where his voice made me shiver. Where his touch brought me to life. I could not deal because all of that *okay* meant Aaron was not. That he was gone, really gone. That my heart, instead of staying broken and bent, had somehow begun to beat again.

"That was the deal," I told Winston somberly. The cat had given up grumbling after Tracy, who was gone with not even a can of tuna left to console him. He'd curled up on my lap, head resting on my knee. One plump ear twitched back toward me at the sound of my voice, the first time I'd spoken since the door had shut behind her. "I was supposed to mourn him forever. Because I loved him, I was supposed to stay that way. Like the fairy tales, you know? I was supposed to wait."

Apparently Winston wasn't very interested in what I had to say. He jumped lightly from the couch, stretched, and rumbled a yawn before he sashayed his way out of the room.

"That was the deal," I repeated, more softly. Brady's scarf was lying against the sleeve of Aaron's sweater, two blues, deep and dark against pristine sky.

Because if I didn't wait, if I didn't love him, then what kind of person was I? What did my whole life mean if I wasn't Aaron's anymore? If he wasn't mine?

The days passed slowly. One by one, petals falling off a withering plant, until it was Thursday, until the week had left me without so much as a by-your-leave. I hadn't called him. Tracy had, Annabeth told me, no recrimination in her gentle voice. Tracy had told him my head was up my ass. Brady apparently hadn't disagreed. Nor could I, really.

I sat and watched the sun make an arc across the wall, and I made promises to myself. When the light hit that crack, I would move. When it hit the doorway, when it slanted across the clock, when the fingers of golden-tinged pink, now, came to rest on the table, I would get up. I would re-engage the world.

But the heaviness never left my limbs. I watched and each marker the sun passed would find me sitting, still. Only when the world had gone dark would I move, aching and slow, and stumble into my bed. The next day started all over again. So the week slipped past me, and I never realized until I woke up on Thursday to a steady drumming at my door.

Somewhere along the line I'd showered, somewhere I'd eaten, but I couldn't quite remember when those things had happened. If it'd been yesterday or three days ago or in fits and starts somewhere in between, I couldn't have said. What I did know was that Brady's scarf was still around me, and I clung to it as I wobbled to the door, looking beat up and as exhausted as if I'd fought a battle I couldn't seem to win.

Brady stood there, looking perfect, hair in place, jacket tight around himself. He stood and he looked at me; I blinked owlishly at him, confused. My brain was still in bed, still watching the sun wander across my walls, and it took me a long time to form words.

"Why are you here?" My voice rasped, sandpaper against silk, and I scratched at the stubble on my chin.

"You're kind of an asshole" was his pronouncement, and he swept into the apartment past me, past any protests I had, none of which found voice.

I frowned at the now empty hallway, then down at Winston, who was sitting next to me all solemn and fluffy. "He's not wrong," I told my cat. Winston meowed up at me.

After getting myself together enough to shut the door, I followed after Brady to find the man in my kitchen, unloading a sack of groceries. A hanging bag was over the back of a nearby chair, and all at once I remembered tuxes and talk of a ball and rainstorms and soup. "Christ," I mumbled, rubbing a hand across my face. "Your charity thing. Did I miss it?"

Brady's face was completely inscrutable as he sniffed the milk in my fridge. He pulled a disgusted face and proceeded to dump it out and replace it with a container from his groceries. "It's tomorrow," he said briskly.

The coffee pot was put on, Brady moving around my kitchen like he owned it. Like he fit there, like he belonged, all his long limbs and graceful motions filling the place up. "Go put some clothes on," he told me. "Shower, shave, whatever."

Again, a frown creased my forehead, and I glanced around at his whirlwind of movement, stupefied. "Why?" I managed. It was the only question I could think of to ask.

Brady's hands stilled on the box of rice before he determinedly put it away. "Why shower? Because you stink like you've been in bed for days, which, judging from how you look and the fact that you've completely stopped answering your phone or going to work, I assume is true." He turned on me, in those perfectly polished boots, eyes holding mine.

It was then I realized he wasn't impassive. He wasn't remote. He was hurting, he was angry, he was a thousand things all at once, all reflected in the wide brown depths of his eyes. There was gold in them too, I remembered. Beautiful gold flecks that lit up when I touched him, that caught the sun and made him shine.

"Or are you asking why I bothered to show up when you so obviously don't give a shit?" His voice was steady and low, but he'd balled up the cloth bag from the groceries in his hand, gripping it tightly. "Because honestly, Quinn, I don't know if I can answer that. Maybe this is it. I'm just purging you out of my system."

A painful ache flared in my chest, and I found myself taking a step forward, searching his face. "Brady...." But I trailed off, because I still had the same problem as I'd had a week ago. What the hell did I say to him? "It's just Aaron—"

He cut me off. "I know," he barked, arms folding tight across his chest, eyes dropped. "God, I know. You're grieving. You're confused. I get that, Quinn. I'm *okay* with that."

I shook my head. "Then why are you so angry?"

"Because *this* isn't grieving, you dick." Brady's lips were thinned out, color high on his cheeks. And even though it was confusing, even though I felt like I was fighting through a fog to understand what was happening, all I could really think was how stunning he was like this. How alive. How he made *me* feel alive. "Having sex and then disappearing, acting like I'm nothing? That's not grief. That's just a shitty thing to do."

"I didn't know what to say." It sounded so flat. Sighing, I rubbed a hand through my hair and went to find a coffee mug, desperate for something to jolt me awake.

"You could have said that." His voice was soft, that harsh, angry edge fading. "Jesus, Quinn, you could have told me you were upset. That you thought it was too much. I could understand any of that. What I don't get is how you could just write me off, like I didn't even matter. I really thought—"

I knew what he didn't say, what was in the heavy sigh the words trailed off to. He'd thought we had something. Something tentative and new. Something born in borrowed scarves and peach pie. Something that meant hands and kisses and his mouth around me, my touch sliding along his skin. He'd thought we were more.

So had I. We *were*. That was the problem.

"I'm sorry." It didn't seem like enough, but I said it, fingers wrapping gratefully around the mug of coffee. "Jesus, I'm just so fucked up." Swallowing hard, I forced myself to meet his eyes, to see the pain there, the hope, the confused anger. I'd done that. I'd been selfish and I'd caused that. The least I could do was look at it.

"You told me once I kept jumping to the end." I took a sip of the coffee, needing that hit of caffeine. "I do that. I get all wrapped up in my own head and I don't look at where you are, where I am, what's actually happening. It was just... I really liked what we did, Brady. And that scared me. I shouldn't. I shouldn't want to be around you or crave touching you. I shouldn't *feel* the way you make me."

"Why?" he asked, frustrated, reaching out to cup my cheek, to push back my hair. His fingertips touched the scarf I was wearing. "Why do you keep freezing yourself off?"

"Because I loved him." My jaw tightened and I shook my head, wanting both to be closer to him and to shove him away. "I'm supposed to wait."

"Wait for *what*?" Brady gripped both of my shoulders, holding me there like he could somehow make himself see what I did. "He's gone, Quinn. He's never going to exist outside of the two of you, together, but you have to. You lived. And I know that sucks sometimes. I know you feel guilty you did, but the fact is, you can't wait for him. You can't stay there where he is. Every breath you take, every moment, it's going to push you further down the road from where he is. He lived his whole life with you. He was yours until the day he died. But that's his story. Not yours."

I'd started crying somewhere in there. Angry tears, horrible, wrenching sobs I kept behind tightly pressed lips, behind a throat that wouldn't give them voice. Shaking, I jerked myself away from him. "I'm not just going to *move on* and forget him."

"No one is asking you to!" Brady threw his hands up, pacing away and then back to me. "God, Quinn. It's like you died, too. It's like you wrapped yourself in his grave and you hunkered down and that's it. And fine, okay, you're grieving. I'm not going to stop you, I'm not going to push you. But there's a difference between going through grief and *wallowing* in it. Letting yourself become less of a person. You treated me like crap and you couldn't even see that."

"I lost *everything*." I was yelling, now. I couldn't remember ever *yelling* about this, ever screaming it out. My sorrow had been quiet and contained, had existed inside my head, inside the walls of my own mind. Now Brady was yanking at the scabs, making me bleed, and I lashed out. "You have no fucking idea. You just walked in with your perfect hair and your smile and some *stupid* peach pie and, what, I'm supposed to forget? I'm just *magically* supposed to stop hurting? Brady Banner's perfect dick going to cure me of my grief, is that it?"

"No, you *idiot*."

He moved forward, those beautiful brown eyes snapping, mouth tight and tense against more words. He was holding back. I didn't have that restraint. It was like something in me had been torn open, some dark, aching wound had been forced to the light. God, it hurt. I was raw, a nerve exposed, because he wasn't backing away. That much pain, that much grief, people tended to turn from me, to hide from the sight of it. Like I was a reminder of what would happen to us all, of the fragile, horrible possibilities. But Brady was looking at me, *seeing* me, all the hurting parts of me.

"I hate you," I whispered, but he didn't flinch away. "I hate you so much."

"No, you don't." There was hurt in his gaze, in the lines of his face, but he held firm. His fingertips went out, touching the soft fabric of the scarf around my neck. "I don't believe that."

"I do hate you." Moving a step closer, I was shuddering, almost sobbing. "Before I met you, I didn't care. I was numb, do you understand that? I was locked up and it was *fine*. But you came in and I *wanted*."

"Why is that so bad?" Agony, then, in his voice, rounded out and barely breaking through. "God, Quinn, why won't you just *listen* to me?"

"Because he's gone!" Why was this so *hard*? It should be the easiest equation in the world. It was me and Aaron. If you subtracted Aaron from that, it was only me. It *should* only be me.

Brady growled in frustration. "And you're still here! God*damn* it, Quinn, no one—" He grasped my arms, ducking to meet my eyes. Forcing me to see, like he did, to *look*, to connect. "*No one* is telling you to forget him. But if you stop living, then what the fuck is the point of breathing in and out?"

"I don't know!"

And with that he kissed me, hard, angry, our lips bruising together with a force I didn't even know I was capable of. I grabbed him and hauled him in when he dared to pull back; his hands wound up in my hair, and my back hit the wall with a thud. The fury, though, faded. Our lips softened, his tongue sought mine, and instead of grabbing hold I just melted into him.

"I don't know," I repeated, tears salting the taste of him.

Sighing softly, Brady hooked me into his arms, chin resting against my shoulder. "Then you've got to figure that out, sweetheart." He kissed my neck, my jaw, nudging his forehead against my temple. "Because I can't make you live. I can't push you into accepting your life. Neither can Tracy or Anna or, shit, *anyone* but you. All I can do is tell you there's something more for you than pushing everyone away to sit here with ghosts."

I didn't want to acknowledge that. For two years I'd stayed in my own head. I'd lived with the memories of what we'd had. What I'd once been. To accept even the smallest possibility of something more, of something *after*, was a betrayal. It had to be.

"I didn't mean to hurt you," I finally said, letting out a slow breath, hitching myself further into his arms. "And I really don't hate you. I don't."

"I know," he murmured. Just like Tracy. Accepting my apology, embracing me again, because sometimes I fucked up. Because family let you do that.

"I miss him, all the time," I choked. Pulling back slightly, I gave him a rueful twist of my lips, an almost smile that was too shaky to be full. "But I missed you too. And that's scary."

"It is for me too," he admitted, rubbing a thumb along my cheek. "It's scary that I need you so much, and I know I can't have all of you. That you're still working through shit." Brady kissed away the tears on my cheeks before wrapping me in a hug. "Just don't shut me out again. Even if it's terrifying, even if you're so upset you can't move, please, just let me in."

After a moment I nodded, relief hitting me. I clung to him as tightly as he was holding me, pressing my face into his neck to kiss him there, to whisper a "Thank you" into his skin.

"What for?" he asked lowly.

I kissed him again instead of answering, gentle and sweet, bumping our noses together when we broke apart. "You never told me why you came."

A little smile touched his lips. "Because you needed someone to."

Huffing a laugh, I reached out, pushing some of his wayward curls off his forehead. "Thank you for not giving up," I clarified.

He wrinkled his nose. "Don't thank me for that. I… well, I don't know *what* we are, but I care about you, Quinn. I think you care about me, too."

"I do." There was a lurch in my stomach as I said it, a guilty twist, but it was true. And I had spent the last several days hiding from it without much success. There was relief in Brady's eyes when I finally let the words exist, when I gave them form and substance. Like he'd hoped but wasn't sure.

"So, we don't give up." He shrugged, taking my hand in his. "Even when I want to shout. Even when it's hard."

"No giving up." Gently I kissed his cheek. "I can do that."

After a few moments, he pulled away. "I have to get back to work. I'm swamped with last-minute stuff and I have to spend the night cooking and—" He waved his hand, filling in the rest with an eye roll. "A thousand things."

"Can I still come?" I asked, eyes going to the bag lying across my chair, the tux inside.

Brady's expression softened. "If you want to," he said, looking actually *nervous* for one of the first times I'd ever seen. "I'd like that. I'm going to be busy a lot, but I'll have time to see you."

"Are you going to save me a dance?" I teased.

He laughed then, nuzzling his forehead against mine. "They're all already yours."

IN THE months after Aaron had died, I'd gone to the graveyard every day. Not because I'd thought he'd want me to—in fact, I was pretty damn sure he wouldn't.

My heart—he called me that, when we were close and still, when the world didn't matter, when I painted and lost myself into the stories only I could see—*there is nothing in the ground other than the dust of our shared pasts. Nothing in the air other than the fog of our remembrances. History is for the living: it's how we move forward, not how we stay back.*

He loved that speech. He loved talking about honoring the past, about how everyone was a part of history. *Even me*, he'd say with that infectious grin, eyes dancing. *Especially you.* Because I was his heart and he was my darling and we were in love. I was his future and his history and his present, just as he was mine.

So I went to the graveyard, not because he'd want me to, but because that was as close to him as I could get. Because the moment of laying him in the ground was the last time he and I existed together. Now he was *history* and I was moving forward and neither of those two things made sense. I went and I sat on his grave like my own little Poe story.

It didn't matter. He was never there. Aaron didn't haunt his grave; he haunted my dreams, the corners of my apartment, the way the rain sounded against the window. The graveyard was quiet and still, utterly without him. But I went.

After half a year had passed, Tracy and Anna told me I needed to stop. Aaron couldn't hear me there, couldn't see me. If he stayed with me, it wasn't in the shadows and the dirt of the ground. I believed them. I already knew where he wasn't. So I stopped going so frequently.

Still, sometimes, my feet led me there. I missed him like a fire, like a pull on my gut. So I went and I sat with him because what else could I do?

History was what moved us forward. I didn't want him to be history. I wanted our *present* again, our now.

I hadn't been to see the grave since I met Brady. Since we shared kisses after being soaked in the rain. Maybe I knew, even then, what would happen when I woke up once more. What it meant that I had so cautiously reached out. Shame had kept me away, perhaps, and fear.

There is nothing in the ground other than the dust of our shared pasts.

That evening, I went to Aaron. To where I put him to rest, where I'd stood, shattered and desperate, and watched him lowered into the ground. He was at rest, here, but I was the opposite. Restless, needy, completely *without*, I went to his grave.

I laid flowers down, fussing over leaves that had blown against the headstone. "There," I murmured to him, to the wind and the sky, to nothing at all. "There, that's better." His grave was clean again, fresh flowers almost garish against black polished stone. "That's better now."

It was quiet in that place. I could think. Only the dead were there to keep me company, after all, and they had nothing more to say.

"I'm not sure what to do." I wasn't sure how long I'd sat, only that I was cold now. Only that the clouds had rolled over the dying light of the sun. "It seemed so simple before, you know? It was you and me. It was only ever supposed to be you and me."

My fingertips slid along the stone, tracing the outline of his name.

Aaron Paterson

Beloved

"I feel like if I could just… if I could only take a step *back*, you know?" I laughed, shaky and low, jaw so tight I felt my teeth ache. "Just one step backwards and it'd all be right again. Like you're right there, behind me."

There was no answer. The wind whipped around me, making miniature whirlwinds of leaves and sticks and dust. But I couldn't hear his voice.

"But you're not, are you?" My voice cracked and I shut my eyes against the sudden rush, the sick, swaying ache in my throat. "God, you're not even *here*. You're in that bed, where I lost you. You're back there, two years ago, and I can't go back there. I can't ever get back to you."

I rubbed my hand along the curve of his gravestone. I watched my fingers tremble against dark stone. "I love you."

I'd said it a thousand times before, laughing or teasing or soft and still. In a hundred times a hundred ways, in mornings while we hurried around the kitchen, in the quiet space between kisses, in the sleepy, secret place under sheets and against his skin. It was a goodbye, said without thinking before we hung up the phone; it was a hello after a long day. It was our language, the two of us, the touchstone of a decade together. And not once, not ever, had I said it and not heard it back. No matter how upset, no matter how busy, no matter what else was going on, it was our call to one another. It was the voice that brought us home again.

I love you.

I love you too.

But now there was nothing. My words died in the air; they hung there in puffs of steam from my breath before falling into nothing.

Aaron couldn't love me back. He wasn't here. This was a marker, a place to lay my grief down. But it wasn't him. He *wasn't* any longer.

He had loved me until his last breath. Our last words had been that, just that, whispered with tears and desperate strength into the gasps of his dying.

I love you, my heart.

I love you too, my darling.

And then it'd been no more. He had loved me with his last strength, and I had loved him with everything in me. But he couldn't love anymore. Or, rather, the love he had for me was not one that could be felt or seen or experienced. It didn't make up a life.

Wherever souls went, wherever good, pure, brilliant people found rest, Aaron loved me. I had no doubt about that. But that love wasn't here. It wasn't in the ground, wasn't in the walls of my apartment or the ghosts of what had once been. It was, it existed, but it wasn't in his arms around me. It wasn't the sound of my name on his lips. And it was no longer one step behind me, just out of my reach.

Aaron was gone.

And I remained.

Lying against the cold ground, face buried in dying grass, in leaves and earth, I cried. I wept for him, for what I'd lost. For a life that hadn't been full enough, for that *one more day* we'd never had. He wouldn't want me to. History was for the living, was how we moved forward, and there was nothing in the ground for me now. But I wanted him, still. I wanted nothing more than to wake up and have the nightmare be over.

When the last tears coated my cheeks, when I was only huffing out quiet breaths, exhausted, spent, I finally let go. God, it hurt. It hurt to even imagine that tomorrow there would be no ghosts. No past I was clinging to.

Then again, the ghosts weren't real. The past was already beyond me. The only thing I'd been holding onto was pain, was that sick, sour guilt.

I finally moved. Brushing leaves off of me, eyes still red, throat still so tight and aching, I stood in front of Aaron's grave.

"I'm never going to stop loving you," I promised him. I promised myself.

Maybe that love could exist where his did. In that soft *after*, in the place where we'd find rest together. Maybe I could believe that.

I bent, kissing his name, pressing lips to cold marble and resting my forehead against the stone. "I love you, my darling," I whispered.

I love you too, my heart.

Chapter 6

"I LOOK like an idiot."

Standing behind me, Tracy rolled her eyes, smoothing her hands across my shoulders. "You look like someone who has a suit that didn't come off the rack twelve years ago." She turned me, fussing with the tie. "Don't be nervous."

"Why would I be nervous?" My voice, I was slightly ashamed to say, had ticked up into a register I normally didn't reach. "I'm just going to a ball. Wearing a tux. To see a guy who I think I might be dating now, even though I'm crazy. Also, I will probably have to dance. This is, like, a three on the nerves scale. Right under yoga. Totally Zen, here."

"You're babbling," Annabeth pointed out, finding the cufflinks I'd been certain had gotten eaten by Winston. Instead, the damn cat had apparently batted them under the dresser. Annabeth stood gracefully, taking one arm and helping me get the cuffs on straight. "You babble when you're nervous."

"You just hush," I told her with a glower. Apparently it wasn't very intimidating, though, as she just smiled at me and held out her hand expectantly for the other arm.

Tracy was messing with my hair now. She'd involved some kind of gel, and I already was pretty sure I was going to look like a twelve-year-old going to his first school dance. "Seriously, it's going to be fine," she assured me, brushing my hair back out of my face. "Brady will be busy working, so you can just relax and drink wine and watch all the fabulously rich people."

Fidgeting, I turned from them to inspect myself in the mirror. With my hair held back with gel and the perfect fit of the suit, I almost didn't recognize myself. I definitely couldn't wear this getup to sell comic books. "What if he's still mad at me?" I asked, voice so quiet, nervously playing with my tie.

"Then kiss him until he forgets about it," Tracy advised me sensibly. "Or dance with him. It's very hard to be angry at someone when there's music and dancing and formal wear."

"Is that a fact?" Anna was smiling, wrapping her arms around her wife's waist, kissing her shoulder. "I'll have to remember that the next time I forget to lock the back door."

"I'm telling you, we're going to wake up one morning to a hobo sleeping in our sunroom," Tracy grumbled, but she was grinning, turning to catch Anna's lips in a slow kiss.

They swayed together softly, beautiful and in love, and it almost hurt to look at them. But the ache was more bittersweet now. I'd had that once. The thing was, I was beginning to dare to hope I might find it again. I wanted to feel guilty about that. Instead, all I really felt was a twinge of nervous anticipation.

I got a white box out of the fridge and Tracy arched an eyebrow at me. "Did you seriously get him a corsage?" she asked, barely hiding a laugh. "Like you're going to the prom?"

"You are a terrible person. Also, it's a boutonniere," I informed her archly. She started giggling again, Annabeth doing her best to remain straight-faced. I ignored them both. Crazy women.

"Come on, we'll drop you off." Tracy's arm slipped in with mine, Anna on my other side, and we headed out, fumbling with coats and scarves against the chill. The night was clear and perfect, stars painted across velvet black. Shivering, I tucked the beautiful blue of my scarf— Brady's scarf, really, but somewhere along the line I'd stopped thinking about it like that—tighter around my neck.

"You really don't have to drive me," I tried to protest. "The bus goes right past the library."

"Hush," Anna told me with a grin, sliding into the driver's seat. "Like we're going to miss a chance to see you off. Don't ruin my fun, O'Malley."

"Yes, ma'am." I climbed in the backseat, careful not to squish the box. Tracy kissed Anna before they pulled out into traffic; it was a silly ritual to anyone who didn't know Annabeth, sweet but forgettable. Six years ago, though, we'd almost lost her. She and Tracy had been fighting, some stupid thing after a date, and Anna had taken off into traffic angry. The other driver had come out of nowhere, slamming into the passenger side of the car, nearly taking one of my best friends with it. Everyone walked away; the cars had been totaled, but some form of grace had been with Annabeth that night. Tracy never let them go anywhere without a kiss, like it was a talisman to ward off the worst. Like love could wrap someone up and hold them safe.

I, better than anyone, knew that wasn't true. But I also knew how important it was to believe it could be. Besides, how could anyone ever argue against love?

The outside of the library was a blaze of light. There were tiny twinkling bulbs in the branches of the trees that lined the path, fat blazing lights hanging from the eaves, and the whole thing looked like a reflection of the night sky. Annabeth parked a short way away, and both women turned around to give me reassuring smiles. "This is going to be fun," Tracy said and Anna nodded seriously. They both were so *earnest* it made me laugh, rolling my eyes heavily at the both of them.

"I'm not a kid you're trying to convince to eat his vegetables," I complained, but I reached out to squeeze both of their hands. I was indescribably thankful for their presence. This was something more than beyond my comfort zone. This was tuxes and dancing and *dating*, real dating, where I was actually going to try and think about tomorrow. It hurt, every inch of it, stretching painfully, uncertainly. It felt a bit like I'd started sprinting without remembering to warm up, like bits and pieces of me were coming to life again.

I ached. But I wasn't numb. So that was a start.

Leaning forward, I kissed both of their cheeks. "Get out of here." I bopped Tracy's forehead with my own, and she carefully tugged at a strand of my hair, being sure not to mess up her work. "I'll be fine."

"Call us if you need a ride." They settled back into their seats, and I stepped out into the chill night air, hugging my coat around me. The engine sputtered back to life and their car pulled away. I was alone.

Right. Okay. Nothing to it. Just one foot in front of the other until I walked into the *formal ball*.

Christ, I hoped I didn't fall down.

The room was awash in candlelight, soft music playing. I walked down the stairs, gripping the railing, desperately hoping I wasn't about to make an idiot of myself. There was an orchestra in the corner, tables with opulent coverings scattered around a space obviously intended for dancing. At the moment, people were mingling, masks on, sipping on champagne and wine.

"Are you Quinn?" A man appeared at my elbow, dressed in white and black with a deep burgundy bowtie. Blinking, I nodded, confused as to how I'd given myself away as a pretender so soon. He just smiled, though, and handed me a box. "Brady said to give you this and show you to your table. He's busy in the kitchen, but he should be free as soon as the second wave of hors d'oeuvres comes out." The guy was friendly, holding out his hand, which I took in an awkward shake, juggling the box from Brady and my own. "I'm Conner, by the way. Gotta say, bunch of us were definitely looking forward to meeting you."

I followed him, dodging around people in dresses and suits that cost more than my rent. "Why's that? I promise, my dancing isn't *that* bad." The joke was weak, but I was feeling more than a little out of place. And nervous, I'd admit it. A *lot* nervous to be out like this, to be so far removed from quiet nights at home or long days spent in a comics store. This was kind of not my scene. Even before, I'd hardly been a *party* type of guy, much less a *ball*.

Conner shot me a look, barely hiding a smirk. "You are the guy who's been driving Mr. Smooth Operator absolutely crazy for the past month. We even had a pool on whether you'd show up at all."

Oh. I looked down at myself then back up at Conner, shrugging. "Did you win?"

He laughed, holding out a chair for me. "Fifty bucks. Don't tell Brady, though."

"Don't tell me what?" There was that drawl, that cool voice that tugged at my gut, both sent butterflies twisting through me and made my shoulders finally relax. Brady came up behind us, clapping Conner on the shoulder, stooping to kiss my cheek.

"What an industrious and valuable worker I am," Conner returned easily, flashing us a grin. "It goes to my head."

He was gone then, twisting around the people like it was a dance in and of itself, disappearing into the back. Brady was dressed in that suit with the tails, a black mask just covering the top half of his face. He looked dashing and mischievous, hair a riot of waves above gorgeous brown eyes, and I found I couldn't help smiling back up at him. "Hey," I said, almost embarrassed at how easily he slipped into a world I was gaping at.

"You made it." Brady looked happy enough to make me not care that the shoes were pinching my feet. That didn't matter at all if it helped make his face light up like that. "Have you opened your box?"

Right. Boxes. I slipped him the one I'd brought him shyly while I opened mine. Inside, nestled in tissue paper, was a delicate blue mask. It had painted silver swirls, the whole thing looking stunning, like a piece out of a rich Renaissance painting. I put it on and tipped my head to the side, smiling. "So?" I asked, glad he'd chosen one that left my mouth exposed. The full-face masks just looked claustrophobic. "How do I look?"

Brady proved the benefit of our masks' designs, leaning in to kiss me lightly. "Perfect," he told me and I blushed, but the compliment was nice. Not even half as nice, though, as the feel of our hands lacing together. Giving me another sideways look, Brady opened his box.

It was silly, maybe. Overly sentimental. But I'd gone to a local florist and had them create a small, subtle boutonniere that had leaves instead of flowers. Fall leaves, red and gold, like the one he'd tucked into my coat the second time we'd seen each other. Definitely a bit cheesy, sure, but sometimes I got like that. And I was hoping he'd get it, that he'd see I *wanted* to be there. That I was choosing to spend time with him.

"Quinn," Brady murmured, long fingers carefully brushing over the leaves.

"If it's stupid, you don't have to wear it," I hastened to assure him, but Brady hushed me with a grin, immediately fastening the boutonniere onto his suit.

"I love it," he told me softly, drawing me in for another kiss. "You're amazing."

"Yeah, I really think you're the only one here that qualifies for that." I huffed out a little laugh, looking around the room. "This is truly incredible, Brady. I mean, God, it looks like something out of a fairy tale."

Brady smiled at the praise. "Good," he said, crossing his legs and leaning back. "That was the hope."

He looked damn good in that suit too. Everything about him seemed so refined, so cool and in control. Brady had always seemed that way, but here it was like he was so much *more*, like he'd settled into his element. I liked him mussed and on my couch, in my kitchen, but I was a little surprised to find how much I liked him *here*, too. How much that confidence fit him.

"Brady." A young woman appeared beside us in the same sort of uniform Conner had been wearing. She flashed me a smile, polite but busy, and I relinquished my hold on Brady's hand. "We're having a minor quiche crisis. Do you want to—"

"Serve take-out burgers? You have no idea, Gwen." Brady sighed, giving me an apologetic look. "Sorry, sweetheart. My magic fingers are needed elsewhere."

"Too bad." I tried for an innocent look. "I had plans for those."

I'd admit, it still felt strange, teasing like that. Talking about intimate things, things that were meant for between sheets and skin and panted kisses. But the uncomfortable twist in my stomach was pushed to the side in favor of the warmth, the connection. Brady's look was unsure, but his lips twitched upward, a hopeful expression hovering on his face. The last time I'd reached out, I'd also retreated just as completely, and he was hesitant. That was okay—so was I.

"I'll make sure to keep them safe for you," Gwen smirked, taking Brady's elbow.

"Give me ten minutes," he promised me. "Then I'm going to try and convince you to dance."

"Ten minutes," I agreed, catching his hand to squeeze his fingers lightly with my own before he strode back toward where I imagined the kitchen to be.

Left to myself, I dared to wander, coasting along the outside of the main group. It was like someone had swept the autumn leaves inside, the bright colors flitting around the floor in succulent fabrics, rich reds and golds and greens caught up in candlelight. The music was slow and sweet, an undertone for the ebb and flow of conversation that wrapped around the room.

It was enchanting. And Brady had created it. Every detail, from the heavy linen napkins to the gold-rimmed glasses, had come from his imagination. It was a side of him I hadn't seen yet, and I was suddenly grateful I'd decided to come. All the awkward dancing in the world was a small price to pay.

I found myself at a small table tucked toward the back, taking in the room. I liked to watch the people, to see how they mingled. One by one, in drops and trickles, couples moved to the dance floor. Champagne was being offered by waiters and I gladly took a glass, sipping it slowly as I waited. It'd been more than ten minutes, but it didn't matter. Brady was busy orchestrating all of this, and I was perfectly content to sit and let the party wash around me.

I did wish for a pen and paper, though. Something about the deep colors, the people in their best clothes and masks, made me want to try and capture it all. To attempt to find the story in the lines and curves and tones. Like many things, the idle thought turned into an obsession and I was mentally cursing the fact that men didn't carry purses. If I had a bag with me this wouldn't be an issue.

After a few moments, I decided the off chance of me actually *drawing* something other than dirty stick figures was worth a little inconvenience. Moving around the edge of the room, I found the door that seemed to lead to where all the servers and staff were coming and going from. This was a library, after all. Surely *somewhere* around here was some paper and a writing utensil.

The hallway was dimly lit, the noise from the party muffled. I could hear the music echoing in the walls, a muted memory of sound. Standing aside for another wave of servers with trays full of delicious-looking finger foods, I followed the trail, bright lights behind swinging doors beckoning me.

It was a kitchen, loud and brash after the hushed softness of the hall. The lights were bright and stainless steel gleamed everywhere. The kitchen normally served sandwiches and coffees to the cafe the library had added on a few years ago; now, though, it was a three-ringed circus. At the center of it, jacket off, sleeves rolled up, bow tie loosened, was Brady. He was barking orders and moving like a dancer, gracefully stepping around a woman at the stove, darting in to taste everything, chopping with such finesse and speed I couldn't stop staring. There was poise there, and command; there was elegance and strength. It was Brady as I'd never seen him, as I'd always known him, in his element.

He was beautiful, this man.

I found a corner, out of the way, and I watched. Instead of the candles and luscious fabrics out there, here there were pots clanging and the scent of things cooking. Here there was chaos that was controlled so finely, so gently, you almost couldn't see the steps. Every move was choreographed, though, every moment deliberate. They all danced together with Brady in the center, in a thousand places at once and each one exactly as they needed him.

There was an abandoned yellow notepad on the table, a few pencils. The first pages were filled with notes, but I flipped past, fingers aching to draw. To let the lead soar across the page, to capture a scene that was drawing me in more every second. I let myself go. I forgot the ball, the shoes that pinched my feet, the tie. I sat on the table, unnoticed by those in the kitchen, and I drew. It was bliss, to rip off the binding scar, to finally, *finally* pour myself out onto paper again. To see lines and blobs morph into something more.

I sketched with abandon, just like they cooked. Pages filled but I hardly noticed. There were smudges on my fingers, probably one on my nose from where I'd absently rubbed it, but I was lost inside the art, the creation, the moment. Hands resting on my legs, a voice saying my name, brought me back.

Blinking, I looked around. The bustle had faded a bit and Brady was in front of me, smiling in a way that sent my stomach into flips and knots. "Hello," he murmured in that low drawl, honey and milk. "Sorry, that took way more than ten minutes. I got into crisis mode and all neglectful and—"

Impulsively, I leaned forward and kissed him. It was sweet and easy at first, a gentle press, but then my fingers hooked into those intoxicating curls and he slid forward between my legs; his tongue teased between my lips and he was devouring me then, with a drawn out groan.

"Get a room, Banner." One of the cooks sailed past us, already tapping out a cigarette from her pack, giving both of us a look halfway between a smirk and a scowl. "Jesus, there's food in here."

"You're just mad because *your* boyfriend didn't show up in a tux and kiss you," Brady shot back, and she snorted, not arguing the point.

"I'll be back in five," she nodded at us, which I took as a greeting. "Don't burn the place down while I'm gone."

She disappeared through the swinging doors and Brady grinned. "That's Susan. Hell of a cook, even if she is prickly. If you listened to her talk, apparently my whole line would lay down and cry without her."

"Would they?" I asked, chasing Brady's smile with my fingertips.

"I refuse to inflate her ego any more than necessary" was his answer as he gave my fingers a playful bite, as he slid his arms around my waist. As he came home, and I was right there, was *there* with every part of me.

It ached, yes. Ripping off scabs always did. But after the blood was gone, after you'd cried and bled out and hurt, wasn't that when you healed? I had to believe there was something good after all that pain.

I think Brady could sense the difference, the way I was trying so hard to be present, because as he kissed my chin absently, his eyes were on mine. There was hope there, yes, wary and fragile. We were perched on a soap bubble, teetering between solid ground and nothing. What I'd done had hurt him, I realized all at once. Not just a little, not just an annoyance—waking up alone in that bed, having me shut him out, had hurt far more than just angry words and a rant. He didn't know if he could trust me.

There was a drop in my stomach, a frown creasing my forehead. "I'm sorry," I told him softly, tracing a path across his cheek with my fingers. "About before."

"Quinn—" He tried to stop me but I kept going, stubbornly.

"It was my fault. How I handled things was shit."

He sighed. "I know. But we already talked about this, Quinn. It's okay, we're… moving on." He nodded a little, trying for a smile, this one less brilliant than the ones I treasured. "And everyone is going to make mistakes. I do, all the time. It's human. We are human, nothing more."

I rolled my eyes, teasing him. "You're disgustingly sweet." But he laughed and I kissed him again, hooking my hands lightly around the back of his neck. It was getting easier.

The graveyard was still with me; Aaron's ghost was still there, yes, but this was so solid and real I was beginning to let myself see the difference. To feel what it was to be alive.

"You drew?" Brady was surprised as he saw the notepad and the evidence of my efforts. Flipping through the pages, his eyebrows raised, studying each sketch intensely. There were dresses made of butterflies and kings dancing with nymphs, but in the middle of it all was the god of the sun. He was brilliant, and he orchestrated the world around him with deft movements; his smile took over the page, beaming light down on the masses. "This is really good, babe."

A bit uncomfortable with his praise, I shifted, rubbing the back of my neck with one hand. "They're sketches," I dismissed, but he shot me a look.

"They're good," he insisted simply, flipping to the next one, a simple picture of him in the kitchen. There were plates and bowls flying around him, but he was calm, commanding, a captain at the stern of his ship. Brady laughed quietly, holding it up to study it in better light. "This one especially," he kidded, nudging a hip against one of my legs. "Excellent subject matter."

He was teasing. I wasn't, though, when I murmured, "I thought so."

God, that look again. The hopeful, worried, hesitantly pleased one. It seemed so out of place on Brady's face, like he'd gotten too skittish to be really sure of anything anymore. Instead of making me afraid, though, I found myself wanting to take care of him. To show him he could trust me to be careful, to match his strength. I wanted to be better because of him.

"I need to go and check on things out there." Brady took my hand and I laced my fingers with his, squeezing them lightly. "Can I interest you in some hors d'oeuvres and my charming company?"

"Who could say no to an offer like that?" I slid off the table and took his arm; we walked back out into the hallway. It was a rare moment of stillness: the music playing, trembling around us, the conversations muted. The staff was out in the main room and we were alone.

I stopped him there, and when he turned to look at me, eyebrows tilted upward in question, I took his hands and tugged him in to me. My arms went around his neck, his fingers curled around my hips, and just like that, just that easy, we were dancing. His startled look faded into a smile and I leaned up to kiss him, slowly, as we moved together.

"I thought you didn't dance," he murmured.

I nipped his lower lip and buried the noise he made into another kiss. "I'm feeling inspired to try new things."

His forehead rested against mine, and we stayed there, in the dim light, in the soft sway of music. I touched his cheek and he smiled; his arms slid around my waist and I leaned into him, loving how he felt, wanting nothing more than the strength of him, gentle and sweet.

"Come home with me tonight." I wasn't sure how long we'd danced—the music had moved on to other songs, the chatter outside the door had risen and fallen, and he'd relaxed completely into me—but my voice broke the quiet between us. He raised his head, looking startled by the offer.

"Quinn...." He trailed off into a sigh. "Last time didn't go so well," he reminded me, regretful, thumb rubbing along my lip. "And this is good, babe. You and me, we're so *good*. I don't want to ruin that."

"I'm not jumping ahead," I told him seriously. "I'm right here."

"What happens in the morning?" It was a valid question, and I made myself stop. I made myself acknowledge the tight hurt in my throat, the nerves that were skittering along under my skin.

"I probably will be a little sad," I admitted, cupping his cheek. "But I'm going to make you pancakes and coffee. We'll read the morning paper together and I'll steal the funnies and you'll suffer silently while I read the ones out loud that make me laugh. I'll miss him, Brady, but I want to learn how to do that while I fall for you." I met his eyes, wanting him to hear this, to hear all of it. Needing so badly to say it all out loud. "Because I am. Falling for you."

Taking in a low breath, Brady didn't move. His gaze flicked up to mine and then downward, those brilliant brown depths troubled. After a long moment where I was so sure I'd broken this beyond repair, he offered, quietly, "I've already fallen."

My heart tightened, joy and fear all together making my whole being constrict painfully. But it was good; it was terrifying and wonderful. Just like love should be. Just like I already knew it could become.

Leaning up into him, I kissed him. While the music played, with his arms around me, I kissed Brady Banner. It was scary and exhilarating and complicated, but it was *us*. And I was beginning to wake up and see the world enough to want more.

"CAN I interest you in a salmon and crab cake with caviar?" Conner was at my elbow, flashing me a smile as he held a tray in front of me. "Or perhaps a fingerling potato and steak bite with truffles?"

I gave the man a look. Conner had been given strict instructions to make sure I didn't get neglected, and he'd taken to the job with glee, making sure I got tastes and sips of everything that was flying out of the kitchen. "I think we've established the rules for the evening, Conner," I told him sternly, eyes wide as I took in the offerings. "I want everything. Let's not be bashful. Bring on the truffles."

Conner laughed, handing me both appetizers and flopping down in the chair next to me. He'd been working the room all night, making sure everyone was fed and happy. "I hate these cocktail focused things," he complained. "Sit-down meals at least have downtime. My feet are going to hate me tonight."

Brady was back working, and I'd insisted he not worry about me. Conner seemed to like having someone to come by and talk with every so often, exchanging gossip about the other staff and some of the guests, refilling my glass, and checking that I was never lacking for something delicious. I'd also met the rest of Brady's crew, one by one, throughout the night.

They were a good group, all of them fiercely loyal to Brady. I could see why; other than the stolen moments with me, he was working just as hard as any of them, ensuring the event went off without a hitch.

"So, am I what you expected?" I asked, almost dying of bliss at the first bite of the crab cake.

"Have to admit, you're not Brady's type." Conner gave me a critical look. "He seems to be more into that high-maintenance gym bunny thing."

Now this was the good dirt. "Oh really?" I asked, sipping my wine. I'd have to stop after this glass unless I just wanted to fall asleep once I got home. Look out, wild man on the loose—two glasses of wine and I took naps. "Who says I'm not a gym person?"

Conner laughed. Loudly. "Yeah, okay," he smirked, gathering his tray again. "I'm just so sure you're on the treadmill every day."

I thought about being insulted. I was too busy shoveling my food in my mouth, though. "This is all natural," I told him with an arch look. "And you really should only run if something is chasing you." Fiddling with my glass, I cut a glance over at Conner, venturing, "How do you know what Brady's type is?"

Conner hesitated before shrugging. "Because *I'm* Brady's type. We used to be a thing, a long, long time ago."

Oh.

Awkwardly, I just kind of blinked at Conner. He laughed again, patting my shoulder. "God, don't look so scared. I'm not going to go all crazy ex on you. Seriously, we dated for, like, three months a hundred years ago. We worked for the same catering company. He was fresh out of college. It was a thing. We were *so* bad together. Trust me, we're way better friends."

It was strange anytime to meet an ex-boyfriend. Even weirder to know it was the guy who'd been bringing me food all night. But I never would have guessed there had been anything between the two of them. It wasn't like I was suddenly boiling over with raging jealousy. I just wasn't sure how to respond to that.

"So *you're* high-maintenance." I decided to go for teasing, keeping my tone light. Conner gave me a flat-out grin.

"I'm totally worth it too," he assured me, hefting the tray back up on his shoulder and heading out into the room again.

Huffing out a laugh under my breath, I watched him go, contemplating. I felt Brady come up behind me before I heard him speak, and I leaned back as his hands came to rest lightly on my shoulders. I'd put my mask aside for the moment, as had he, and we smiled at each other in greeting. "You look serious," he mused, sitting beside me. I drew his hand into mine, resting them on my knee.

"Conner." I shrugged.

"He's been taking care of you?" Brady's gaze was sharp as he scanned the room. "I swear, I will kick his ass if he left you to starve. He's probably flirting with someone and letting his food get cold."

"Nah, he's been good," I assured Brady, raising his hand so I could kiss his palm. Brady's expression all but melted, and I got a warm jolt all through me at the sight of it. "He just told me you two used to date."

Brady blinked, startled, before he gave me a sheepish grimace. "Christ. I was going to tell you about that, but then I was busy and I didn't think and...." He winced a bit further, studying my face anxiously. "I swear, it's been years. And it wasn't even a *thing* so much as, you know, working late and going out a lot and way too many shots of tequila. There were a couple of months there, but it was—"

I cut him off, tugging him in to kiss him quiet. "Brady," I told him, holding his gaze. "I don't care that you dated someone however many years ago. You're not sleeping with him now, right?"

Giving a mock shiver, Brady shook his head. "Definitely not."

"So, it's fine." And then, quieter, "I believe you were going to tell me. It's an ex, Brady. We both have them." There was one question, though, that I hesitated in asking. But finally, I ventured, "Why did you ask him to bring me the box? And food and stuff?"

Rubbing a hand across his face, Brady paused. "He's one of my oldest friends," he told me frankly. "Whether or not I've seen him naked, Conner and I have been friends for nearly a decade. I trusted him to make sure you were alright while I worked."

It wasn't malicious or a test or anything like that—not that I'd seriously thought it could be. Brady might be a lot of things, but discovering he had a thing for men who worked out did not mean he was suddenly manipulative or cruel. Still, I relaxed at the confirmation. This was the guy who patiently stayed with me even while the specter of my dead partner lurked over the relationship. I could handle him being friends with a former boyfriend. I wasn't *that* insecure.

"I dated Tracy once," I informed him, arching my eyebrows over my wineglass as he snorted out a laugh. "It's true. We were in fourth grade, and she was the only girl I didn't think was icky. We kissed on the swing set, and then she stole my cupcake. I left her for my crush on Rudy Morten, who is now a dentist."

Shaking his head, grinning at me, Brady pulled me in for a hard kiss. "You, sir," he told me in a murmur, "are dancing with me. Right now."

We did. He made me feel like awkwardness was for other people, and I could feel him relax into us, into my arms, as we moved around the floor. I laughed as he described the process of making sure five hundred mini chocolate soufflés didn't fall even while your pastry chef was so tired he kept whipping the mayonnaise instead of the egg whites. He introduced me to everyone as his boyfriend, his hand on the small of my back and mine around his waist as we mingled and mixed, as we drank more wine and I didn't once wish for a nap. But mostly, we danced.

It was perfect.

CRASHING back against the wall of my apartment, I grabbed at Brady's suit coat and shoved it unceremoniously to the floor. His mouth was on mine, hot and hungry, devouring me while I was helpless to do anything but moan. I slid my hands down his back, palms flat against the soft fabric of his shirt until I could shove them down under his waistband. I curled my fingers around the gorgeous curve of his ass, nails digging in, and jerked him closer. He groaned into our kiss and my tongue tangled with his, both of us panting for breath when we pulled away.

His lips were flushed and swollen, his eyes dark with want. I stared at him, knowing I looked just as needy, that I was practically vibrating with how much I was turned on. His fingers fumbled at my belt and I helped him, our eyes locked on each other, tendrils of heat curling into my gut, hooking me up into dizzying heights of arousal.

With a low groan, he shoved my pants down; I kicked them away, leaving puddles of clothes behind. My shirt, his shoes, our belts, all scattered across the floor as we stumbled our way toward the bedroom. He was kissing me like I was oxygen, hands sliding across my skin.

After yanking off my shirt, he tossed it away with a laugh, with that beautiful grin, and I teased my lips across his. "You're gorgeous," I murmured, fingers mapping the curves and ridges of all that wonderful bared skin.

"God, Quinn."

We fell across the bed, Brady blanketing me. Heavy and warm and solid, he rocked against me, my moan lost in another endless kiss. His hand slid down my arms, playfully pinning them above my head before he moved to mouth his way across my chest. "Please tell me you're going to fuck me," he breathed, and I felt a shot of heat clench at my gut. "Because you're so damn beautiful, and I think I'll go crazy if you're not inside of me right the hell now."

With a laugh, a breathless, aching whimper, I rolled us over. This time I pinned his arms, biting his neck, his shoulder, loving the way he responded. I'd never even thought about *biting* before, but with the way he moaned and moved under me, I couldn't help myself. "I need you," I told him, resting our foreheads together. I did. In that moment, in all the moments since I'd met him, that had become truer than anything else I could say. I'd grown to *need* Brady in terrifying, heart-stopping ways.

"I'm right here." His voice was a low breath of sound against my ear. His hands painted trails down my back, his mouth busy drawing maps along my collarbone. "I'll always be right here."

It was a promise no one could keep, but it seemed so *possible* right then. So close with his hands on me, with our kisses panted between moans. I reached out and found the lube, the sad little bottle I had left. Honestly, I hadn't really thought much about this, about the necessary things; it'd been so long since I'd wanted anything like this.

"Shit." I pulled back, heaving in air, realization dawning. "Condoms. I don't have any condoms." It'd been nearly a decade since Aaron and I had needed them and until that moment, feeling the hard press of him against my thigh, the coil of want tight in my belly, I'd forgotten all about them.

"My wallet." Brady arched up to catch my lower lip between his teeth, smirking lightly when I shuddered. "Back pocket. I have two."

"We'll need to get more later," I murmured, and he smiled, fingers threading through my hair while I kissed my way down his body, reluctant to leave him alone. Finally, I made myself stand, him sitting up with me to keep touching me as I dug through his pants, as I found his wallet. Brady grabbed my hips and nuzzled into my cock; every muscle in me jumped at the contact. His tongue, clever and quick, teased around the base, darted up to the head, found the slit and sent me moaning.

Easily, I pushed him back, and he went happily, legs spreading as I ran my hand along his thighs. I eased one of my fingers inside of him, slick with lube, warming from his body. Christ, he was tight. I kissed him as he rocked back against me, eager and wanting. It took a great deal of effort to hold back, to make myself go slow. I didn't know how long it'd been for him, but this was something far bigger than *sex*, than just fucking. This was us, for the first time; it was me in the moment.

Aaron wasn't there. He hadn't been the last time, either. The difference was, this time I wasn't looking for him.

Two fingers, now, scissoring in and out of him. I watched his face as he moaned for me, as his head fell back, as his body arched into me. It was intoxicating. He was lean and long, the blond trail from his belly button to his cock becoming my new favorite thing to tease my teeth against, his legs spreading wider, as if he could take all of me in. As if he wanted nothing more than this.

I kissed his thighs and he groaned my name. "I'm ready," he panted, teeth gritted together. "Fuck, Quinn, I'm ready. Stop teasing."

I laughed. Startled and, God, so *free*, I laughed, feathering kisses against his hips. "So impatient," I murmured, and he growled, but his hands running along my shoulders were gentle. His eyes, when I met them, were achingly sweet. He wanted me, just like this. He wanted us.

God, I did too.

Easing inside of him, I almost lost it altogether. He was heat—more than heat, he was fire. He was the god of the sun, burning me up with need. Every inch I sank into him, I lost myself more into the glorious joining of *us*. I gave myself up to worshiping him. "You're perfect," I murmured against his neck, panting hoarsely, scattering kisses anywhere I could reach. "God, Brady."

His legs wrapped around my waist and we moved together, slow at first, gentle rocks of our hips as he turned his head to find mine, as we kissed, as his tongue teased into my mouth and I was utterly his. The languid pace, though, couldn't last. Not with Brady looking the way he did, feeling as tight and hot. He hands urged me on, fingers digging into my back, and I moaned against his lips.

Bracing my arms on either side of his head, I moved faster. Harder. Deeper. I took him and he took me, and looking down, I wasn't sure which part was only mine and which was only his any longer. Every second pleasure raced deeper. Every moment it was like I was burning up with need. He was kissing me, I was lost in the sensations, and the bed was shaking with how hard we were fucking together.

He came with a near-silent cry, a whimper as his head fell back, eyes falling shut. I watched as the blush coiled along his skin, as his legs shook and his hands grasped at my shoulders. He tightened around me and I couldn't help but follow.

"Brady."

I sagged down against him, heart racing, lost in the blaze of pleasure, the pounding bliss of the aftermath. We sank into one another, arms wrapped tight, barely able to move. For a long time, there was nothing but that, but sweat-slicked skin, but his breath stirring my hair, but the bass throb of my heart and the little jolts of pleasure through my veins.

"Christ." I barely managed to roll off of him and Brady followed me over until we were lying side by side. We just *looked* at one another, and I contemplated the flecks of hazel in his eyes, the satisfied curve of his lips. My fingertips explored his cheeks, his jaw, the crinkles at the corners of his eyes.

I didn't feel guilty. I felt sad, a little. More than a little. Like I'd shut a door I couldn't bear to see left behind. But Brady's arms were around me, and he smiled, just for me. And the sadness wasn't unbearable. It simply was, the pull of a scar, of newly healing skin.

"Hey," I whispered and Brady huffed out a little laugh, quiet and still, kissing the tip of my nose.

"Hello, sweetheart."

Chapter 7

SUNLIGHT, warm and golden, flitted across my eyelids. Slowly it coaxed me back to wakefulness, the haze of sleep being gently replaced by the weight of a certain enormous fluffball on my feet, by the comforting press of someone tight against my back. Brady's arm was slung across my waist, his head buried into my shoulder, and the man was still sleeping soundly, filling my bed with his solid presence. There was warmth, there, and weight; there was the undeniable idea that *I was not alone.*

Smiling faintly, I turned, grin growing as Brady snorted irritably, as he nuzzled into my chest and his arms tightened around me. Apparently Brady was not a morning person. Kissing his forehead, I amused myself with teasing the wayward curls back from his face, studying him as he slept. His features were relaxed and content; he sighed softly, a smile easing across his lips.

We were there, in bed, to greet the morning. The other pillow was rumpled, the sheets were tangled around us, Brady's legs were laced with mine. It was so achingly normal, so perfectly domestic, and I wanted to soak it in.

Winston heaved out a long-suffering meow and nudged his way up between us, rudely shoving his face into Brady's. I choked back a laugh as Brady woke with a start, blinking widely and staring around himself. Winston chirped at him, nudging his face again, then mine, before prancing off.

"Morning," I murmured, kissing his startled expression. I could feel his smile bloom under it and he trailed his fingers through my hair, happily turning us so I was sprawled underneath him while he deepened the kiss.

"You're here," he whispered, lips trailing along my jaw, back to my mouth, before he rested his forehead against mine, eyes drinking me in.

"I'm here," I agreed, brushing my fingers along his cheek. "As is my cat."

Brady snorted out a laugh, nuzzling his nose against mine. He was sleepy and warm and cuddled close; I couldn't find too many things to complain about at that moment. Even my giant prissy diva of a cat was a special kind of wonderful right then. We kissed again, slowly, and morning breath didn't seem to matter so much. Not when I felt so decadently lazy. Not when Brady's fingertips were sliding along my side.

"Are you sad?" he asked quietly, pulling back just enough to see my face.

I considered the question. I'd told him I would be; whatever else I'd learned over the past few weeks, I knew hiding myself away was the least-favorable option. Brady, for reasons I hadn't quite grasped yet, *wanted* to be here. With my ghosts, with my grief, with my cat and my haunted apartment, he wanted me. I wasn't going to take that lightly.

"Yeah," I admitted, lips curved up ruefully. I let the next kiss linger, though, nudging my forehead against his. "But I'm starting to be happy too."

His smile was quiet but I clung to it, the soft, sweet swell of sunshine hovering between us. "You make me so happy, Quinn. Just like this, I'm happier than I've ever been."

"Even if I still miss him?" I knew the answer, I thought. I just needed to hear it, while we were like this. I needed to know Aaron was still a part of me, even if he wasn't the whole any longer.

"Babe, you wouldn't be you if you stopped missing him completely." Brady's hand gentled through my hair to land lightly curved around my neck, thumb stroking just under my jaw. "He was part of you. You'll always feel that loss. I just…." He trailed off, worrying his lower lip. Insecurity seemed so strange on him, so utterly foreign after his graceful confidence. "I don't want to push you. But I'm selfish, Quinn. I want a part of your life. I want…." Brady breathed out a quick, helpless laugh. "Shit, I want *this*. I want us. There has to be a way for you to be both things. To be someone who misses him and someone who… someone who wants me too."

There was an instinct to rush to reassure him. To make him promises, to press pretty words between us and hold them there. But I could feel that tightness at my throat, the ache that hadn't died down no matter how much I'd wished it to, warring right alongside the urge to gather Brady close and hold on. Aaron had been the largest piece of me for so long; even if I wanted to give that to Brady, I didn't know if it would be that simple. If it *should* be that simple.

"I can't promise I'll be easy to live with," I finally began, eyes down on our hands, which had laced together, before coming back up to his face. "And I can't promise I won't have moments, days, when missing him is all I can do. I lost my way, Brady."

"I know," he started, but I shushed him with a kiss, needing to say this. Desperately wanting to.

"What I can tell you," I murmured, forehead resting against his, eyes closed as I sorted through every word and made sure all of it was true, "is that I want you. That when I said I was falling for you, I meant it. That I need you in my life, more than I think you realize. And I'm going to mess up. I'm going to stumble." Sighing softly, I cupped his cheek. "I went to the graveyard the other night. After you came to see me."

He pulled back a little, startled, searching my eyes. "Are you all right?" he asked, so tenderly I nearly drowned in it. In him.

Nodding, I tightened my hold on his fingers. "I… I needed to tell him. He's not there, I know he's not, but I don't know. I needed the symbolism, I guess?" One shoulder lifted in a shrug. "Before, when you and I were together, I felt like I was cheating. Like I didn't deserve to feel happy with someone else. And you needed someone better than that, someone who could be more."

My words were thick around the sharp hurt in my chest, the tight grasp the past and the scary prospect of the future had on me. But I didn't flinch away. "I think I stayed there, in all the grief and... and everything. I think I did it because it was easier. It's easier to wallow in that than it is to wake up in the morning and realize he's not coming back. And it's easier to say *that* than it is to finish the sentence." I touched my fingers to his cheek, his jaw, looking for the light in those beautiful brown eyes that said he understood. "He's not coming back, but I have to keep going."

Brady exhaled slowly, eyes closing for a moment before he wrapped me up in his arms. "I love you," he whispered, and I shivered at the words, at what they meant. At how big and huge and terrifying, at how small and simple and hopeful.

Before I could try and say anything, before I could sort through the rush of emotions, Brady nudged my shoulder lightly with his chin. "Don't even think about it, O'Malley," he murmured, and I could feel his smile against my skin. "I just wanted to say it. I don't need you to say anything back."

Relaxing into him, I nodded. I couldn't yet. I wanted to. I felt myself craving that word, knowing Brady was worth giving it to. But not yet. I was still too raw to offer that part of me.

We wound up eventually moving out of the bed after Winston had come to complain at us a second time. He curled up happily in Brady's arms as we padded out to the kitchen, Brady's boxers slung low on his hips and definitely a nice sight to wake up to. I showed Brady where the cat food was and he took care of the obviously starving to death drama queen while I started up the coffeemaker and banged around for a large pan.

"What are you doing, Mr. Industrious?" Brady's arms wrapped around me, his chin resting on my shoulder as he watched me carefully mixing flour and sugar and eggs. "Why I do declare"—his Southern accent was terrible, but he did it with gusto—"are you *cooking* for little old me?"

"I promised you pancakes," I reminded him archly. "Coffee should be ready soon. Is His Royal Butterball fed?"

"Apparently he was only minutes from wasting away," Brady informed me seriously. "We were lucky, this time, to save him from a food coma."

"Yes, he is so neglected." Said abused cat was currently winding around our legs, purring loudly. His squished face turned up to me, eyes blinking closed as he kneaded the ground, doing a little happy wiggle. "And he's definitely not getting pancakes."

"You're such a hardass." Brady kissed my neck and I leaned back against him, taking a moment just to bask. I liked basking.

"That's me." Nudging him toward the coffee, I laughed at his pout, turning to brush my lips against his cheek. "Go. Have coffee. Let me cook."

It was quiet and simple, the two of us. The sun was warming the room, shining through the window. There was the soft clink of dishes as Brady made coffee for us both, as I dropped the pancake batter into the heated pan, and I felt content. I felt like I'd woken up, finally, like I could see a life that was bigger than haunted rooms and empty beds.

I felt like maybe Aaron was with me, arms wrapped around me, nudging me forward.

History is for the living, my heart.

My pancakes were, as promised, horribly misshapen. But Brady ate four and proclaimed them delicious. Winston wound up on his bare feet as we sat at the table, happily sleeping. Brady stole the paper but granted me the funny pages first, grinning at me as I laughed. Our hands wound up twined together as we sat in comfortable silence, as we greeted the day together.

A loud ring blared into the stillness, startling me. Brady cursed, nudging Winston up, digging through the scattered piles of clothes for his pants. "It's probably my crew," he said, finally finding his phone. "Yeah. Hang on, babe, I need to take this."

He walked a few steps away, just enough to give himself a little privacy. I caught the soft hum of the conversation, but I let it wash over me while I gathered our dishes, as I refilled our coffee. He came around the corner, looking positively sheepish. "I'm so sorry. I need to go in."

"At…." I checked the clock, a little surprised by how early it was. "Quarter after nine on a Sunday?"

"Yeah, well." He looked embarrassed, rubbing the back of his neck. "Normally, after big events there's a lot of cleanup, but I kind of, you know. Left early last night. With you."

I paused, mug halfway to my lips. Quirking up an eyebrow, I studied him. "That's kind of horribly adorable," I decided, fingers curling under the waistband of his boxers to tug him forward into a kiss. "You are the worst boss."

"I really am." His breath caught in his throat when I nipped his lower lip, and he took my mug out of my hand to set aside while he backed me up against the counter. "I'm such a slacker."

I nodded in agreement, brushing our mouths together again, grinning widely when his hands slid under my boxers to curve around my ass. He pulled me into him and we met in a long, slow kiss. Brady bent me back over the counter, and I wound my fingers into his hair, tasting syrup and coffee and *him*.

"Crap." He pulled back but I moved with him, feathering kisses along his jaw, his lips, the curve of his nose. "I actually do need to go. But, uh…." He kissed me again and for another few moments that was all there was. "Dinner tonight?" he managed, breathless, and I nodded.

"My place or yours?"

That beautiful smile bloomed across his face, and he rested his forehead against mine. "How about mine? I've got the makings of a frittata and a bottle of white I think you'll like. Maybe about six?" His phone rang again and he pulled away with a groan. "Okay. I'm going to go use the shower, if that's okay?"

"Towels are in the linen closet," I agreed. "Though I kind of think you're going to be overdressed?" A quick laugh escaped me at his crestfallen look; his tux had been incredible last night, but probably showing up to work in it would send the wrong message.

I playfully pushed him toward the bathroom. "Go. Shower. I'll get you something of mine to wear."

My closet, though large enough to fit a dresser in along with lots of shelves Tracy had helped me install, was slightly better than disorganized. I did manage to find a pair of jeans and a T-shirt I was pretty sure would fit Brady. He was a little taller than me, but my shoulders were broader, and I thought they would do in a pinch. Shifting through my drawers for clean boxers, I paused.

There was a box on my dresser labeled "Aaron's Clothes." A few of his cardigans hung next to my own sweaters, but the rest of his things were packed away. I'd tried so hard when I first moved in to get rid of them. The best I could do was put them away in the closet and try not to give in to the urge to pull them all out again. To bury myself in the remnants of him.

Eyes closing against the sudden burn, the twist in my throat, I tried to remember to breathe. To not break down. It seemed so *stupid*, to be standing there holding clothes for the guy I was now seeing while Aaron's things were in a box. It seemed impossible I could begin to be happy without him. It seemed petty and wrong.

Could he wear the clothes, though? The things I'd packed away? As much as it hurt, Aaron was beyond any of that now.

Clutching the clothes I'd found for Brady, tears in my eyes, I very firmly shut the closet doors.

THE day passed slower than I would have thought possible. After Brady had left for work, I'd gone into the store, moving some inventory around and helping my cashier ring up Sunday afternoon shoppers. It was busy enough I thought for sure the time would fly; after the sixteenth time I'd checked my watch, though, I had to reassess that assumption. Even reorganizing the racks didn't seem to help the hours slip past. But I was now sporting a paper cut and my shirt was speckled with dust, so I had that going for me.

After a while, the crowd died down and I slipped to the back with my things, intending to find the Thanksgiving decorations I'd bought years ago with the best of intentions and never remembered to bring out. Aaron had thought the giant paper turkey was hilarious. I wanted to dress him up like a superhero, with a purple mask and a bow and arrow. TurkeyEye. It'd be fantastic.

Tossing my bag onto the couch, I began digging through boxes. Christmas decorations were at the front, since that was the one holiday I usually managed to get organized for. Behind that were some Halloween things I'd forgotten existed, and I got tangled up in a fake spiderweb for a moment, nearly falling over as I tried to beat it off of me. Turned out fake spiderwebs felt far too close to the real thing.

My hip bumped an easel and I struggled to maintain my balance. Cursing loudly, I grabbed at the canvas before it fell, managing to keep myself and everything else from hitting the floor. Now I had an armful of paints and canvas and was standing in the middle of my studio with the easel teetering accusingly at me.

After a moment, I barked out a laugh. I didn't believe in actual ghosts, in spirits lingering after death. But if I did, I'd be tempted to blame Aaron for this.

"Okay, okay," I muttered, putting the canvas carefully back into place. "Bossy."

The sketches from the other night were in my bag, and I got them out, carefully smoothing the creases out of the paper. For a while I just stood there, heart hammering, chewing on my lower lip in uncertainty. It'd been so long since I'd picked up a brush, I half expected to not remember which end to use. Hesitantly, I dug around in my supplies for the charcoal. My paints were no good now, but I didn't want to use that as an excuse. If I was going to plunge back into this, I had to just take a breath and jump.

Finding a large sketchpad, I settled myself at one of the tables. Charcoal in hand, I considered the blank paper for a long moment. I nearly gave up right then, put the sketches aside as wine- and dancing-induced craziness and moved on. But, jaw set, I dashed a curved line across the paper, marring the perfect white expanse.

The hours slipped by me almost unnoticed. My fingertips were smudged all over with charcoal, my head was bent over my work, and one by one, the papers piled around me. Over and over I drew Brady, his eyes, his lips, the curve of his back. The strong lines of his legs. The gentle grace of his fingers. I knew that form. I'd grown to know it, and it eased me into something more. Eventually, Brady merged into the sun god I'd sketched before. Not him any longer, though I took his curly hair, the bold tilt of his lips, the confidence in his shoulders. I made it into something new.

And I had a story.

My phone rang loudly, startling me. Blinking, dazed, I looked around the room, fumbling for my phone and nearly knocking over half the things on the table. Finally, I managed to pull my cell out of my bag, snapping it open just before it would have rolled over to voicemail.

"Hello?"

"I'm going to try really hard not to be offended at the fact it's now nearly five and you haven't even called me." It was Tracy's voice, heavy with teasing impatience, heaving out a long-suffering sigh I knew all too well. It was the "of course you can have the last of the coffee or the final cookie I don't need it at all I'll just sit here in caffeine withdrawal and silently, stoically starve" sigh. Sadly, it didn't work on me any longer.

"Wait, what? It's almost five?" Crap. I really had lost all track of time. I started to bundle up my sketches, the ones of Brady put aside. The others, though, the story that had been working itself out in smudged charcoal across paper, I hesitated in tucking away. Instead I spread them out on the table, humming quietly to myself as I started to see the order of them.

Tracy was talking. Damn it. I tried to focus, frowning as I struggled to jump back into the flow of conversation.

"I mean, no one called me crying or angry or drunk, so that's got to be good, right?" Tracy paused and I obviously was supposed to chime in there. Sadly, I had absolutely no idea what she was asking.

"Sorry, I was in the middle of something. Still haven't gotten my head out of it." I deliberately turned my back on the workbench, giving Tracy my full attention. "Give that to me again, Trace?"

I could practically feel her rolling her eyes at me over the phone. "You went home with Brady last night, I assume?" she asked.

"Oh." I felt heat hit my cheeks and squirmed in my chair, suddenly wishing I hadn't picked up the phone. Talking about this was so much easier over a few drinks or a pastry. "Yeah."

"And you feel...," she prompted me, and I could hear her grinning.

I paused, worrying my lower lip. "A little upset," I admitted. "Just, you know. Aaron. But mostly.... Tracy, it was *really* great. Brady was perfect and it was amazing and God, the way he kisses."

"Oh my God, I am so happy for you." There was the noise of Tracy's footsteps in the background, the quiet beep of her unlocking the car. "And it's normal for you to be upset, hon. It is. The important thing is you're not stopping there. You feel it, sure, but then you let yourself be more than that. I'm so proud of you, Quinn."

"We had breakfast together," I said, smiling to myself as I turned lazily on the stool. "We're having dinner tonight. I think... he said he loved me."

She was quiet; the engine started, the noise faint, but I could tell she was just sitting in the car. "What did you say?"

Shrugging, I fiddled with a charcoal pencil. "I don't know, yet, Trace. I mean, I'm definitely.... It's all *possible* right now, you know? When I let myself look past Aaron and everything, I feel all those things, that rush and the want and all of that. Love is just a huge word for me right now. I'm not sure I can go there yet."

"Please tell me you didn't freak out when he told you," Tracy said, only half kidding. "I totally did when Annabeth told me, and seriously, I still feel guilty about it."

"No freak-outs," I assured her. "Amazingly. He told me he knew I couldn't yet, and that was okay, and okay, seriously, Trace, how is it possible he's, like, a prince? Because I know I'm crazy—I can feel how crazy I am sometimes—and he just keeps showing up."

"We are both very lucky to have found sane people who are completely taken in by our charms," she agreed somberly. "Some days I'm pretty sure Anna has to be, like, the reincarnation of a saint or something. Joan of Arc."

"Mother Theresa."

"Francis of wherever, the one who talked to animals."

I barely kept back the snort of a laugh. "I think you're thinking of Doctor Dolittle."

"Wasn't that the chick who got English lessons from the singing professor?"

Honestly, I couldn't tell if she was kidding or not. "That's *Eliza* Doolittle."

"Whichever. Anna's all of them. Even the singing one."

"Yeah," I agreed with a little smile. "She is."

"So is Brady, hon," Tracy said simply. "You got lucky twice. God knows why, because you're kind of a brat."

"Oh, no, what's that? You're going through a tunnel?" I was grinning by then, even as Tracy laughingly shouted her protests that she was still parked. "I'm losing you. Oops, you're gone." Ending the call, I stared down at the sketches. For a long time, it was just me and them as I listened to the story they were telling me. The potential they had.

I paged through my contacts to find one other number. "Hey, Anna? Your wife is crazy. Also, uh, do you still have that opening at the gallery next month?"

I WOUND up at Brady's door only a few minutes after six. He'd mentioned wine, my usual default contribution, so I'd stopped at the bakery just down from my shop and picked up a couple of red velvet cupcakes. I'd also indulged my need to be an absolute idiot and gotten a bouquet of sunflowers. Which I'd wavered on, back and forth, the whole taxi ride over to Brady's apartment. I'd very nearly just given them away to a random person on the street, but when Brady opened the door, I was still holding them, sheepishly handing them off to him with a "Hey. Uh, sorry I'm late."

"No problem. I just opened the wine." He was grinning at me. "Did you bring me flowers?"

I rolled my eyes and laughed when he caught my arm to kiss me, happily sinking into the embrace. "Yes," I admitted, though I wasn't sure how I could pretend I wasn't a giant dork. "They just looked so happy when I walked past. I couldn't resist."

He ushered me inside, hand at the small of my back. There was this warmth on his face as he fussed over the flowers, arranging them in a vase, shooting little smiles over at me the whole time. It was kind of incredible. Like if I could capture even a hint of that and bottle it up, I'd be able to heal puppies and make rainbows out of gumdrops. It was a good feeling, just watching him. Knowing I'd managed to do something right.

"I also splurged on dessert," I told him, flipping open the bakery box.

"Oh my God, red velvet." Brady swiped some of the frosting, waggling his eyebrows at me as I batted his hand. "You are a terrible tempter, Mr. O'Malley."

"You enjoy it far too much, Mr. Banner," I returned, catching his hand with mine and kissing his knuckles.

We were easy together. It always had been *easy* with Brady, but now that I was remembering how this went, how the steps could work, it felt *good*, too. It felt like we were settling into something.

"You're a mess." I looked up at Brady to find him inspecting my hands, nose wrinkled. "What is all over you?"

Glancing down, I laughed, a short burst of noise. "Oh, crap. I thought I got it all." I moved to the sink and washed up while Brady followed me with a frown. "It's charcoal. I get it everywhere, but I thought I'd managed to look a little less like a hobo."

There was a beat, and then Brady caught my shoulder, turning me back to him. "You were drawing?" he asked, feeling his way, careful not to pry too hard. He absently picked up a dish towel and dried off my hands for me. It was an impossibly sweet gesture, and I smiled up at him for it.

"Yeah. I, uh, got inspired last night. Figured I might as well give it a try." Pausing, rolling the words around in my head first, I offered, "I, um, I took Anna up on her offer. Of a show? I'm taking two weeks next month."

The grin that broke across his face was absolutely breathtaking. "Oh my God," he said softly, a thrill in his voice. Wrapping his arms around me, he whooped, loudly, spinning me around. I was laughing by the end of it, stunned by his reaction, but his excitement was far too infectious. "Oh my *God*, babe, this is so great! This is… okay, we are *so* not staying in tonight. You and me, we're celebrating."

"Brady," I protested, but it was hard to with my arms around his neck, with his exuberance spilling out into my own smile. "Trust me, staying in with you is my idea of a perfect evening."

"Well, we have to do something," he insisted.

"Um, hello. I brought cupcakes." I arched an eyebrow at him, because obviously cupcakes were a celebration in and of themselves. Brady merely snorted a laugh, though, and kissed me deeply until I was leaning back against the counter and I'd completely forgotten what we were talking about.

Damn him. That was a far too effective method for changing my mind.

"There has to be something we can do to celebrate." He was giving me that slow, mischievous smile, the one that made heat surge from my gut straight south.

"Well," I drawled, doing my best to look innocent. "I do need some more paints."

He paused for a beat before huffing out a laugh, the sound growing as I tugged on his lower lip. "You are mean," he pouted. "I'm doing my best to be all charming and sexy."

"Oh, you are," I assured him, hands slipping around his waist, teasing in under his shirt. "I just really need paint."

"Well, far be it for me to deny you anything." Brady put the cork back into the wine, checking the oven and then turning the heat down. "We've got about forty-five minutes before this goes from warm to rubber. Think we can make it?"

"There's an art supply store two blocks over." I tugged my gloves back on, and Brady wrapped the cashmere scarf around my neck, pausing to kiss me lightly as he did so.

"Then we have our mission." Holding out his arm for me to take it, he led the way out the door. He locked up behind us and tugged his phone out of his pocket as we headed down the stairs. Off my questioning glance he just smiled, dialing while we made our way onto the sidewalk.

"Anna, it's Brady. Quinn just told me." Brady's arm tightened around my waist and I leaned into him, letting the wind curl around us. We walked through piles of drifted leaves, footsteps crunching a path. "I know, it's freaking awesome. We're heading out right now to buy paints."

I could hear Anna's laugh, like church bells, and I nudged Brady with my shoulder. "And we have cupcakes," I reminded him quietly. "Don't forget the cupcakes."

"How could I forget cupcakes?" He sounded scandalized, our fingers tangling together, resting against my hip as we dodged around a woman walking her dog, as the wind played catch with the autumn leaves. "Anyway, Anna, who do you have doing the event that week?" Apparently whatever name she said was not impressive to him. Brady's nose creased up and he shook his head. "Okay, here's what is going to happen. You are hiring me that week. Whatever you're paying that schmuck with a hard-on for pastels, you're knocking off twenty percent and that'll be my fee."

Shocked, I pulled back a little. I knew Annabeth's gallery. It had an impressive array of artists, mostly through Anna's hard work, but it was fairly minimalist. She wasn't one for splurging on events. And I'd seen what Brady did. He was kind of out of Anna's league.

"Brady," I started, but he just leaned into my side, kissing my cheek. "You don't have to do that."

Annabeth was saying the same thing on her end of the phone. "Both of you hush. My boyfriend is not going to have some raggedy cheese tray and cheap wine at his opening. I want to do this." He fixed me with a look, arching an eyebrow. "Seriously, babe. This is kind of my thing. Let me do this, okay?"

After a beat I nodded, and Brady beamed at me. I admit it was kind of ridiculously sweet he wanted to make a big deal about the opening. Of course, it just made me worry I was going to bomb out big time—it'd been more than two years since I painted. What if I sucked? What if I'd always sucked and now everyone would know it? I'd had shows before, sure, but for some reason this felt like I was doing it all over again for the first time—same nerves as I'd had when I was eighteen and managed to convince a gallery owner to give me two feet of space to display my work.

But Brady's arm was warm around me, and he kept smiling as he and Anna discussed particulars and he talked about fabrics and menus. That cold knot of worry in my gut eased, just a little. I could do this. Aaron used to tell me I was never more *myself* than when I was creating, when I had a brush in my hand. When I painted he could see the entirety of my soul laid out bare in colors and strokes. For so long I'd been convinced whatever spark I had was taken with Aaron, had withered and fallen with him. Now, though, I thought I had just been waiting for a new story.

The art shop was nearly empty, and we spent a good twenty minutes just poking around, Brady happily carrying the basket while I hunted for just the right materials. I loved this smell, the oil and turpentine, the heavy weight of brushes between my fingers, the rough white expanse of canvases begging to be used. When we headed back to Brady's apartment under our heavy load of bags, I felt *good*. I felt like the jagged pieces were finding a new way to fit and maybe, maybe, I could recapture a little bit of what I used to be.

I set my things aside while Brady fussed over the frittata. Wine was poured and we settled in, comfortable together, enjoying the meal. I put on some music, and Brady told me about his day, about upcoming projects, about meetings and menus and developing a bacon-wrapped cod entree for a wedding. I loved to listen to him; there was such excitement in his voice as he described his events, a kind of easy happiness and confidence in what he was doing. He was a storyteller, just as much as I was; his canvases were rooms and plates, but his art was no less vivid.

And he'd been right, all those weeks ago. I was completely smitten.

The memory made me laugh and Brady paused, fork halfway to his mouth, fixing me with a look. "Everything alright, Quinn?" he asked, confused smile curving up one corner of his lips.

"I was just thinking about what you told me, the night we first met." Reaching across the table, I brushed his hair back, expression soft when he turned to catch my fingertips in a kiss. "You were right. I am smitten."

The grin that crossed his face was nothing short of breathtaking. Pushing my plate back, I tugged him to stand with me, ignoring the dishes and the half-empty glasses of wine. Eyes on his, I pulled him back toward his bedroom, my own smile growing while his turned positively wicked.

With a laugh he pushed forward, catching me, our breaths mingling into a kiss. Clothes were tugged off and left behind, bare skin found its match, and both of us forgot everything for a while. The strands of music mingled with panted gasps, with moans, with the quiet cry of ecstasy. I came with his name on my lips, his mouth around me, my hands threaded in beautiful blond curls. And for a time, for an endless hour, it was only the two of us. And I was happy.

WE'D eaten cupcakes in bed, and I painted frosting trails down his stomach and licked him clean. The memory still made a jolt of heat hit me; Lord knew I'd never look at a cupcake the same way again. He'd laughed, God, and it felt like the world was all right. Like all that grief and mourning I'd buried myself in was melting, bit by bit, dripping away in the light of his spring. He'd been sensual and sweet and I responded, I'd been carried away in it.

Sleep had come easier with him beside me. Waking up next to him had made the whole morning seem better. Such simple domesticity was almost painfully dear, now that I knew how it felt to lose it all.

Making breakfast, splitting the last cup of coffee, discovering he liked enough cream in his to turn it pale but no sugar—"Moderation," he'd teased, with a sleep-tousled smile—every moment of newness was becoming a favorite. How he clutched the pillow in his sleep; how we used the same shampoo; how he warmed my towel in the dryer while I showered; how much we seemed to *fit*. I'd wanted to stay there forever, to compare childhoods and favorite meals and watch old movies until we fell asleep again. But sadly, reality had intruded.

Now he was at work and I was back in my studio, charcoal sketches pinned around me, materials at hand, and a blank, accusing canvas staring at me. Waiting.

"What are you looking at?" I muttered to it crossly, fiddling with first one brush and then the other. Trying to find the perfect one.

I was stalling. There was nothing more terrifying than a completely empty page, than an untouched canvas. All the *possibilities* of what I could imagine were still out there, until that first stroke. Before I began was when I was most afraid; it was when all the half-formed ideas and imaginings were still clamoring to be heard.

Picking up the phone, I dialed Brady's number, patiently waiting through the rings. When he answered I asked, without preamble, "I need you to yell at me."

There was a pause and he huffed out a laugh. "I don't suppose you're going to provide a topic?"

"I'm just sitting here, looking at the canvas. I need to be motivated." I settled onto my stool, contemplating my brushes again. "So you should yell at me."

Brady hummed an agreement; I could hear him moving, the sound of a door closing. Then, loudly, he commanded, "Quinn O'Malley, get your pert ass in gear and paint *something*."

I'd jumped at the volume of his voice, nearly knocking the paints to the ground. Okay. That was definitely yelling.

"Did it work?" he asked.

"You're very authoritative," I assured him. The ice had been broken, though. The tense, horrible knot of "I can't" had faded a bit, and I chose my brush, dipped it into the blue mixed with a bit of white, and slid the bristles across the fabric in front of me. It was a beginning, a humble one, but with that the floodgates were opened. I absently put my phone on speaker and set it on the table while I worked.

"And you aren't even listening to me anymore, are you?" Brady's voice came from the cell, and I merely made a quiet noise of agreement, moving to a red-gold next. "Fine," he continued. "I can take a hint. But keep this Thursday open. I told you I'm going to be hugely busy for the next few days, but Thursday night, my family is going to be in town. I want them to meet you."

Wait. What?

I fumbled for the phone. "Brady?"

"Don't worry," he assured me. "It's just my mom and dad and my sisters. We'll go out for dinner, and you can even leave early if you want. Just pop in to say hi. Okay?"

Crap. I wasn't good at *families*. Mine had just been me and my parents, and when they'd died I'd been alone. I didn't get siblings or big Christmases or Sunday dinners. It had been a really long time since I'd even had to think about things like that. Aaron had been disowned by his family when he'd come out, and I'd never even spoken to them until the funeral. Meeting the folks was definitely a new experience.

But it was what people did. So I took a deep breath and nodded. "Yeah," I added, when I realized he couldn't see me. "Okay. I'll just stop in for dessert, maybe? Low-key."

"I can do low-key," he promised. "But really, hon, you don't have to worry. They are going to adore you."

I nodded again, worrying my lip.

He sighed at me. "I can hear you fretting from here," he teased, gently. "Listen, how about you call me tonight when you get home? I'm going to be working late the next two days, but we'll talk on the phone before you go to bed and we can decide what you want to do. All you need to do now is concentrate on painting. My parents will keep if you don't think you can meet them yet."

"Yeah." I studied my brushes, the bright swaths of colors already forming the outline of the first piece. "Hey, come on. Families are good, right? And they made you, so they're probably good people." I smiled a little, still nervous, but sure about this part at least. "I'll call you tonight. But tell your mom and everyone I'm looking forward to meeting them."

"You're kind of amazing, Quinn," Brady told me, fondness in his voice.

I just smiled, murmuring, "You're not so bad yourself. Now leave me alone, slacker. I'm trying to create."

He laughed and hung up. Turning back to my canvas, I blew out a slow breath. Right. Families were easy. Piece of cake.

UNFORTUNATELY, when Brady said he'd be busy, he meant it. I hadn't thought I'd mind—really, I did understand work was important; I wasn't *that* needy. But I did miss him. We talked on the phone every night, even if it was only for a few minutes, and he texted me when he could through the day, but I missed *him*. The presence of him, the way he smiled. How he kissed me in the morning. Things I'd just begun to get used to I already was craving.

Still, it did leave me with ample time to both run the shop and paint. It was strange I'd been so apprehensive about starting. Once I'd made myself begin, once the paint had coated the canvases, it was like I remembered what it was like to *breathe* again. All those possibilities I'd held inside, all those ideas and half-formed stories, they were rushing from my fingertips like a wave.

In three days I'd completed one piece and started a second. Which was ridiculously fast, but that first one had been so liberating I'd barely put my brush down. It'd purged the cobwebs from me, the stale air from my lungs. Now I'd settled into the second of the series, and I felt like I'd gotten my sea legs back a bit.

That night, I was meeting Brady's parents. Just a casual dinner at a nearby Italian place he liked. They did have the best marinara sauce in the city. I'd also had their leeks and prosciutto in cream sauce over pasta once and had promptly changed my will to insist I be buried in a vat of it. Even if the night was terrible and awkward, at least I'd eat well.

My phone chirped a few times before the noise penetrated. I'd been painting the dawn, the god of the sun emerging from the sea, and the delicate blush of rose against the water had captivated my attention. I hadn't noticed the time slipping past, much less the sound of my phone. Reaching for it, I paused to stretch. I never realized how stiff I was until I moved again.

There were a series of texts from Brady, showing him and his sisters around town. They'd gone to the zoo today and shopping. His sisters looked like him, tall and gorgeous, with the same curl-ridden hair. His younger sister had freckles, though, but all three of them had the same infectious smile.

Miss you today. Can't wait for tonight.

I smiled at the text, rubbing my thumb across the screen as if I could touch the sound of his voice, could capture the warmth seven simple words gave me. I sent back *"me too"* and set the phone aside. Cracking my neck, I lifted my arms above my head, absently stretching, studying my progress. Just a little longer, I thought. A little bit more before I stopped.

Hours passed in a blur, the sweet-sharp smell of oil paints as familiar and welcoming to me as coming home. When Aaron had died, I'd honestly thought my inspiration had gone with him. I was not a technical artist, not one of the greats. When I painted, when I found my stories, they seemed to spring up from some deep well of emotions, of sensations that begged to pour out and over. With Aaron gone, I'd simply dried up.

I wasn't going to pin my resurgence of creative desire solely on Brady. That wouldn't be fair—to give one person that much responsibility, to shoulder him with the burden of *my* life, of *my* hopes and wants—but he'd breathed into me again. He'd warmed me, thawed me, like I'd been wrapped in ice and he was fire itself. The dawn breaking, perhaps, to go totally poetic.

When I finally pulled myself away from my work, I only had time to scrub the smears of paint off my skin and change before I was due at the restaurant. It was a short walk away, and I relished the bite of cold in the air, the crisp smell of snow. The fall was dying out, spreading withered brown leaves across the streets in a blanket, preparing for winter's first hit. There'd been frost on my window that morning; soon the whole world would be a whirl of white.

I wondered if the fireplace in Brady's apartment was functional. I kept meaning to ask. Perhaps after the exhibit was over, we could take a few days and hole up inside, drink hot chocolate and watch movies, make love in front of a fire. Christmas was coming. This year, I decided suddenly, I'd get a real tree. Aaron had been allergic and they'd always seemed like so much work to me, all the needles that would fall, the sap. But this Christmas was my first with Brady, and maybe I needed a little bit of a mess.

The restaurant was warm enough that the tip of my nose burned as I came inside from the cold. Brady wasn't there yet, so I curled myself into a chair in the waiting area, content to people watch. There was a loud, boisterous family there, children settled in parents' laps, wine poured for the adults, sharing bites of huge platters and laughing together. In the corner was a couple, sharing low conversation. Across the room was another pair, much older, their hands laced together on the table as they ate in contented silence.

There was life in the room and I relished it. It hurt, still, to see people in love, to know that Aaron and I would never be the white-haired couple sharing an evening meal. Of course it did. And I was beginning to think parts of me would always ache for him. I was bigger than that loss, though; at least, I wanted to be. I wanted to be endless on the inside, huge enough to hold Aaron close and still love Brady. To find pieces of me that would be only his. People had to be like that. We had to be made for love unending: like parents with children, like friends, like family. There wasn't a limit—three children loved, but not four, six friends held dear, but not seven. So I would always long for Aaron. I would hold myself there with him, in the world that had been ours. But I'd grow and stretch, I'd expand my skin, and I'd take in Brady as well.

At least, I wanted to. I was trying. The growing pains were still there, but there was hope that came with the hurt.

The clatter of dishes and conversations washed around me as I waited. Ten minutes passed, then fifteen, and I began to check my watch. Twenty minutes, and I began to get a sick knot of dread. Brady was sometimes late, yes, but never this much, not without calling. Not without letting me know.

My fingers shook a little as I dialed, but I tried to be calm. I did this. I imagined terrible scenarios and really it would be nothing more than Brady losing track of time while he was with his family, or the stunning lack of available taxis. Or maybe I'd gotten the time wrong. It was going to be a mundane thing, a silly nothing, and I'd feel ridiculous for worrying. Just the other week I'd been *sure* Tracy had been in some terrible accident when she was half an hour late for lunch; it turned out, she'd gotten pulled into a closed-door meeting that had run over. She'd called me with huge apologies, and I'd done all that worrying for nothing. Most of the time, the worst thing wasn't what happened. Most of the time, life was boring and safe and wonderfully dull.

Most of the time.

"Hello?"

An unfamiliar woman's voice had answered the phone, and I recognized the tone of it. It was stark fear. It was a dread that went so deep it dulled every sense. It was an attempt to sound normal when your insides were howling at you to fall apart. I'd sounded that way a lot, when Aaron had gotten worse. When we'd been at the end.

"I... I'm sorry, this is Quinn O'Malley. I'm trying to reach Brady Banner?"

With a quiet sob of noise, the woman breathed, "Oh, God, I'd forgotten to call you. I'm so sorry, dear, I am. This is Brady's mother. There's... there's been an accident. We're at the hospital."

Everything stopped.

People said things like that. *Everything stopped.* In a movie, they would show it, making the outside noise fade away, blurring everything else to white. Pins dropped and hung there, trembling into nothingness. A record scratch or a loud noise and everything literally did just stop.

That wasn't what it was really like. In reality, it wasn't that everything *stopped.* Your heart still beat; you could feel it in your ears, in your throat. Your breath moved in your lungs, ragged, painful, and the thunder of your pulse combined with it until you were certain everyone else could hear. The world around you didn't go still; it sped up until it didn't matter anymore. You weren't in it. You were in the *next.* You were desperately clinging to the *before*, the wonderful normal that existed only three heartbeats ago. And trembling, sick, you would be thrust into the after. Into the world where whatever terrible thing actually existed.

Cancer.

An accident.

Such stupid, weak words, to invoke such a reaction.

"Brady?" I asked, barely getting his name out.

"We've only just arrived ourselves," Mrs. Banner was saying, but her voice was so tinny and far away I couldn't quite grasp hold of her meaning. "The doctors are with them now. You should come, dear. We're at Saint James. Do you know it? I'd never heard of it, but the taxi driver, he was such a nice boy, he got us right here."

She was rambling now, just needing to talk. To have someone else who felt it too, that strange, twisted pulling in your gut, the ache in your throat that tightened so much you could hardly breathe. "Yes. Yes, I know it. I'll be there as soon as I can."

Hanging up, I fumbled my phone into my pocket. Tracy was always going on and on about how I left my phone places when I wasn't paying attention. I'd need that phone if something happened. I'd have to call people. Tracy. Annabeth. I'd need to tell someone what had happened.

Numbly, I went up to the hostess. She flashed me a cheery, distracted smile, obviously busy. "Your party's not here yet. I'll call you when they come in, if you miss them."

"There's... I'm sorry, I need a taxi. I have to get to the hospital." I was having trouble asking the right thing, putting it the right way. She should know the Banner group wouldn't be arriving. She shouldn't keep looking for them all night, eyes going again and again to the door, with their name printed neatly next to 7:30 p.m. She wouldn't cross them out if they never came. Their name would just sit there, frozen, and she'd wait for someone who wasn't ever going to come.

The hostess frowned a little at me, concern tightening her face. She looked nice. I suddenly found myself hoping she had someone to come home to. Like Tracy did. Tracy had Annabeth. I had Winston. It wasn't quite the same. I hoped this woman with the kind eyes had an Anna and not a Winston.

"I'll call you a cab," she told me, and I nodded, shuffling over to wait by the door.

It was raining. Hard pebbles of water were pelting down from the sky, turning the slush of streetlights into blurs against the night. Absently, I realized I was clutching my scarf in white knuckles. Not my scarf, really. Brady's scarf. The borrowed blue one I'd never given back.

"God," I prayed, I pleaded, staring sightlessly out into the street. "Or whoever's out there. Please." That was all I could say. No specifics, no hopes I dared give voice to. Just that one word. "*Please.*"

The cab pulled up, brilliant yellow, garish against the muted, rain-soaked world. I got in and directed the driver to Saint James, sitting back in my seat, wondering at how numb I was. I was acting calm, but inside it was a raging tempest, a churning swirl of emotions I couldn't quite feel. I knew they were there, I could almost taste the panic, the fear, the horror, but I hadn't broken through to them yet.

The hospital was a mess of people, of that calm kind of urgency as doctors and nurses moved through the hallways. There was the squeak of shoes, the sterile sharpness of antiseptic, the steady beep of machines from behind closed doors. It was all painfully familiar, and I had to swallow back bile as I passed elevators I'd ridden up a hundred times and rooms I knew better than my own.

Finally I found the correct station and started to ask after Brady, voice cracking so much I couldn't get the words out.

"Quinn."

It was his voice, strong, steady, relieved. I turned and saw him rushing toward me, stark white of the bandage on his head drawing my eyes. But he was *walking*, he was collapsing into me, arms tight around me, and I felt that numb ache snap. Everything came rushing back, tears pricking my eyes as my stomach flipped with the force of *relief*. I clung to him, burying my face in his neck, taking deep, hungry breaths of him. "Oh my God," I whispered, words cracking around the edges. "You're okay. You're alive." I pulled back to search his face, desperate to see him, to *feel* him, to know he wasn't going to fade away. My fingers brushed against the bandage. "Are you okay?"

He frowned and flicked his eyes upward, like he'd forgotten that was there. "Yeah. Yeah, just a bump. Got a couple stitches, nothing major."

I guided him to sit down, my hands going over his arms, his chest, winding up cupping his neck. Letting out a breath I swore I'd been holding since the phone call, I tugged him in, kissing him, hard, joyful, greedy for him. Wanting him close.

"I love you," I told him, voice thick. "I mean, I do, this isn't just… God, I thought you were gone. That's not the only reason I'm saying it, but…. Fuck." I kissed him again, wrapping him up in my embrace as tight as I could, holding on. "You're okay."

As I got my brain back in order, as I cupped his face and searched his eyes, I realized Brady wasn't smiling. There was a pinch to the corners of his mouth, a paleness to his complexion. His gaze dropped from mine and he shook his head, looking close to tears. "Yeah. But my sister was driving. Bea, she's…. They don't know, Quinn."

Just the way he said it broke my heart. I shoved everything else aside, everything except Brady. Taking his hand, I gripped it tightly until he looked up at me, eyes red rimmed, expression breaking. He leaned into me, head resting against my forehead; I gathered him as close as we could on the uncomfortable molded chairs of the waiting room, fingers threading through his hair.

"It's going to be all right," I whispered. "I'm here. I'm right here, sweetheart."

THIS wasn't how I'd envisioned meeting Brady's parents. I'd wanted to be poised, to try and *prove*, somehow, that I was worth their son's time. That I could do the whole family thing. Instead, I shook his father's hand and hugged his mother tightly in the waiting room of the hospital. I went with his sisters, both looking wan and wrung-out, to find coffee. I held Brady's hand as we all sat and numbly watched the television, no one caring at all what happened to be on.

It was just the noise, I'd theorized a long time ago, on one of my midnight trips with Aaron into the emergency room. At the end, he'd found it so hard to breathe sometimes. Even a little cold could be devastating. That was what had done it, the doctors told me. A cold. Cancer, yes, but also a stupid cold, and Aaron had been gone.

A driver hadn't stopped, Beatrice hadn't been familiar with the intersection, and now this beautiful family was sitting in the hospital, waiting. Watching the TV just to hear the noise. To have the lights flicker. To get close to a parody of normal. Such a stupid thing, to bring down so much life. To cause so much fear.

"I'm sorry." Brady's mother interrupted the silence, turning to me. Her name was Claire. Her husband was Bruno; he was a big man who looked hollow, now, staring at the doors behind which things were happening he couldn't change. He couldn't fix this, and he was a big man with big hands. He probably fixed everything. Not this, though. I knew how that felt. "I'm sorry, Quinn, but I can't remember what Brady said it was you did."

Brittany and Belinda, the two older sisters, were huddled together on the other side of Brady. They looked over at me with interest, Brittany clinging to Brady's other arm. All eyes on me, I cleared my throat, suddenly nervous. "I, uh, I own a shop," I told them, smiling slightly, expression mostly in my eyes. "I sell comics and graphic novels. I'm also an artist, of a sort. I paint, mostly. I used to draw my own graphic novel, but I, um, I got out of it for a while."

"He's preparing for a show next month," Brady said. He sounded exhausted, but there was pride in his voice, and he squeezed my hand, head tilted to rest against mine. It was like I was holding him up, literally, like he'd just sag to the floor in a puddle if I didn't hang on. So I did, smile softening when I looked at him.

"Yeah. It's at a friend of ours' gallery. Brady is doing the event, actually, so at least that part will be excellent." There was pride in my words, too, shining in my eyes.

He nudged me, adding, "See? Told you you'd change your mind about party planners."

I kissed his cheek. "Definitely."

His mom was looking at us with a content expression, her own hand stealing over to her husband's. Bruno gave me a once-over and grunted, but he asked, "Own your own business, then?"

"Yes, sir." I nodded. "It's not much, but it pays the bills."

Bruno nodded at me. "I like entrepreneurs. Built my own carpentry business when I was a little younger than you boys. Bea is going to take it over…." That rumbling, strong voice just shattered like heated glass, showering around us all as Bruno heaved in a huge, trembling breath, mustache twitching as he swallowed back tears. "Bea is going to take it over," he repeated more firmly, like he could will that to happen. Defying fate to take his daughter away.

"And you, ma'am?" I asked Mrs. Banner, and she tutted at me, though a pleased expression stole across her face.

"You just call me Claire," she told me. "Lord knows the first man my Brady introduces us to is not going to call me *ma'am*. Makes me feel old." She fussed with her purse, pulling out some tissues and dabbing at her eyes. "I was a schoolteacher, before I had Brittany. And then again once they were all older. Just retired last year, and Bruno and I are going to go traveling this summer. To France. Brady and the girls surprised us with a trip for our anniversary."

Of course they did. Belinda offered, "They deserve a vacation. I can't remember the last time they took one."

The coffee from the machine was bitter and lukewarm, but I took a swallow, using it to hide the fact I was studying them all intently. They were just so... *comfortable*. They loved each other, that was evident, and in their worry they were all literally leaning on one another.

Whatever disagreements they might have—and I was sure there were some, every family had them—they were a unit. A clan. I felt like a kid with his nose pressed to the window, taking it all in before I was dragged away.

"Brittany is an accountant," Brady told me. "And Belinda is a teacher, like Mom. Her husband, George, is driving in with Britt's boyfriend, Clint. So it's about to get much more crowded."

I nodded. "Good." He gave me a look and one corner of my lips tilted up, a bit ruefully. "You should have family here, Brady. It's good they're coming."

"You're not going to get overwhelmed?" he asked me.

"How about you don't worry about my delicate sensibilities." I kissed him lightly, just the corner of his mouth, and nudged my shoulder against his. Turning back to the room at large, I asked, "Okay, so George belongs to Belinda?"

"He's an art teacher," Belinda told me, smiling, tired but genuine. "You two will get on wonderfully."

"And Clint's mine," Brittany told me, shoving her hair back and absently rubbing her neck. "He is a marketing consultant who really wants to be a fireman. Which is why he and George didn't come with us. Clint's a volunteer firefighter, and he had his on-call shift this week, and George had classes."

"Are you coming to Christmas?" Claire asked me, and I froze a little. "I don't know how much Brady has told you, but we have a little farmhouse a few hours upstate. It gets gorgeous once the snow comes, and the kids always come and spend the week with us. We'd love to have you, Quinn."

"We hadn't talked about that yet, Mom," Brady said, sighing. But he was smiling at his mom and Claire hardly seemed deterred.

"Well, we're all just sitting here. Might as well talk about it now."

I couldn't argue with that logic. "I, uh. I hadn't really thought about Christmas this year," I told her honestly.

"Then it's settled." Which wasn't exactly how I remembered things going, but I just breathed out a laugh at her self-satisfied smile. "I'll have Brady give you the details. We'll put up an extra stocking."

"Don't fight it." Brittany leaned across Brady to squeeze my hand with a smile. "She did the same to Clint and George. You're pretty much doomed."

"How do you feel about children?" Claire's question set off a chorus of *"Mom!"* and she just looked innocently around. "What? It's a perfectly legitimate question."

The mood had eased slightly and I shook my head, amazed. Brady was giving his mother a look. "How long have you been sitting on *that* question?" he asked her.

"I'm simply pointing out I'm not exactly getting any younger. I'd like to hold my first grandchild before I'm too frail to lift them." Claire gave me a pleading look, but the whole thing was ruined by Bruno snorting, fondly wrapping his arm around his wife.

"I always said my Claire could talk an Eskimo into skinny-dipping," he said, and I couldn't help it. I laughed. The pall of worry that was hanging over everyone lessened a bit, and Brady leaned into me, shaking his head and kissing my cheek, chuckling softly. Even Claire was laughing, Brittany and Belinda giggling together. It was a slightly hysterical kind of laughter, the sort that came when you were stretched too thin to do anything else, but it felt like a form of release.

The swinging doors flipped open and a doctor strode out, blood on his scrubs, tugging a face mask down. The laughter died as suddenly as it started, and I was left sitting as the family surged forward, surrounding the man. I didn't watch them, though. I knew this game. I studied the doctor's face instead.

Internal bleeding.

Surgery.

Unconscious.

Wait and see.

Brady turned around and met my eyes, his whole expression crumpling. I just nodded. The doctor's demeanor told me more than the words—the careful, clinical neutrality, the way he hedged his bets. It was bad. Whatever the medical details, it was bad.

The family went in to see Beatrice. I puttered around the waiting room, throwing away half-empty Styrofoam cups, rearranging magazines. Twenty minutes later, Brady came back, scrubbing a hand across his face. He just looked so tired. I hauled him into a hug, resting my chin on his shoulder.

"Mom and Dad are staying the night," he mumbled into my neck, hands fisted into my shirt. "Britt and Bel are waiting for the guys, and then they're going back to the hotel."

"What do you want to do?" I asked.

Brady heaved out a low sigh. "Just take me home."

WE WOUND up back at my place. If not for Winston, I would have had the cab take us to Brady's, but in the end, I thought it might be a good thing. The fluffball could be good for comfort, if nothing else. He'd had enough practice at it. Winston was there to greet us at the door, fat tail waving as he weaved between our legs. He followed Brady into the living room, plopping happily down on his lap when Brady collapsed onto the couch.

I kissed his forehead and took his coat, shaking out the rain and hanging it up next to mine. "Relax," I told him. "Are you hungry? You must be hungry."

One shoulder lifted in a shrug. "My head kind of hurts," he admitted. "I'm just feeling a little woozy."

"Did they give you anything for the pain?" Worried, I sat next to him, nudging Winston aside with my hip. The cat gave me a grumbling meow, turning around a few times to get comfortable, resting on Brady's stomach as the man slouched back on the couch.

"Nah." His hand caught mine, holding on tightly. "They just said regular aspirin would be fine." He searched my face, those beautiful brown eyes troubled. "I really am okay, Quinn."

"I know." I didn't, though. I knew he was there, with me, and I was clinging to him hungrily. But he wasn't okay. Of course he wasn't. Giving him a slight smile, I went to the kitchen to dig through my cupboards, searching for food. Where Brady could whip up homemade bread and delicious fresh pasta, I was lucky most days to work my can opener without major injury. I did manage, though, to get some soup in a pan. Tomato with toasted cheese sandwiches, I thought, would be mild enough to tempt him.

It wasn't the homey Italian meal we'd been planning on. There would be no wine, no family introductions over garlic bread. But it was soup while it was raining out. It would be warm and filling. It would be comforting. That was really all I could hope for.

Waiting for the sandwiches to toast, I looked across the living room, out the window that had seemed to catch Brady's attention as well. It was still storming; no thunder or lightning, though. Just a monotonous, relentless gray stream, dredging the world in colorless wet. It was wearying, the hard pellets of water pounding down onto the earth. No beauty or magnificent outpouring; no Thor with his hammer. Just the rain.

I dished up the food and carried a tray carefully into the living room. We curled up together, Brady's shoulder tucked under mine as I encouraged him to eat. He looked so *quiet*, so very small, that bold exuberance that he wore so well faded into worry.

"What happened?" I asked, finger-combing some wayward curls off his forehead.

Sighing, he dragged his spoon through the soup, watching the path of it, the creamy red liquid folding in on itself in the wake of it. "We were all carpooling to the restaurant. Mom and Dad and them went into one car, but we wouldn't all fit, so Bea asked to drive mine. It's just...."

His face crumpled slightly and I hastily reached out, putting the bowl aside, gathering him in close. "One second everything was fine, but this truck came out of nowhere and then we were upside down." Shuddering in a breath, he buried his face against my chest. "Oh, Christ. My car. I don't even know where my car is."

"It's okay," I soothed him, sliding my hand through his hair, my cheek tucked against his. "I'll call around in the morning. You're okay, sweetheart. I've got you right here." I could feel him taking in deep breaths, his shoulders rising and falling with each one. For a while we just sat there, me rocking him, back and forth, the thrum of the rain against the windows whispering into a gray noise in the background.

"Can I just stay here tonight?" he asked me, voice muffled.

"I'm insisting on it," I told him, kissing his jaw, just under his ear, sighing softly when I finally could sense him relaxing into me.

A few beats later and he pulled back, hair in disarray, lips curving downwards. "You said... at the hospital."

Ah. I'd kind of wondered if he'd even heard, honestly, and with everything else that'd been going on, I'd put it aside. Whether or not Brady and his family were okay was far more important than declarations. Rubbing my thumb across his cheek, I tried for a smile, feeling nervous. "I did."

His eyes searched mine. "Did you mean it?"

I didn't answer flippantly. He wasn't asking lightly, and I knew if I told him *I don't know*, he'd accept that. I'd been so scared, so frantic, and then he'd been there. Not lost, not still and small and gone, but *there*, and Brady would write off what I'd said as just relief. So I thought about it, searching through my feelings, trying to find the truth of them. Trying to test them, to make sure they were real.

"I love you," I whispered, and a smile touched his lips, relieved and hopeful, absolutely beautiful. "I am in love with you, Brady Banner."

"I love you too, Quinn O'Malley," Brady murmured. The words were nearly lost as I leaned in, as I caught them in a kiss. We sank into one another, Brady's hands curving around the sides of my neck, my fingers buried into his hair. He pulled me toward him and I went happily, the kiss turning from sweet to needy as his mouth opened under mine, as our tongues tangled together in a wet, heated pant of want.

"There's...." I paused, fumbling for the words. "There's lube and condoms in the bedroom. I, um, I got them. For us."

Was this right? Brady's sister was in the hospital, he was upset, there was uneaten soup cooling on the table next to us. Maybe the time wasn't right. Maybe Brady needed something else. But he grabbed my hand and wordlessly pulled me after him. Winston was firmly nudged out of the way as he closed the door, as he looked at me with an expression I couldn't quite read.

Wonder, I realized all at once. He looked *awed*. Heat flushed my skin, and I reached out for him; Brady met me halfway and we came together in a kiss so sweet and soft it made me ache. I moved to undo his pants, and Brady kicked them aside. His shirt followed, and I stopped him when he went to undress me in turn. "Wait," I murmured. "I want to see you."

He was gorgeous. Stomach just barely defined narrowed down to hips and legs that were almost a shame to cover up. His shoulders were broad, his chest absolutely lickable, and as I nudged him to sit on the bed, as I knelt between his legs, I found a faint constellation of freckles along his ribs I tasted with my tongue, following them down to his thighs.

Shuddering out a low breath, he murmured my name restlessly. I answered by kissing the head of his cock, smiling as he gasped at the contact. I wrapped my hand around him and stroked slowly, teasing my mouth down further along the delicious thick length of him. He was velvet smooth on my tongue, and I loved how I could feel him hardening under my attentions. Brady's leg shook and his head fell back, lips cupped open into a perfect *O*.

I wanted him inside of me. In every way possible, I wanted Brady in me, to feel him grow and swell and come buried so deep I couldn't help but be swept away in it as well. Kissing his thighs, his knees, the curve of his stomach, I grinned as his eager hands came to tug off my shirt. I helped, shucking my slacks off into the corner and sprawling on him. Our hips slid together and we were both moaning at the friction, kisses turning frantic and hungry as he turned us, as I hooked both legs around his waist.

"Lube." My grin was positively wicked as I bit his lip, as I mouthed my way down his neck. "First drawer on the nightstand."

Brady fumbled a bit, cursing as his knuckles hit the wall, but he managed to grab what we needed. I was absorbed in mapping out the dips and contours of his collarbone, teasing kisses against his skin. I felt his hands paint down my back, fingertips brushing along my ass and then down to my thighs, gently tugging my legs further apart.

"Are you sure?" he asked, breathless.

Looking up at him in the dark of my room, his hair in wild curls across his forehead, I couldn't find the words. Instead I tugged him down for another kiss, parting my lips under his, moaning softly as his tongue swept inside my mouth. Nodding, I grabbed the lube and managed to slick one finger, then reached between us to press inside myself.

It'd been a while. A fact which came rushing back as the pressure overwhelmed me, as I had to pause and grimace at the tightness. Brady was right there, soothing me with soft kisses, his hand stroking my cock, helping me relax. "Slowly, babe," he murmured, ducking his head to suck lightly on my neck, finding that sensitive spot just at the hollow of my throat. "Let me help."

Together we opened me up; together we turned pain into anticipatory pleasure. My finger alone at first while he teased along my cock, while he sent arousal in waves through me. Then his finger joined mine and the two of us together fucked me. Brady was so gentle I nearly forgot how long it'd been, that we'd never done this together, the two of us. He coaxed my body into bliss, and I was begging him by the end, rocking back against his hand, my arms flung around his shoulders as I groaned for more.

Brady pulled back and I grumbled, reaching for him. "Patience, grasshopper," he teased, and I managed to make a face at him, though my eyes, dark with need, might have made it a little less effective.

Our gazes met, his nose brushing against mine, his breath a hot pant against my cheek. Leaning over me, he thrust inside, watching my every expression. I winced and I could feel my body tighten. He was beautifully big, but I couldn't stop myself from tensing as the pleasant hum of arousal faded and the tight burn took over. Brady kissed me, stopping completely and rubbing the small of my back until I managed to melt again into the warmth of his body, into the delicious taste of his mouth.

Inch by inch he eased inside, and when I finally took him all, I gasped a little when he moved, eyes fluttering shut. "God, Brady," I moaned, biting my lip, concentrating on how he felt. How every rock of his hips sent jolts of pleasure through me.

It didn't take long before I was pressing back with every thrust. I wanted more. He met my eager motions, hitching one of my legs up further around his hip. The change in angle rubbed his cock along my prostate whenever he fucked into me, and I gasped his name, my fingers digging into his back as I desperately moved with him.

We found our pace, our rhythm, and there was nothing other than us. The entire world faded and ended around us, falling down in gray streaks against the window, and all we knew was the heat of skin, the sweat-slick movement of our bodies, the way Brady filled me up completely. The mattress squeaked under us as I hooked one knee over his shoulder and he moved faster, taking me, giving me everything I was begging for in breathless moans.

He was over me and inside of me, and I was wound up in him so tightly it felt like our hearts were beating as one. My moans teased out into his whispered words, his endearments and dirty pleas and promises for a thousand nights of this. We were writhing together on the sheets as the rain tumbled down outside, as the day and the years washed over us and were driven out by our need.

I came nearly silently, arching up into him, hand thrown back to grab at pillows, to clench and shudder with the force of how deeply I felt him. He moved through it, and every jolt of pressure, every delicious rub of friction, catapulted me higher. I touched stars and they were in his eyes. I caressed the moon of his lips, the endless heights of his skin.

Brady followed after me and I could feel his every sigh and shake. We collapsed together, heaving in breaths and tangled in one another.

And I loved him.

I WOKE before Brady, spread across half the bed, Brady's arm flung across my back. Winston was crying outside the door, sounding as though he were inches away from dying if someone didn't show him some attention very soon. Sighing, I studied Brady in the low light, and I smiled faintly. He slept with the same abandon he lived life; he was deeply asleep, limbs sprawled everywhere, taking up most of the pillows and definitely more than his fair share of blankets. I liked it, though. I liked the way he filled up the empty space of the bed, of the room, with so much ease. Rubbing my fingers along his cheek, I kissed his shoulder and eased out from under his arm.

Padding to the door, I opened it and stepped back out of the way of the pale streak of fur. Winston hopped up onto the bed, grumbling the whole time, turning in a delicate circle and huffing out a breath before he collapsed. Shaking my head, I went to the kitchen to find a drink of water, treading lightly in an effort to not wake Brady.

The sun was just barely starting to creep in under the curtains, pale and wan, no warmth at all in it. It was too early to be awake, and I sluggishly poured myself some water, contemplating my bare toes against the chilly floor. I waited to feel the aching sadness that seemed to tinge my mornings now. And it was there, in the back of my mind, that quiet grief, but it wasn't all there was. Like before, like Brady had slowly thawed out pieces of me, I felt more than sorrow. There was contentment, too. Hope. I was worried about Brady's family and concerned over how he'd handle things. I wanted to call Tracy and Annabeth, I wanted to work, I wanted to take Brady out for lunch and make him laugh just to hear the sound of it.

I wanted. I wanted things and places Aaron had never been. I wanted people he'd never met. There were stories in me he'd never hear. Yes, it hurt. I was stretching beyond my old skin, my comfortable existence, and it hurt. Brady was in my bed, in the bed Aaron had never lain in, and that was new and beautiful and terrifying and sad. It was more than just grief; it was bigger than who I'd been before.

I loved him. Not the same as I'd loved Aaron, but not *less*, either. It was Brady's love, only his, and Aaron's love only belonged to him. I held them both in my heart, in my very breath, and I wasn't torn apart from it.

I was sad, yes. Perhaps I'd always be a little bit sad. But there was more to me than the sorrow.

I padded back to bed and collapsed in with a sigh, shivering a bit from the cold morning. Tucking myself back under the blankets, I curled up into Brady's side, Winston sleeping between our legs. Brady smiled, half-awake, sleepily dragging his lips along my arm.

"Good morning," he mumbled.

I kissed his cheek. "Good morning, sweetheart."

For a few moments, he looked content. His fingers found mine and he tugged me in closer. We were all wound up in one another, warm and lazy, and Brady seemed happy. A frown flickered across his face, though, and he drew in a ragged breath, remembering. The bandage on his forehead, the ache in his neck; I could see the realization trickle in bit by bit.

Reaching across him, I grabbed his phone and handed it to him. I sat up against the headboard, tugging him with me to rest against my chest, wrapping him in my arms as tightly as I could. "No messages," he told me, quiet worry thrumming in his tone.

"That could mean they're still sleeping. It's pretty early." I pressed a kiss to his shoulder. "Why don't you go shower? I'll make some coffee and call us a cab."

He nodded, grimacing as he touched long fingers to his forehead. "I should probably rewrap this too," he said, apologetic.

"There's gauze in the medicine cabinet." I fussed over him, easing us out of bed and going to the closet to find him clothes. "Do you remember where the towels are?"

"Yes." I heard a faint smile in his voice and looked over my shoulder to find him watching me. "What would I do without you?"

I swallowed the sudden lump in my throat. No answer seemed good enough, so I went to him, sat on the edge of the bed, and drew him in for a long kiss. "We take care of each other," I finally managed. "That's what we do. Pie crust and filling, remember?"

He sighed, pulling me in for a hug. "Pie crusts and filling," he agreed.

"You know," I told him, rubbing a hand through his hair before getting up and going back to digging through my drawers, "you really should keep some stuff here or something. I'm not sure if these jeans are going to be long enough for you." I held them up to myself, frowning down at them. They were a little too big for me, so maybe they wouldn't look ridiculous on his longer legs.

"Maybe I will," he ventured, and I looked up to find those brown eyes studying me intently.

Taking a slow breath in, I held his gaze for a moment. Yeah, I realized what the implications were. What it would mean. But I could do this. More than that, I *wanted* to. So, casually, I scooped out some T-shirts and put them into another drawer, emptying the top one in the dresser. "So you have room," I told him, suddenly unsure. God, it'd been a while since I'd done anything like this. What if I was messing it all up?

But Brady smiled at me and moved over to stand behind me, slid his arms around my waist, and propped his chin on my shoulder. "That's a good drawer," he rumbled and I laughed.

"Only the best for you," I told him solemnly. "Can't have you using an inferior drawer space."

He kissed me, slowly, and I reached up to cup his cheek. The embrace sent warm curls all through me; the kiss left tingles on my lips as he pulled back. "I love you," he told me seriously, eyes sweeping my face like he was trying to memorize every expression.

Drawing him back in, it was my turn to instigate the kiss, to slide my tongue along his with a soft moan of contentment. "I love you too," I assured him, feeling his smile against my mouth, chasing it with one of my own.

We finally untangled from one another, Brady went off to shower, and I went to make us coffee. Winston, grumpy that his human heating pads had abandoned him, sashayed after me and bitched until I appeased him with some wet cat food. Mug in my hand, I slid down to sit on the floor next to him, back resting against the fridge. There I sipped my coffee and petted the cat. I thought. Dreamed. Imagined a drawer of Brady's stuff next to my own, a second toothbrush in the bathroom, his shoes by the door.

It was a good mental picture.

When Brady came out, all damp hair in curls and sleepy smiles, I passed my mug to him and went to take my own shower. We got dressed and drank coffee, and by the time the cab got there, some of the pinched lines of worry on Brady's face had eased. We held hands on the silent ride to the hospital, but I hung back as we walked onto the floor where Beatrice was when Brady went to greet his family with tight hugs.

"She's not awake yet," his mother was saying and I wondered if I should stay. If this was too personal. Last night had been a flurry of fear and needing to be close to Brady, but now, perhaps this wasn't something I should intrude on.

That thought died a quick death when Claire hauled me into a hug as well. "I'm so glad you came," she told me, and Brittany was next, hugging me tightly, followed by Belinda. Even Bruno shook my hand. I was introduced to George and Clint, and we all huddled down together, Brady sitting with me, holding my hand. Clint brought everyone coffee and then hauled Brittany in close, arms around her while she rested her head wearily on his shoulder. Belinda was holding George's hand, texting with the other, updating us all on what aunts and cousins and uncles were saying. Bruno and Claire were slumped together, Bruno's arm around his wife's shoulders. It was like we needed that. They all needed someone close, someone to hold on to for reassurance.

And I was that person for Brady. It made me feel… good. Needed. Like I was part of this, of this messy, loud, beautiful family.

The hours passed with a numbing slowness. The updates we got were all the same—Beatrice was still not awake, her vitals were stable. We were waiting and hoping for the best. After calling around to figure out where Brady's car had wound up, I finally tracked it down in a police impound lot across town. Dutifully scribbling notes, I made arrangements for it to be released to a tow truck to take it to a local garage, after which I called Brady's insurance company and put him on the phone. That conversation was a ten-minute distraction, after which everyone fell into a kind of stupor once again.

Tracy and Anna were texting me back and forth. I'd let them know what was going on that morning, and now the both of them were checking in every half hour or so, wanting to know if Brady was all right, asking after Beatrice. I tilted the screen to let Brady see each one, and there was a flicker of a smile, an acknowledgement, but it was short-lived. What did you say to "are you all right" over and over again? The answer would always be "no" until the Banners knew if Beatrice would recover.

I'd packed a few things to bring. If there was one thing I knew how to do, it was hole up in a hospital. So I had a deck of cards, some books, some magazines, my sketchpad; I offered them to the rest of the group.

"I didn't even think to bring anything," Brittany admitted, taking the cards.

"I've spent a lot of time in this place," I shrugged. "You get to know some tricks along the way."

I could feel the questions they weren't asking. Belinda picked up a magazine and flipped through it before setting it aside in favor of the game of *Go Fish* Brittany was starting. "Were you sick?" Belinda was the one to finally voice it.

Brady's arm went around me, and he looked like he was going to shut down that line of conversation. But I answered it, because Brady had a drawer, now, and I was invited to Christmas. They should know. "No. My partner was. He had cancer, and towards the end he got sick a lot. So I kind of learned how to make the time pass a little better."

They were quiet while I flipped open my sketchpad, trying not to look like a widower or a man who was going to die alone and be eaten by my cat, as Tracy had warned me about so often before she'd set me up with Brady. Brady tugged me a little closer, kissed my temple, and I gave him a slight smile.

"I'm so sorry, dear," Claire said, and I looked up to find sympathetic expressions all around.

"Thank you," I told her sincerely.

After another beat of awkward silence, Clint picked up a book of crossword puzzles. "What do you say, Mama Claire?" he asked, waving it around. "I bet I can beat you in these."

"Those are crosswords, hon," Brittany told him with a smirk, putting down another card while George pretended not to be stealing a look at her hand. "I don't think they're a competitive sport."

"Oh, just you watch," Clint informed her with a grin. "Come on, Mama Banner. Best two out of three? Bruno can time us."

We all settled back in, Brady paging through a magazine, sprawled out on the seats with his back pressed to my side. One of my arms was draped around him, and he played idly with my fingers as he read about the latest celebrity gossip. I drew, slowly at first, absent doodles. But gradually they turned into sketches of the family, of the sadness and worry under their smiles, of the strength each of them wore like a cloak. We hunkered down, this gorgeous family and me, and we waited, as I knew how to do. The waiting I had much experience in.

No one was hungry, but George and I went to get sandwiches at noon anyway. George was a nice guy. We talked in the elevator down to the street. He taught art to kids ranging from fifth graders to high schoolers, and by the time we returned, arms loaded with subs and sodas, I was laughing at his impersonation of a twelve-year-old trying to assure him the reason his sculpture was falling apart was *not* because he had done it the night before and it wasn't dry, but because he was attempting a homage to Picasso.

George was an easy guy to like. He clearly loved his wife, his family, and his job, and he approached all of them with a steady calm I thought would go well with what I'd seen so far of the Banners. We distributed the sandwiches and I settled back in next to Brady, giving him a sideways look. "Eat," I commanded him. He grumbled, but obligingly unwrapped the sub and took a bite, shifting so he was back resting against my side.

"So," I started, hesitantly, "tell me more about Christmas."

There was a beat and then Brady grinned at me fully, squeezing my hand. "Oh, man, you are in for it," he decreed and Claire was beaming at me across the room. "Mom goes all out. Tree, lights, the whole thing. And it's never not snowed. Even if it's only a dusting, Mom always gets her white Christmas."

"It's just not Christmas without snow," she informed us, looking pleased. "I think Quinn will have a wonderful time with us. Bruno, we'll have to get him a stocking. Remind me to find a nice pattern once we get back home."

"Mom knits all our stockings," Brady explained off of my puzzled look.

"Mine has a fire engine on it," Clint told me happily. "And a Dalmatian in a Santa hat."

"We have a whole week of things to do," Brittany said, stealing a bite of Clint's sandwich once she'd finished her own. George and I exchanged a grin—he'd told me she'd do that. "Sledding, if we can, or going for a sleigh ride. Sometimes we even carol, if the weather's good enough. We string popcorn and we bake. It's kind of like Norman Rockwell, only we drink more."

"Brittany!" Claire interjected, sounding scandalized.

"Well!" Brittany was laughing, leaning back against her sister. "We do, Mom. Your eggnog is lethal."

"It's *Christmas*," Claire defended. "What's the point of Christmas if you can't have a little nip of eggnog?"

"You'll love it," George assured me, arm easily looped around Belinda's waist. "Brady's Christmas Eve dinners are legends."

"Then I definitely can't wait," I said with a smile, squeezing Brady's hand.

The swinging doors opened and a woman in scrubs stepped through, going up to Claire and lightly laying a hand on her shoulder. "Claire." She smiled. "I heard you and your whole clan were here. That's good."

"Everyone," Claire introduced, "this is Sara. She's the nurse on duty for this floor and she's been taking care of our Bea." We all nodded, but no one's mind was on pleasantries. Sara had news; I could sense the breathless waiting as we watched Sara's face carefully.

"She's awake," Sara said with a smile. "Very groggy, but awake. I was coming out to bring you in to see her."

Claire clapped both hands to her mouth, closing her eyes and swaying a bit, gratitude and tears tracing across her face. "Oh, thank God," she whispered, one hand going down to firmly grasp at Bruno's. "Oh, thank God, our little girl."

"Follow me," Sara told them gently. "Probably not all of you at once, but I'll bring you in in groups, if that's all right?"

"Yeah, sure," Brady said, gripping my hand so tightly it ached. His voice cracked a little at the edges. "Mom, Dad, go give her a kiss from us. We'll come in a minute."

The rest of the family sagged back into their chairs, watching as Claire and Bruno made their way through the doors and out of sight. Hugs were exchanged, relief so palpable it felt like it'd taken a seat next to us. Brady dragged a hand across his face, and I leaned into him, resting my chin on his shoulder. "It's going to be okay," I told him softly.

He smiled at me, taking my hand. "I know."

I STAYED behind in the waiting room while the rest of the family had their moment with Beatrice. Brady had invited me to come, but I felt strange intruding on that. There would be time enough for Beatrice to meet me when she wasn't groggy from surgery and being embraced by a whole whirlwind of giddy, relieved relatives.

Settling back into my chair, I returned to my sketching. The soft drag of pencil lead against paper was soothing, and I relaxed into it, legs hooked up over the arm of the uncomfortable bench seat, head pillowed on mine and Brady's jackets. It was only when I felt a dry kiss to my forehead that I realized the family had all filtered back in, sharing smiles and clinging to each other's hands like children after a long storm had passed.

"She's talking," Brittany told me, smile beautiful in her relief. "Cracking jokes, the jerk. We're all going to grab some dinner and then take shifts tonight."

"I signed us up for the late night watch," Brady told me, a question in his eyes. Unsure if he should have. I just nodded.

"Sounds great. I'll show you the best place to steal coffee. The answer is always 'bribe the nurses'."

Brady chuckled and held out his hand to help me up. We shrugged on coats and he wound the scarf around me, the blue soft against my cheek. It had been his, been a part of him I kept close. Now it was just mine. Like he was. Like I was to him. We belonged, in a way that hadn't been simple or easy at all to navigate through, but it had been right. It had fit, even when it hurt. We fit together now, his arm draped across my shoulders while we walked, his family bumping around us, surrounding us completely.

There was a little diner across the street and we all filed in and helped the waitress push tables together until we had enough room for us all. I wound up sandwiched between Brady and Belinda, and the two of them play fought over the basket of bread we were brought until I stole the last roll with a triumphant grin.

We ordered soups and salads, huddling together over our coffee mugs and talking about absolutely nothing. George's class stories and Clint's news from the firehouse mingled into Claire and Brady discussing the perfect way to cook a turkey and Bruno insisting his clam and sausage stuffing was the real star of the show. They'd relaxed, some of that tense, horrible worry fading into familiar smiles and old stories dragged out again to remind them they were still whole. The family was still as it once was; bigger, now, in fact, instead of smaller.

Loaded up with to-go cups of coffee, kissing and hugging everyone good-bye, Brady and I went back to the hospital. "Mom wanted first watch," he told me, gloved hand curled around mine as we watched the floors ding past in the elevator. "But she and Dad look so tired."

"It's good," I told him. "I'm glad we're staying."

He smiled at me then, softly, and we kissed before the doors slid open. He kissed me and I felt like I was coming home. Or finding my way to someplace new, someplace I was learning to feel comfortable in. It was different from Aaron and me. Not better, not worse. It was Brady's, and I couldn't begin to compare the two.

Beatrice was asleep when we crept in. There was a long sofa that folded out into a bed; we climbed in under the sheets, curling up together. By some unspoken agreement, we got ready for sleep in silence, winding up with my arms around Brady, our heads resting on the same pillow.

"She looks like you," I whispered after a long moment watching as Beatrice slept. She had the same cupid-bow mouth, the same golden curls spilled out around her.

"We look like Mom," Brady murmured back. "Britt and Bel look like Dad."

"It must be nice. Having siblings." I sighed and shifted a bit, resting my hand across his stomach. "I like your family."

"I'm glad." His voice sounded exhausted; I could see the tense weariness in his shoulders, in the set of his jaw. "They like you too." Pausing, he turned in my arms to face me, a crease in his forehead. "You didn't have to say yes to Christmas, if you didn't want to."

"I know." Kissing the tip of his nose, I smiled at him. "I wanted to."

He smiled at me. I loved it when he smiled. Brady's face seemed made for it, and it eased something inside of me, some tense, ragged edge smoothing away at the sight of it. "I think you'll really like it," he assured me, fingertips tracing a path across my cheek. "It's peaceful and we'll take over the attic. Dad installed huge windows up there, you'll have loads of light to paint by."

"That sounds perfect."

"And there's cranberries." The creaky voice broke in and Brady sat up, immediately climbing out of the bed to go to his sister. Beatrice was smiling wearily at both of us, lids heavy as she blinked, trying to keep her eyes open. "The cranberries are the best part."

"I wouldn't know. *Someone* hogs them every year." Brady sat on the edge of the bed, fingers combing through his sister's hair. "Hey, sleepyhead. How are you feeling?"

"Like I got hit by a truck," she responded, but she managed to stick her tongue out at Brady, patting his knee clumsily. "And like I can feel you fretting from here. Don't worry, Brady, 'm just fine."

"Sure you are." Brady leaned down to brush his lips against her forehead. "You're a regular superwoman."

"Invincible," Beatrice agreed. Her gaze went to me and she smiled again, holding out one hand. "You must be Quinn. I've heard a *lot* about you."

I stood, a bit awkwardly, but I took her hand in a gentle shake, shooting Brady a look. "Have you? I'm not sure if that's a good thing or not."

"Oh, no, trust me." Bea settled back against her pillows, a mischievous glint in her eyes. "It's *very* good. You're the first guy whose last name I've heard."

Brady groaned. "Okay, sis. Enough talking. You should rest."

"Come on, resting is boring. I want to talk to your boyfriend." Beatrice smirked up at Brady and I was struck all over again by how similar they looked. Brady had given me that teasing look more than once. It must be a family trait. "So, you're doing Banner Christmas, huh?"

"Yeah," I returned, sitting on the opposite side of the bed. Brady's hand found mine easily, an almost unconscious gesture. "I'm all in for chestnuts roasting on open fires and something nipping my nose. The whole nine yards."

"You know, you're going to be the first guy Brady's even introduced to Mom and Dad, much less brought home for the holiday."

Beatrice wrinkled her nose at me, smiling. "So, you good enough for my brother?"

"Bea...." Brady protested, hiding his face in his hand. "God, you don't just *ask* stuff like that."

"What?" She was giving Brady an entirely innocent look. "I just suffered a *trauma*, Bray." Those wicked brown eyes went back to me, Bea folding her hands on her lap expectantly. "Well?"

"Probably not" was my answer, and it seemed to please her.

"Is Brady your first boyfriend?"

"Come on—" Brady's expression was kind of hilarious, really. I shared a grin with Beatrice.

"No. I had a partner for a little more than ten years. His name was Aaron and he died about two years ago. Before that, I dated three men, none of them for more than a couple months."

She absorbed that and nodded, considering me. "You want to get married again?"

Hesitating, I nodded, and she immediately followed up the question with, "What about kids?"

"She really is just like your mom," I muttered to Brady, who had given up trying to interject protests and was sitting there looking resigned.

"You don't have to answer her," he informed me, shooting her a glare. "She's being nosy."

"Well *someone* has to ask these things," she returned haughtily. "This is a big deal."

"I like the idea of kids," I answered into their bickering, and both of them turned to look at me. Brady's face softened, and I found myself smiling a little at him, shyly. "Aaron and I didn't because we never got around to it. We were both busy. But I think we would have. And I think I'd like it, *if*"—I arched an eyebrow at Beatrice—"I was involved with someone like that again. I wasn't really married to Aaron, not legally. It *wasn't* legal when we were together. So marriage is kind of... I don't know. I think it'd be nice, to have the piece of paper and all that."

"You were married," Brady murmured, squeezing my hand. "Paper doesn't mean anything, not really."

It was my turn to smile at him, and I shrugged. "Well. He was mine and I was his. So I guess that's a marriage. And yeah, kids, if I got to have that kind of relationship again."

Beatrice was watching us both with a little smile. She leaned back against the pillows, looking satisfied. And exhausted. I was tired just watching her fight to keep her eyes open.

"Okay. I guess maybe I'll share the cranberries with you."

I laughed. "Thanks."

Beatrice nudged her brother. "You promised you'd come home early so I can help you design office furniture. Don't forget."

"Bea is a great craftsman," Brady told me.

"Craftsperson," Bea corrected him sleepily.

"Right, craftsperson." Brady smiled, running his hand through her hair. "She creates the most beautiful things. She's going to make me a desk."

"And wooden bowls, but that's a surprise," she mumbled, head listing to the side as her eyes drifted, finally, closed. "With dragons."

"Dragons?" I asked, amused, but she was asleep again.

"I love fairy tales," Brady explained as we stood, as he tucked the covers more firmly around his sister. "My sisters used to tease me that I really just wanted to be a knight when I grew up." He shot me a little smile. "They weren't wrong."

As we climbed back into the bed, the springs creaking under us, the sheets too thin to be truly comfortable, I couldn't find it in me to complain. Beatrice was alright. She'd been talking and laughing. She didn't have that hollow, pale look of the nearly gone. And Brady was right there, his body curled around mine, arm slung across my waist. We were together and everything really was going to be fine.

Chapter 8

"TRACY! I can't find my tie. Do you know what I did with my tie? And my shoes. And oh, God, my notes. Anna wanted me to give a speech and I can't find my notes or my shoes and—"

Grabbing my shoulders, Tracy forced me to stop pacing around the small back room. "Quinn. Breathe," she snapped at me.

I tried to obey, but it felt like a thousand panicked butterflies were beating their wings against my stomach. Pressing my hands to my chest as I heaved in air, I stared at her, wide-eyed. "I think I'm having a heart attack."

Tracy, good friend that she was, rolled her eyes at me. "You are not, you big baby." Finding my tie draped over the back of a chair, she hooked it around my neck and tugged it straight so she could tie it. "Okay, repeat after me. You are going to be fine."

I gave her a skeptical look, but Tracy simply arched one eyebrow at me, waiting. Giving in, I muttered, "I'm going to be fine."

She nodded, tying the knot in my tie, making sure it was perfect. "You have worked hard on this show."

"I have worked hard on this show," I parroted back dutifully.

"It's going to be a success," she prompted.

I sighed, again giving her an exasperated expression, but Tracy simply met my gaze. "It's *going* to be a success, Quinn," she told me again.

"Fine." Shaking my arms out, trying to disperse some of that nervous energy, I nodded. "It's going to be a success."

I wasn't exactly brimming with confidence about that fact, but Tracy fussed over my jacket, making sure the collar was even, and she looked so damn *calm*. Everyone had looked calm, even Annabeth, who kept breezing in and out of the room, telling me how much longer I had until I needed to make an appearance. How the hell Brady had managed to put this all together while doing his normal jobs and with Beatrice still in recovery, I'd never know. He was superman. I was lucky I'd finished the last piece two nights before the exhibit.

Speak of the devil. Brady poked his head in with a grin. "Knock, knock."

"Your boyfriend is freaking," Tracy greeted him dryly. "And I need to go make sure my wife doesn't need anything. Can you take over?"

"I've got him," Brady smiled, kissing her cheek. She patted his shoulder affectionately and took off, black dress swishing around her knees, heels clicking across the wooden floor. Brady himself was in a charcoal gray suit and a green tie; all together his outfit made him look indescribably good. I kind of wished my whole art show was just him on a pedestal. It'd be the most beautiful thing in the room by far.

"I have to give a speech," I told him miserably.

Brady chuckled softly and ran his hands down my arms. He'd insisted I get a new suit for the occasion. I thought I looked ridiculous. He said purple brought out my eyes; the plum tie and waistcoat, though, I was pretty sure just made me seem like a kid who'd wandered into his dad's wardrobe. "You have to say a few words, that's all. Hi. Thanks for coming. Try the veal."

"There's veal?" I worried.

"It's a joke, babe." Brady kissed the bridge of my nose. "Take a deep breath." He waited patiently while I did so, his hand rubbing my back as I slowly let it out again. "Good. Okay? This is going to be fine. There's wine and food and pretentious people all ready to talk about how brilliant you are."

I wrinkled my nose at him, but some of that tight panic was easing out of me. Brady was good at that. "I'm glad you're here." I leaned against him with a quiet sigh. "I'm not good in front of groups."

"I'll be right in the back where you can see me," he promised, lips brushing against my ear. "If you get nervous, just look at me. Pretend like you're only talking to me."

I nodded, tipping my head up to catch his lips in a slow kiss. "I like talking to you," I murmured, feeling him start to smile.

"I know." He nipped playfully at my lower lip. "I'm very charming."

"It's true. Will my charming, very handsome boyfriend be coming by tonight?" I wrapped my arms around his waist, liking how Brady would shift closer when I did so. "And you do, by the way. Look absolutely handsome tonight. Kind of unfairly gorgeous."

"Thank you." He grinned. "You look rather amazing yourself." We kissed again, soft and sweet, and the butterflies in my stomach beat for a different reason altogether. "I'm going to the hospital tonight to sit with Bea, though. I might be late."

"So be late," I shrugged. "Or I could go with you?"

The smile he gave me was brilliant; it crinkled the corners of his eyes and lightened up his face, sending a warm ache all through my chest. "Yeah," he agreed, lacing our fingers together. "If you want to."

"So long as I'm not being a nuisance." Our foreheads bumped together and Brady huffed out a quiet laugh.

"You, Mr. O'Malley, will never be a nuisance." He teasingly tugged on my tie. "She's getting released day after tomorrow. I had to convince Mom and Dad not to drive back out here as soon as they heard."

"I'm still kind of amazed they left at all," I admitted.

"Well, I promised to watch out for her." Brady shrugged. "And Dad had some jobs to finish. I don't think they'd ever have walked out of the hospital, much less gone home, if I wasn't here."

"We'll go see her tonight." I liked Beatrice. We'd had an epic Scrabble game the other night, and I had to go back and try and earn back my dominance. "When are you going to drive her home?"

"Day after Thanksgiving." He grinned. "She's excited about spending the holiday with us. I think she's under the impression I'm actually going to let her make the stuffing."

"This is a Banner thing, isn't it?" I guessed. I was right, judging by Brady's sheepish look.

"The stuffing is very important," he informed me wisely, and I nodded, somber, trying to keep the teasing gleam out of my eyes.

"Good thing my entire contribution will be the wine. I wouldn't want to get in the middle of that competition."

A quiet knock at the door interrupted us. "Everyone decent in here?" It was Conner in his waiting suit, empty tray tucked under his arm. Giving me a smile, he turned to Brady, voice lowering to a hush. "We've got a slight"—he saw Brady's eyebrows wing up and emphasized again—"*slight* ricotta ball crisis. It seems our oil is not getting to temperature and frying them results in, well. Mush."

Eyes closing briefly, Brady sighed. "Mush," he repeated. "Fantastic."

Oh, Christ. People were out there eating mush. They were going to eat mush and then they were going to hate me before I even showed my pieces. "I don't even know what ricotta balls are," I told Brady, panicked again.

"Hey." His hands cupped mine and he smiled at me, calm. Everyone else was so *calm*. "It's okay, babe. I've got this. Everything is perfect. *You* are perfect."

I filled my lungs with slow, deep breaths over and over, and nodded. "I'm glad you're here," I told him again earnestly.

"I wouldn't be anywhere else." Brady tucked a strand of my hair back and rubbed his thumb across my cheek. "Alright. I'm going to go make sure everyone's eating and happy. Do you want some wine or something?"

"I can grab a glass," Conner volunteered, but I shook my head.

"No. No, I'm fine. Thanks." Kissing Brady softly, I repeated, "I'm fine. Go, be awesome. I'll see you when it's over?"

"Definitely. Remember, I'm going to be in the back, watching you be amazing."

They both left me alone. Pacing the room again, I closed my eyes, muttering to myself. I knew what I wanted to say. How I needed to present my work to the crowd. It was just so much *harder* to do with everyone staring at me. I'd never been good in front of people. Knowing they were all shortly going to be judging my art only made it harder.

I could hear the murmur of voices growing louder. I was expecting twenty people at most; really, I hadn't done anything in two years, and I hadn't exactly been Ansel Adams before that. Anna was good at her job, but even she couldn't promote me that well. It was a week until Thanksgiving, people already in holiday mode. There was a reason she hadn't found anyone else to showcase these two weeks. But even twenty people were more than I thought I might be ready for. Hell, no one but Annabeth had seen the work yet.

God, I was going to make myself sick.

"Hey." It was Anna, poking her head around the door. "Come on, Van Gogh. Time to introduce your art."

"I don't think I want to be the guy who cut off his ear," I protested faintly, fingers flying up to nervously smooth my tie.

"But he did such beautiful work. And who really needs an ear?" Annabeth was teasing me, taking my hand and drawing me in for a tight hug. She smelled like oranges and lavender, her dark hair up in a loose bun. I took a deep breath and tried to relax, resting my chin against her shoulder.

"I wish Aaron was here," I admitted, very quietly. It felt wrong, to want that. Wrong for Aaron, wrong for Brady, to want both of them, to have one on either side of me. Aaron had been my rock for so long, and now Brady was so steady and sure and wonderful. God, how fucked up was I to want Aaron here when I had Brady?

But Anna just smiled at me, a little sad, fussing with my hair. Long, cool fingers smoothed across my forehead. "I think you're always going to want him here, especially at things like this," she mused softly. "Remember my first exhibit here?"

Breathing out a quick, stuttered laugh, I nodded. "You were too nervous to pronounce that artist's name right. So Aaron just started clapping really loudly and drowned you out and everyone thought your speech was over."

Annabeth grinned at me. "He was a force of nature. I loved having him come to these things because even if it went horribly or no one liked the art, he'd always make me smile."

"He was one of a kind," I agreed. We smiled at one another, and I missed him again. I missed him so much it hurt to breathe in, it hurt to keep myself from crying. But then Anna cupped my cheek, bringing me close to nudge her forehead against mine.

"And he's always going to be here. You remember him. I remember him. Trace remembers him. That's how we live forever. In the stories and the memories we leave behind. We love him, Quinn, and that means something."

Nodding, scrubbing at my eyes, I blew out a shaky sigh. "Is it totally after-school-special of me to just want him to be proud?"

Anna clucked her tongue at me, hauling me back in for another hug. She gave really good ones where she just held on tight and you felt like, really, everything was going to be fine. "He is, hon. I know he is. He loved you so much."

He had. God, he had, and that was something I knew for sure.

"And Brady's here," Anna told me, rubbing her hand up and down my back. "He's crazy about you."

"I think I love him," I mumbled to her. "Well. No, I know I do. He's just…. He's a *really* good guy, Anna. He's smart and funny and so sweet, and he's kind and…."

"And hot," she added, lips quirking upward.

"*So* hot," I agreed. We were smiling again, and I'd scrubbed away my tears. She leaned up to brush a kiss across my cheek.

"So both of them are here," she said simply, lifting one shoulder in a shrug.

Maybe they were. Maybe that wasn't as weird as it sounded. Sure as hell comforted me.

"I love you, Anna," I told her, hugging her tight.

She smiled, lightly bopped the back of my head with one hand. "Love you, too, you big teddy bear. Now come on. Let's go get this show on the road."

Hand in hand we walked out into the main room. I'd come in the back that evening because Annabeth had this weird thing about artists not touching her displays. And, I'd admit it, I was kind of a perfectionist. I probably would have spent an hour rearranging everything only to have it back the way it started and then obsessed the rest of the time over half an inch one way or another. I'd been expecting the typical white room Annabeth had her studio as, with black trim over the doors and windows and a pristine light wood floor. It was an empty canvas, she'd explained to me, and since I'd shown art a few times here, I knew I appreciated the fact that the room didn't detract from my pieces.

Then again, in expecting nothing to be different, I'd apparently forgotten who my boyfriend was.

Everything was bathed in a beautiful golden glow, like the sun was just rising. Waiters moved with trays among the crowd, serving all circular food and sunny champagne. Light flecks of blue were the accent color, just subtle enough that it all melded together into this gorgeous backdrop. I knew without even unveiling my first piece the room was perfect.

"Goddamn, he's good," I breathed, wide-eyed.

"Yes, yes he is." Anna looked very self-satisfied. And she should be—the room was *packed*. There had to be at least fifty people milling around.

"Holy crap, how did you do this?" Looking around, I felt that jump of nerves in my gut again. "Where did all these people come from?"

"A magician never reveals her tricks." She smirked, squeezing my hand. "But I will say, there are a lot of people who are happy to hear you're back doing shows. Now get up there and tell them what they're about to see."

She nudged me forward and I stumbled a bit, managing to walk up to the microphone she'd provided without falling down completely. Clearing my throat, I stood there, awkward and unsure, while conversation around the room died and eyes turned toward me. There were people everywhere, and for a very long moment, I couldn't think of anything I wanted to say. I couldn't even breathe.

There was a flash of blond hair at the back of the room and then Brady was right there, in my eye line, smiling at me. That beautiful, brilliant smile that was like the sun coming up, like warmth unfolding. I took a long, deep breath in, and I began to talk.

"Welcome to my show. Uh, my name is Quinn O'Malley, and I'd like to thank you all for being here." My eyes caught Brady's and I smiled back softly. "The series I'm about to show you is called *In the Chill of Dawn*."

I nodded and Tracy moved to unveil the ten pieces.

"It's the story of the sun god, who fell from the sky and found a world encased in ice." One by one, the paintings were revealed. The story flowed from one to another: the golden god tumbling to earth, ice clinging to his wings. The man he discovered, buried deep in the heart of the world, frozen. "And how he burned up the stars just to get to his love."

By the time the last canvas was revealed, the crowd was murmuring, some moving a bit closer to the piece they were near to examine the details. "It's the story of love and redemption. I hope you enjoy it. Thank you."

There was light applause and then the people were released to edge around the room, to study each piece at their leisure. I looked up and found Brady again; his hands pressed over his heart as he smiled at me and I nodded, a soft expression touching my lips. I was whisked away by Annabeth to talk to various people, to smile and nod. The waiters flowed around us again and Conner pressed a glass of champagne into my hand with a wink before he disappeared on his way.

Eventually, I made my way to the back of the room and leaned against the wall, feeling exhausted. There was a press of someone's shoulder against my own, and I looked over to find Brady there, eyes scanning my face. "You're incredible," he told me quietly.

I snorted lightly. "I hate these things." I tugged at my tie, loosening it. "Honestly, I think I'm just lucky I didn't fall over or set myself on fire."

"Is that a danger?" he asked, amused.

"You have no idea." A tray of food went by and I reached out, stopping the waitress, who I recognized as she turned. It was Gwen and she grinned at my hello, giving me a quick hug.

"Oh my God, hi. This is so great." She offered me the tray. "Dessert?"

"Is that...." I'd stopped her because I wanted to be sure. "Is that peach pie with no crust?"

"Yeah!" She handed me one. "It's on a crispy sugar cookie base, and then the pie filling on top. Just supposed to be one sweet, perfect bite. The whipped cream has basil in it, which sounds weird, but it's delicious."

It was. I popped it in my mouth and closed my eyes, humming lightly in pleasure. "Holy crap," I mumbled around the mouthful. "That's amazing."

She laughed and moved to another group of people who'd been eyeing the food. I finished chewing, fingertips touched to my lips. "Brady...."

"What?" He was trying to look innocent, but he kept glancing at me hopefully.

"Thank you." My hand found his and I squeezed it tightly. "This is… I don't know how you did it, but it's perfect. And you made me pie with no crust. I'm just…."

"I wanted you to have a good night." He shrugged, but he looked pleased. "Your work is absolutely incredible."

We wandered over to each painting, hand in hand. Annabeth was standing with Tracy, Tracy's arm around her wife's waist, their heads bent together close as they talked. The room was filled with people who were laughing and chatting and looking at my work, eating Brady's food, standing in Annabeth's art gallery. It was my family, in one crystallized moment. It was everything I loved, here, together.

"I'm glad he found him." Brady was studying one of the paintings, where the sun god was standing above the man frozen in the ice, his wings draped down around him, the air filled with the steam of fire meeting cold. "It must have been terrible, being so numb and frozen for so long."

He glanced over at me and I nudged my shoulder against his. "I'm glad he did, too," I murmured.

We stood there, Brady's fingers laced with mine, and I felt like Aaron would have been proud. Like he was proud, up in the stars, or wherever good souls went to rest. Like the memories we carried with us and the memories I was making new were both, just then, happy.

"I'VE got the turkey!" Arms full of bags, I carefully navigated down the steps of Brady's apartment. Beatrice was waiting out by the car, making sure no one took off with the sedan loaded with groceries and, in my opinion, a ridiculous number of pans. I had assured Brady that Tracy and Annabeth did have cookware at their place, but he'd just given me a *look* and handed me a second roasting pan. Just in case, he'd said.

Cooks were kind of adorable, sometimes.

"You know, I *could* help," Bea told me, holding open the door as I struggled with the huge bag holding the bird.

"You're recovering," I reminded her with a grin. "And Brady would kick both of our asses if you lifted something bigger than a spoon."

"Not even that." Brady's arms were loaded with a huge box full of produce. "I'm going to feed her like a baby bird."

Beatrice gave him a grossed-out face and he laughed, sticking out his tongue at her and dodging the playful kick she gave his leg. "You're disgusting, big brother," she grumbled, but she was smiling and so was he. They'd had this fight now five or six times. Beatrice insisted that she was much better, Brady seemed to think she was made of glass. And I just tried to stay out of the way; the whole sibling thing was something I was still trying to get used to.

"Okay, is that everything?" There was barely enough room left in the car for us. I stuck my head in the back door, checking through the bags. "Babe, did you remember your little fire gun thingy?"

"The torch." He was grinning, his hand on the small of my back as he looked in the car with me. "And yes, it's in with my spoons. I think we're good."

"And does Tracy *know* you're moving into her house?" I teased.

"Well, I volunteered my place, but apparently my dining room isn't big enough." We all piled into the car, Brady making sure we were buckled up before he pulled out into traffic.

"I'm just amazed you didn't try to bring your stove too," Beatrice said with a grin.

"What makes you think I didn't?"

Rolling my eyes at both of them, I shifted the bag of potatoes off my lap and smiled as Brady absently took my hand. This was going to be good. Brady, Beatrice, and I were joining Tracy and Annabeth at their place for Thanksgiving. Brady had tempted me with previews of his menu all week. Apparently he saw the opportunity to create a Thanksgiving dinner for his adopted family as some sort of challenge to see if he could kill us all with a food coma. I, for one, was looking forward to the task of eating my body weight in ridiculously good food.

Tracy and Annabeth greeted us at the door. Between us we managed to haul in all of Brady's supplies. "You do realize I have pans, right?" an incredulous Tracy asked, holding up two skillets.

"It's a cook thing," I told her with a grin, kissing her cheek and bringing the last of the groceries in. "Trust me, it's cuter if we just think of it as a quirk and let it go."

Brady and I moved together easily in the kitchen. I put things away—onions and carrots on the counter, butter and heavy cream into the refrigerator—while he got his pans organized, his knives out, ready to begin cooking. Annabeth had pies cooling on a rack, her contribution to the dinner, and several trays of vegetables and dip, crackers and cheese. The women were in the living room, nibbling on those and talking.

Brady pulled out the turkey and began chopping herbs to stuff it with. He was so intense, focused completely on what he was doing, every movement sure, nothing wasted. For a while I just sat on a stool out of the way and watched him. With calm, even strokes he moved through an onion, a bundle of herbs, cubing butter, knife flying with ease. It was a dance he knew every step to.

Six pans were on the stove, the turkey in the oven, before he even stopped for air. I handed him a glass of wine when he finally looked up, and he smiled at me, faintly startled. "I didn't even see you there," he admitted, taking a drink.

"I was very quiet," I agreed with a smile, tugging him in for a slow kiss. "Can I help at all? I feel like I should chop or stir or something."

"Nah." He nipped my lower lip, and I shivered happily. "It's pretty easy once I've got my prep done."

Brady tossed a pan full of browning sausage, glass of wine held loosely in his free hand. I shook my head, giving a soft laugh. "You are so damn sexy when you cook."

He looked over at me, a slow smile easing across his lips. "Really?"

"Oh, yeah. One of these days my legendary self-control is going to fail, and you'll find yourself in a very awkward position."

Lips quirking upwards, he stalked over to me, all long limbs and beautiful grace. His perfectly curled hair became mussed under my fingers as I tangled my hands into it, pulling him in again for a kiss. My back lightly thumped the wall as he leaned in. Our hips angled together, making me gasp quietly. "When I get back," he promised me, throaty voice sending hop-skip sparks of *awareness* down my spine, "I think I'll need to investigate this possibility more thoroughly. Maybe I'll cook for you, and you can do with me what you will."

"That sounds like an excellent plan."

A beeping noise interrupted us and Brady cursed under his breath, moving back to the stove to taste and stir, his eyes darting back to me every so often. Both of us were smiling, that blissful look of the very well kissed. Beatrice wandered in for more cheese from the fridge and glanced between the two of us before rolling her eyes. "Oh my God, you two are ridiculous," she teased.

"He started it," I protested, holding up my hands in innocence.

"Yes, I'm a very wicked man, standing here cooking," he threw back, grinning so the corners of his eyes crinkled.

"Whatever," Beatrice summed up. "Quinn, come out so we can play cards. We need a fourth."

She wandered back out, and I straightened my shirt, sliding off of the stool. "I think it just hit me that you're going to be gone for three days," I told him, fussing with the buttons so I didn't have to look up at him. "This sounds stupid, but I... I'm going to miss you."

After a moment, Brady said, very quietly, busily stirring a pot I wasn't sure needed that much of his attention, "It's not stupid."

Rubbing the back of my neck, I took a hesitant step forward. "I mean, I know you're just dropping Beatrice off. It's three days, it's not a big deal. I'm just... I think I've gotten used to you being there."

He glanced over at me before dropping his eyes again. I could see emotions slide across his face, some too quickly for me to guess at, jaw tightening as he struggled with what he was going to say. "I'll miss you too," he settled on at last. I didn't understand the little jolt of disappointment I felt, like we'd almost reached for something more and then fallen short.

"It's only three days," I said again, reassuring myself and him.

"It is," he nodded, dumping clams into the sausage in a buttery, fragrant waterfall. "And hey, maybe you'll welcome the break, right?"

My hand rested on his arm, stopping him for a moment. He looked at me, the deep brown of his eyes registering his insecurity. "I'm going to miss you," I repeated. "I don't want a break."

Surprise tugged at his lips, but before he could say anything, Tracy called my name, Beatrice as well, laughter rounding out their words. Sighing, I gave him a rueful shrug and left him in the kitchen with his pots and pans and the dance he did so well, with the words I felt like we should have said but didn't quite get out. Too bad I really didn't know what those would be.

Tracy and I teamed up against Annabeth and Beatrice. It only took a few hands, and a few glasses of wine, before we were all laughing, the conversation flowing easily. Brady kept poking his head in, wandering over to check my hand, giving Beatrice tips, or stealing some of my drink. In all, it was cozy and relaxed, just a group of people enjoying each other's company.

"I'll get another bottle," I said, stepping over Beatrice to get to the kitchen. "Since you lushes finished the first."

"Oh, I'm sorry," Beatrice giggled after me. "It must have been someone else who drank your two glasses."

"Damn straight." I grabbed a bottle of white, Brady giving me a look as he pulled the turkey out of the oven.

"Don't get drunk, bunch of alcoholics," he called after me. "Dinner is in twenty."

I twisted out the cork and refilled my and Beatrice's glasses, going to Annabeth and then Tracy. Tracy, however, held her hand over her glass. Her still full glass. Of water. "I'm good," she told me, striving for casual.

Thinking quickly, I tried to remember if I'd noticed Tracy drinking anything at all that evening. Anna was on her second glass, Beatrice was as well, Brady and I had shared one and a half, and I'd just refilled. But Tracy had been sipping that glass since we'd gotten there.

"You're not drinking?" I frowned at her and Tracy very deliberately didn't look up at me.

"Whose deal is it?" she asked.

Annabeth, voice a bit strained, said, "I think it's Quinn's. Quinn, sit down and deal the cards."

"You're not drinking," I said again, eyes going wide. "Oh my *God*, you're not *drinking*." There were only two reasons why someone didn't have a glass of her favorite wine. And she definitely wasn't on a twelve-step program.

"Hush," Tracy told me, but she was fighting a smile. Anna wrapped her arm around Tracy's waist, hauling her in and kissing her forehead, looking unusually emotional. "Look, we were *going* to wait until after dinner, Sherlock, but, uh."

"Brady! Get in here!" I called, an incredulous look on my face. This was so not happening. Oh my God, I might actually die or faint or something horribly cliché and embarrassing.

Brady emerged from the kitchen, a streak of flour on his cheek, looking baffled. "What's wrong?"

"Tracy isn't drinking." Now *I* sounded giddy.

Pausing, Brady shared a baffled look with Beatrice. "Did we bring the wrong wine?" he ventured.

Tracy burst out laughing, fingertips pressed to her lips. Anna kissed her shoulder, resting her forehead against it, smiling so hard I swear she was just going to fly away. There was a sharp ache at the back of my throat, a burn at the backs of my eyes.

"No, I...." Tracy paused, biting her lower lip, pure bliss on her face. "We're pregnant."

There was a pause and then a burst of sound. Brady's joyful exclamation, my shout. We were hugging and I was crying and Anna was kissing Tracy hard, long fingers tangled into Tracy's copper waves. Brady kissed me, then, and then Anna, before hugging Beatrice and twirling her around. It was a jubilant explosion that wound up with us all around Tracy and Anna, arms around each other, laughing and all talking over each other.

"When? I didn't even know you were trying," I asked, grinning at her.

"We didn't want to say anything until we knew, it was so up in the air. There's only a small chance it would have worked, and we only really had the money for two tries. This was the second." Her hand went to rest over her stomach and I choked back another happy sob, hauling her in more carefully this time.

"I can't believe you're going to be moms," I whispered and she smiled, pressing her face against my neck. I could feel her tears, too, and we clung to each other, overwhelmed with joy.

"Okay, well, this calls for a celebration." Brady's arm was around my shoulders and he pressed his lips to my temple; I could feel his smile and it warmed me. It added to my happiness until it felt like I could float away on it, like it was big enough, substantial enough, to bear me up. "How about a huge feast? I just so happen to have something just about ready to go."

Tracy laughed, fingertips touching Brady's cheek fondly. "Well, so long as it's no trouble," she teased. We set the table in a blur of smiles, settling in while Brady brought out the food. There was turkey and the famous Banner stuffing, carrots and a yam tart, and cranberries Beatrice had made and subsequently hogged. They really were delicious.

"I'd like to propose a toast." Annabeth stood, holding Tracy's hand and her glass aloft. "There are a great many things I could be grateful for this Thanksgiving. New friends," she tipped her glass to Beatrice, "and new happiness," a smile at Brady and I; Brady squeezed my hand tightly. "But most of all, I think I'm thankful for my beautiful, brilliant wife and the hope of our child." Her expression was tender as she looked at Tracy, so much love it was almost painful to see. "To many, many more holidays, and so much more happiness. I love you, Trace."

There was a communal *aww*, and we lifted our glasses as they kissed. Brady leaned over to press his lips to mine lightly and I smiled against it, cupping his cheek.

I was happy. Wonderfully, completely *happy*.

It was a very good day.

"I DON'T know, Tracy. Do babies really *need* shoes?" I was flopped across my couch, phone pressed to my ear, Winston resting on my stomach, kneading my chest with rumbling start-and-stop purrs. "Even if they are tiny and cute."

"Well, does anyone really *need* shoes?"

"Um, yeah." I huffed out a laugh, shaking my head. "That's why they have those signs. You know, no shirt, no shoes, no whatever."

"Fine. But our baby isn't going to go into a convenience store, so shoes are more of a want, really." I could hear Tracy shifting on the couch, groaning faintly when she moved. Apparently, her morning sickness was more of an evening thing. Annabeth was at the gallery, and Brady was still up at his parents', so we were commiserating together. "Still, I think I should totally register for them for the baby shower. Seriously, Quinn, they were adorable."

"Yes, there are few things more crucial to an infant's first weeks than pink high-tops."

"You have no soul," she informed me, but she was laughing. "They had *rhinestones*."

"Ah, so they were the unisex ones."

"I don't believe in gender roles, you know that. And neither do you, Mr. Plum-Striped Shirt and skinny jeans."

"Hey," I said, shoulders shaking as I tried not to let my stern voice crack. "You picked that outfit out with me. You said I looked good!"

"Did I?" Tracy paused for a moment. "Hey, Quinn, Anna's on the other line. Give me a second."

"Sure." I tipped my head back, staring up at the ceiling. "It's okay, Winston," I assured the cat, who hadn't really moved other than to knead his paws against my chest or flip his tail around lazily. "You and me, we're having fun, right? Just the two of us? Absolutely. Totally bacheloring it up."

For example, that afternoon I'd chased Winston around the apartment, trying to brush him out and clip his nails, and then I'd eaten peanut butter from the jar while watching shows on the BBC. We were pretty much living the dream.

"Sorry about that." Tracy came back, sounding, just from two minutes worth of talking with Anna, so much happier. "She's about an hour away from coming home and just wanted to check in."

"You are a pretty lucky woman, Mrs. Annabeth."

"Don't I know it," she sighed, content. And then, of course, "Have you spoken to Brady?"

I tried not to feel miserable about it. He was due back the next day; it was hardly like he was shipped off to war or something. I was not going to go all pining, Austen novel heroine.

"He's texted a few times." See? Casual. Breezy. That was me. After a beat, though, I sighed. "I miss him."

"Aw," Tracy said, and I could practically hear her smirk. "You're so cute."

"Shut up."

"No, really, that's adorable. You're all wistful. You should write him long letters about how you're thinking about wandering aimlessly around a moor, sighing his name."

I really shouldn't be laughing this hard. I was trying to be angry and insulted. "What moor? Where is this moor I'm supposed to be wandering?"

"I don't know. I think it's like a field."

"Oh, that's romantic. I'll just go aimlessly walking in a *field*."

"Yeah, that loses something in translation," Tracy agreed. "Maybe you should lock yourself in a tower or something. Or, oh, or you could, like, stand outside his window with a boom box."

"Did you just go from Victorian romance to eighties movies?" I shook my head, rubbing a hand through Winston's fur. "God, you're insane."

Tracy cackled dramatically. "That's why you love me."

"I do," I told her, sobering just a little. "Love you."

"I know, you dork," she said. "Love you too."

"You going to be alright until Anna gets home?"

"Yeah. I've got ginger ale and saltines here, and I'm not moving until she carries me to bed. I'm perfect."

"Okay." I smiled a little, voice getting a bit tender around the edges. "Good night, crazy woman."

"Good night. Try not to fall in any moors."

We hung up and I let the phone fall by the side of the couch, scrunching myself down further in the cushions. "Well," I told Winston, his ear flicking toward me. "I guess we really are alone."

There was a knock at the door. I looked over toward it, eyebrow raising. "That was a little touch of dramatic irony, wasn't it, fluffball?" Unsettling Winston from his spot on my stomach, I padded over to the door, pajama pants slung low on my hips, hair all messy from where I kept running my hands through it. I hadn't actually bothered to shave yet, and I knew I looked completely rumpled and unpresentable, but I figured it'd just be the pizza guy getting lost on his way to the apartment upstairs again. It happened a couple of times a month.

"Hey, I'm pretty sure you want five-thirteen, not three-fifteen," I was saying as I swung open the door. And there was Brady, leather jacket and boots and *perfect*. Oh. Well. "You're not the pizza guy," I said dumbly.

He didn't say anything at all. Just pushed me inside and kissed me, hard, hand cradling the back of my head, arm wrapped around my waist. After a moment of mental flailing, I melted into him, fingers curling into his jacket, yanking him back when he dared to break away for breath.

Eventually we did separate, panting and lips swollen, my eyes searching his face. "What the hell?" I managed, but I was grinning, that uncomfortable ache I'd had since saying good-bye to him Friday morning easing a bit. "I thought you weren't back until tomorrow?"

"I left early. Couldn't stand the thought of another night apart." His thumb brushed my cheek, and he looked so *vulnerable*. So utterly undone. I instinctively leaned into him, forehead bumping against his.

"God, I'm glad you're home," I told him. Brady chuckled, but it was thin, a little strained. I frowned and pulled back, my hands on his shoulders. "What's the matter?"

"Just… I was thinking. I've been thinking since Thanksgiving." His fingers found mine, absently playing with them, a crease in his forehead as he looked down at them.

There was a nervous drop in my stomach, liked I'd just stepped forward only to find nothing under my feet. "Oh, Christ," I murmured, feeling the color drain from my face. "You want to break up."

"What?" Shocked, wide eyes went up to mine. "Jesus, Quinn, no. Nothing like that."

Releasing the sharp, painful breath I'd been holding, I sagged back against the wall, rubbing a hand through my hair. "Fuck." I didn't have any clue what he was leading up to, but God, I was just happy he wasn't trying to find a nice way to let me down. "Then what is it?" I offered a shaky smile. "You're scaring me."

His arms were around me then, just like that. That warm strength circled me and I leaned into him, clinging to his jacket, burying my face into the curve of his neck. "I'm sorry," he told me, quietly. "God, this is not how I wanted this to go. I had this whole... I practiced. On the drive back. I had this speech in my head, but then you answered the door and you're all gorgeous and rumpled and those damn blue eyes and I forgot everything I was going to say."

It was kind of strange, to think of Brady Banner as anything less than fully confident. But that's what he was right then; he was oddly hesitant, slightly awkward. It was endearing in a way Brady hadn't been very often. He looked so unsure.

"Okay." I gently pushed him toward the door. He gave me a baffled look, huffing out a laugh as I closed it in his face.

"Um, Quinn?" His voice was muffled from the other side, and I smiled faintly.

"We're starting over. So you can remember what you wanted to say."

There was a pause and I got a bit nervous he'd just leave. But then he knocked, and I opened the door to find him standing there, leaning against the jam, a fond expression on his face. And just like the first time, he drew me in for a kiss; this one, though, was long and lingering, sweet and utterly overwhelming. By the time it ended, all I could manage was a hazy, "Hey," around the grin spreading across my face.

"Hey," he replied, rubbing his nose lightly against mine. "So, I have been thinking about this for a while. And I know it's going to be big and scary, and I'm well aware maybe this time it's me jumping to the end. But I just... I want to ask you this. To see if you're where I am. Because even if I'm jumping, maybe you're jumping with me."

"Brady...." I shook my head, confused. "Tell me what you're thinking."

"I'm thinking we should move in together." When I didn't answer right away, he gave me this smile, this heartbreaking, hopeful smile. "Here or my place or a new place or, I don't know, in a car under a bridge. I don't care. I just know I want to wake up next to you, and I want to come home to see you every night. I want your socks next to mine in the drawer."

There was this lump in my throat that was making it hard to talk, this aching burn in my chest I couldn't breathe past. But I knew. Yes, it scared me to death to think of packing up the last bits of my life with Aaron and finding a spot for Brady. Something bigger than a drawer, something so much more substantial than pushing back hangers for space in the closet.

It definitely was jumping. But I figured so long as Brady was next to me, the way down couldn't be anything but great.

"Yeah," I finally managed, and he grinned, relieved and beautiful. "Yeah, I think that's exactly what we should do."

Chapter 9

"HAVE yourself a merry little Christmas. Let your heart be light."

Reaching forward, I turned down the radio. "You do realize this is our second straight hour of Christmas carols," I told Brady, eyebrow raised. "If you're trying to start a sing-a-long, you might have wanted to get me drunk first."

"Oh, come on," he teased, reaching out to take my hand, bringing my knuckles up for a kiss. "Get in the spirit, Scrooge. There's snow, our trunk is full of presents, and we are now an hour and a half away from Mom's eggnog and Dad's famous mac and cheese. This is as Christmas-y as it gets."

Winston, in his carrier in the backseat, grumbled at us. He'd spent the first twenty minutes bitching at us, meowing plaintively, and now he'd settled down and just occasionally was making his displeasure known. He would much rather be wandering around the car, but all we needed was a fat, fluffy cat deciding Brady's driving hand was much better used for petting than steering.

"So, tell me what to expect." I settled back in my seat, watching the fat, fluffy flakes of snow drift past our windows. "You said tonight we'd decorate the tree?"

"Oh, yeah. Mom insists we all have to be there. I think Beatrice and Dad were going out to the farm we've gone to since I was a kid to pick out the perfect tree. Britt and Belinda are getting there this afternoon, and we'll be there in time for dinner, so after that we'll crack open the Christmas boxes and string cranberries and popcorn, the whole thing."

"I wanted a fresh tree this year," I mused. "Aaron was allergic, and I thought the pine needles were too much work, but I thought it would be a nice change."

"And, bonus, Winston will love to rub those chubby cheeks all over the branches." Brady glanced back at the cat in the rearview mirror. "Won't you, buddy?"

Winston growled at him. I laughed, twisting in my seat to wiggle my fingers through the bars of the carrier. After a moment, he was shoving his fuzzy face against them, purring rustily. "Oh, shush," I cooed at him. "Big grumpy butt. You love your carrier. You get treats when you get out."

He did love treats. Winston lay back down, plopping himself so his fur was spilling out the front of the carrier. I turned around again and, with a quick smile in Brady's direction, switched the radio back up, just in time to catch another rendition of "White Christmas." Brady held my hand lightly, pulling away from time to time to switch lanes, but he always came back to me, our joined fingers resting on his knee.

We pulled up outside his family's house only slightly delayed by the snow. White lights glittered on the porch in the gradually creeping darkness. Cranberry-red bows were bound on each of the pillars, and a fresh green garland wound around the railing. With the snow drifting, it really did look like something out of a Christmas card. Brady paused, hand on the keys, looking up toward the house.

"Okay," he said, taking a deep breath. "I've never brought anyone home. I've never wanted to. But this is… I mean, you met them. My family is kind of crazy. And loud. And messy. I just don't want you to run screaming."

I huffed out a quiet noise, tugging him in to kiss him lightly. "Brady? Shut up. I love them, I love you, and I'm not running anywhere. Now"—playfully, I shoved his shoulder—"get your ass out of the car, Banner. Someone promised me mac and cheese."

Some of the tenseness that had crept into his expression eased, and he laughed, shaking his head. "Fine. That was your out, O'Malley. Now you're stuck with me."

"Promise?" I grinned over the top of the car at him as we got out, as we gathered our bags and got covered in snow. Winston batted through the front of the carrier at the snowflakes.

Beatrice flung open the door and threw herself at Brady in a giant hug; I was next, and I smiled at her enthusiasm. "Oh my God, we thought you'd never get here. Come on, Dad's just pulling the pasta out of the oven, and Mom's got carols on." She took the carrier from me, holding it up to greet Winston. Hand in hand, Brady and I walked inside the house. It was warm and filled with lights and sound and music. Claire greeted us with hugs; Bruno shook my hand. There was a stocking over the fireplace with my name on it and tiny knitted paintbrushes.

We gathered around the table to eat and talk, to drink eggnog and laugh about old family stories. Claire pulled out the baby pictures, much to Brady's dismay; Winston made friends with absolutely everyone and stole bites of the ham from people's plates. It was perfect in an achy, shuddery way, like I wanted to just sit back and watch, to memorize everything and hold it close enough it would never quite fade. There was warmth there and a welcoming kindness that seemed almost overwhelming.

After wine and more eggnog and fifteen different kinds of cookies, we decorated the tree. The presents got laid out underneath it. Winston had claimed the back corner of the tree skirt for his new favorite napping spot, and it was just Brady and I left sitting in front of the fire. Everyone else had drifted off to sleep in ones and twos until we were there in front of the glittering tree and the dying embers. After George, the last holdout, had dragged himself upstairs, I'd migrated into Brady's lap, his arms around my waist. We were just talking: about childhood Christmases, about favorite presents. About everything and nothing and the electric train set we'd both gotten when we were ten.

"I remember it had this button you could push for the whistle," Brady mused, chin resting on my shoulder. "I'd put on this little striped engineer's hat and plot out routes for the train to take. Every stop, I'd blow that whistle, all important-like. I bet it drove Mom crazy after the fifteenth time, but she never said a word."

"I tried to make it go down the steps." I smiled at him, my fingers absently combing through his messy waves. "Like it was a mountain."

He laughed. "I bet that went well."

"Total destruction," I informed him, soberly. "No survivors."

"Well, those mountains can be tricky." He kissed my arm, smiling. "Lucky you didn't grow up to be a railway builder."

We watched the fire dwindle down to red-hot coals, the room lit now only by the tree. It was one of those moments of absolute contentment.

"I love you, Brady." I whispered it into the near-dark, into the stockings and the garland, into the cranberry strings and the sweet skin just under his ear. He turned to find me, to kiss me softly, there in front of the fire.

"I love you too."

We had the attic, like he'd promised. Stripping off clothes, panting kisses and hungry touches against bared skin, we fell into bed together. The snow fell against the windows, the old, rusty heater kicked on to pump out hot air, and we tangled together, Brady inside of me, my hands braced on his chest. I gasped his name as we thrust together, as I came in a roll and shout of bliss. He followed after me and we wound up sprawled out across a faded quilt, panting and grinning, falling asleep in each other's arms.

The sun slipped across my face. Blinking, I batted in front of me with a groan, like that would magically make it dark again. Brady was curled up on top of me, hugging me close, head pillowed on my chest. I flopped backward, giving up the struggle to sit upright. Much better to laze about in bed with him.

"I smell cinnamon." He mumbled the words against my skin in a slur.

"Good morning to you too."

I could hear the house waking up somewhere below us; voices and the smell of coffee filtered up to our room. We didn't move for a few minutes longer, enjoying the warmth of our bed and the sleepy, soft kisses. Finally, though, I managed to get up, Brady following after. We showered and got dressed, then headed downstairs to find Claire flipping French toast and Brittany adding icing to giant cinnamon rolls.

Clint passed me a cup of coffee, earning him a grateful grunt. We settled in around the table, passing platters of eggs and French toast and bacon. I had two cinnamon rolls and fought Brady over the last taste of frosting. Winston was more than happy to go from person to person, begging with huge eyes, because *obviously* his mean owners were starving him to death. Fat lump got more bacon than should be allowed just with that routine.

It really was a little bit like Norman Rockwell had organized our day. We went for a sleigh ride, sharing it with Belinda and George, laughing so hard I forgot all about the cold. There were games by the fire, and Brady even taught me how to bake the traditional Banner sugar cookies. Which is to say, I stirred things and then wandered off to sketch him while he did the hard part. It was still a great deal of fun.

That night, Christmas Eve, we sang carols around Claire's piano. And when everyone else had gone to bed, Brady took me for a walk. There was a hill behind his house, a long sloping expanse of pure, crystalline white. The snow was powdery, crunching under every step. My nose was red and I was shivering by the time we got to the top.

The view was worth it, though.

"This was my favorite spot," he explained, wrapping his arms around me as we looked out across the farmhouse, lit up and beautiful, across the fields dotted with points of light. And above us were the stars, pinpricks of flashing white against an endless velvet black. The moon hung ripe and low, bathing everything in silver. "When I was growing up, I'd come up here when I needed to think. All my big decisions happened up here. Realizing I was gay, deciding to come out, deciding to drop out of college, to open my own business…." He kissed my cheek, his lips cold against my skin. "This place is a part of me."

I smiled a little, taking a deep breath. "Thank you," I murmured. "For showing it to me."

I could feel him shrug. "Well, you're a part of me now too. I guess I thought it fit."

Turning in his arms, I studied his face. I lifted gloved fingers to brush lightly across his cheek. "Did I ever tell you how glad I am I met you at that bar?"

Brady smiled, and suddenly it seemed like the moon itself wasn't all that bright. Not in comparison. "Me too."

Aaron would have loved this night. He would have loved the snow and the stars, the sense of standing still in a place where history moved all around us. He would have loved me, happy. I hoped he would, anyway.

It wouldn't ever stop hurting. That was part of living, I thought. That was part of loving someone so deeply. They burrowed into your bones, and you couldn't ever really get them out. You didn't ever really *want* to. But I was bigger than one moment, than one loss. I could love the past and have a future. I could love Aaron every bit as deeply and still find new parts of me to give to Brady.

We had a lifetime, however long that was, however scary and unsure and wonderful. That was all anyone had. Only a lifetime. It was all we could do to fill it, to live every moment, to learn how to love better. Brady was showing me that.

And I really wanted to be there.

ALEX KIDWELL, confirmed geek and bibliophile, lives in the Midwest with partner Robin Saxon. Alex relaxes by slaying dragons in MMOs, listening to music that can be sung along with in the shower, and enjoying BBC programming.

Other than writing, Alex enjoys knitting and is currently attempting to learn how to knit in the round. There are plans for a future of cat hats, which Alex is certain will go over well with household-running felines, Starsky and Hutch. Alex also indulges in too many cooking shows, while owning only one pan.

Visit Alex's blog at http://saxonkidwell.blogspot.com/, Facebook at http://www.facebook.com/profile.php?id=100002270719608, and Twitter @kiddingalex, or e-mail Alex at alexkidwellwrites@gmail.com.

From ALEX KIDWELL & ROBIN SAXON

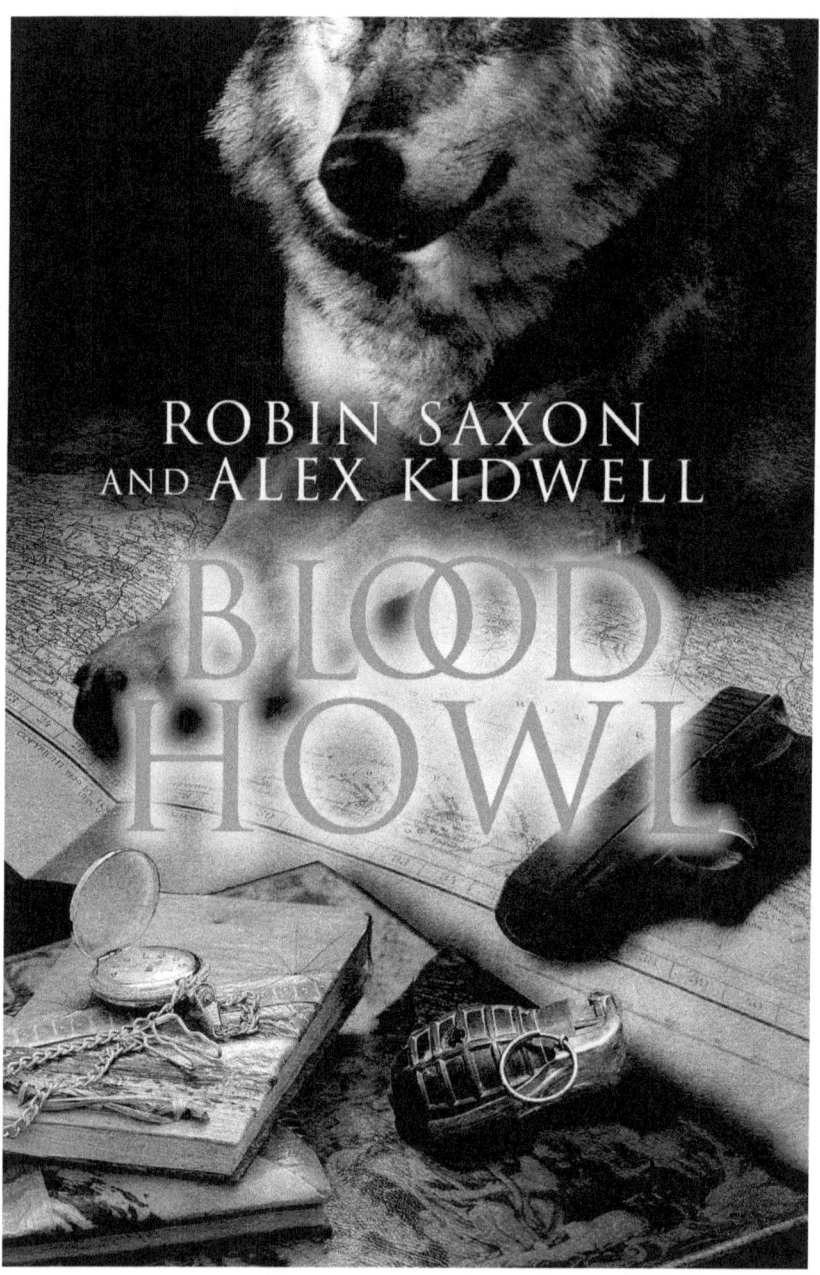

ROBIN SAXON
AND ALEX KIDWELL

BLOOD
HOWL

http://www.dreamspinnerpress.com

From ALEX KIDWELL & ROBIN SAXON

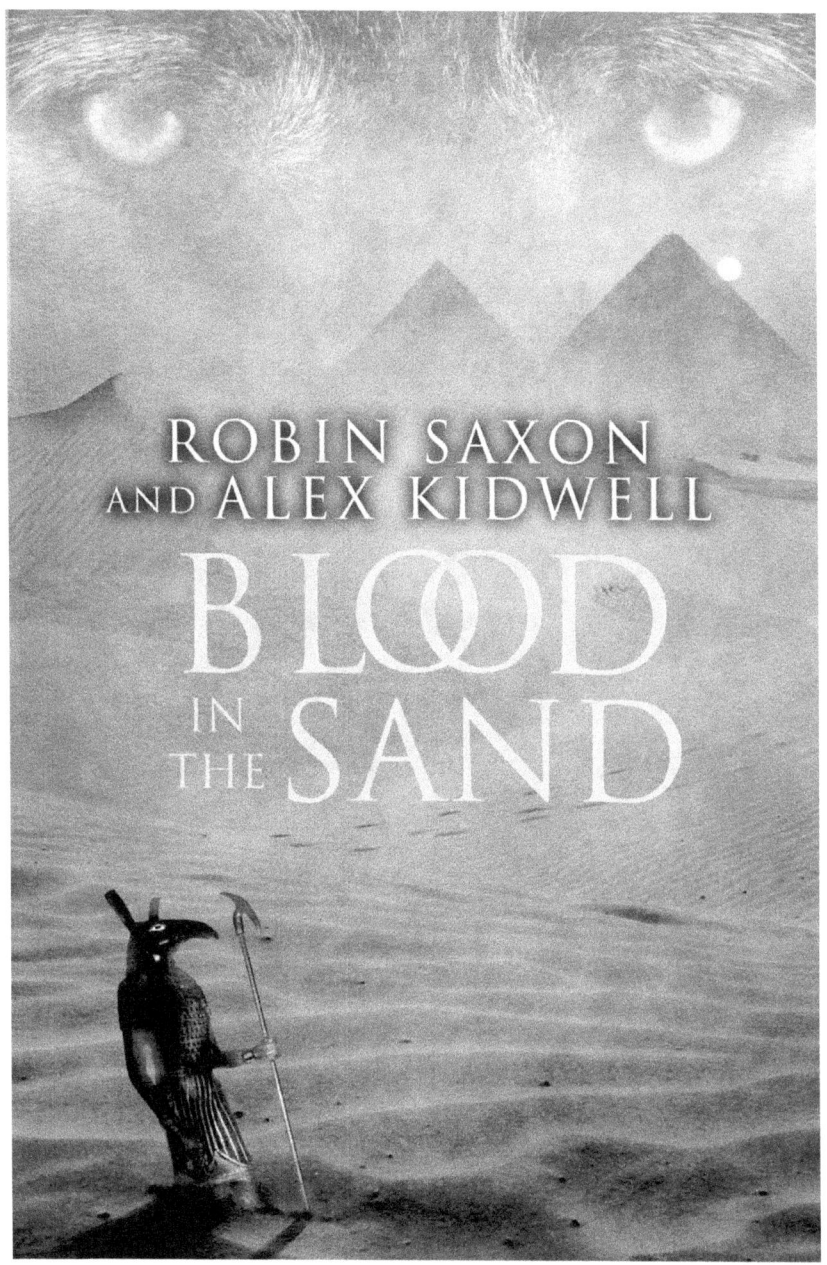

Also from DREAMSPINNER PRESS

CON RILEY

AFTER *Ben*

A
Seattle Stories
novel

http://www.dreamspinnerpress.com

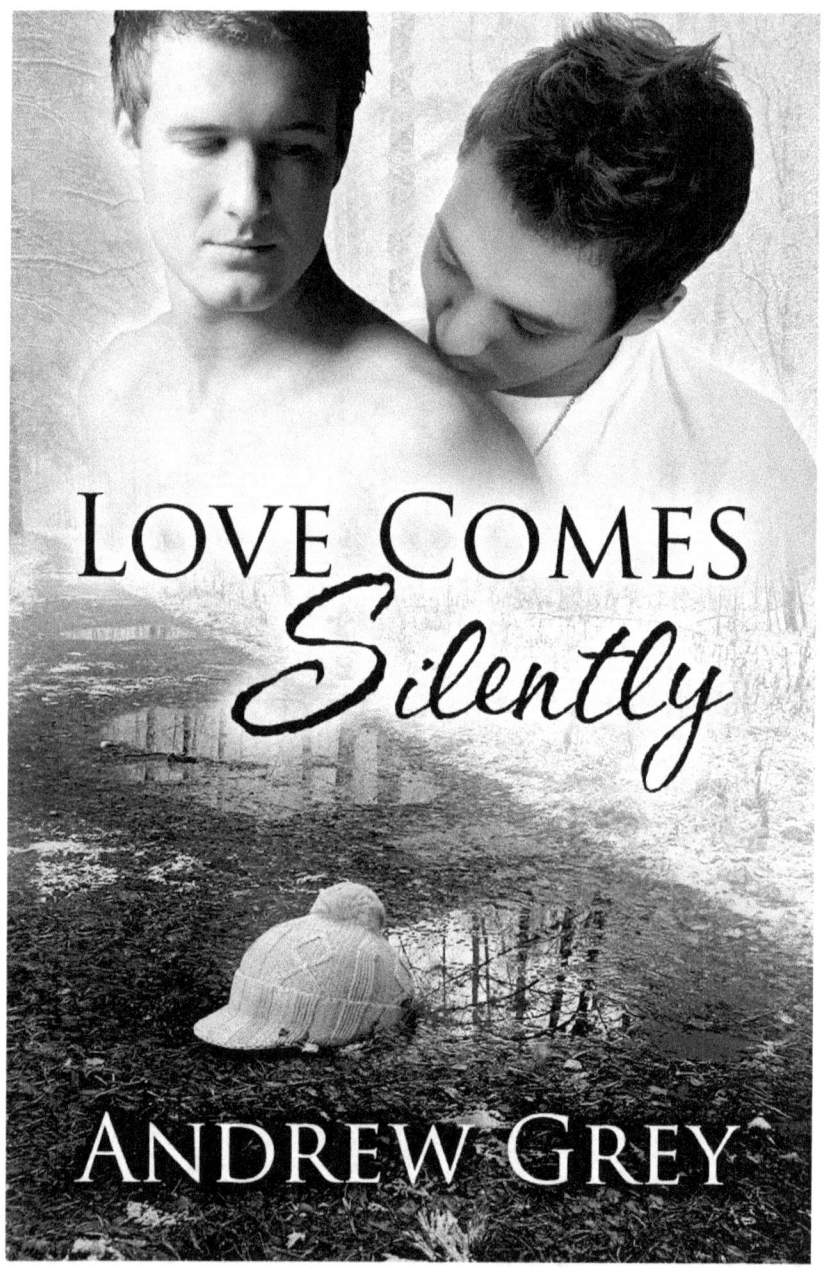

Robin Saxon

The Royal Road

Also from DREAMSPINNER PRESS

The Way You Say

DAR MAVISON

http://www.dreamspinnerpress.com

www.ingramcontent.com/pod-product-compliance
Lightning Source LLC
Chambersburg PA
CBHW060056260626
47160CB00005B/1692